ROOKIE NOIR

12 SHORT STORIES
ABOUT 2 SHORT DETECTIVES

DAVID RADA

First printing: 2015

The Library of Congress Catalog Control Number: 2014922187

ISBN 978-0-9862442-0-9 (Paperback)

ISBN 978-0-9862442-1-6 (e-book)

Juggled Words Publishing
678 Beaumont Elm Street
North Wilkesboro, NC 28659

Table of Contents

Acknowledgements 7

Rookie Noir 11

Two Timing the Comics 29

Third Grade Airforce 47

That Dame .61

Busted Downey Oshun 95

The Cricket Clicker Caper 111

Christmas Ginks 'n' Santa's Elves . . .131

The Spitball Shooter 159

Home of Deranged 181

You and What Army? 201

The Last Bus to Gwynn Oak 223

The Bottle Deposit Mystery 243

Bawlmer Lexicon 263

Hard Boiled Lexicon 267

About the Author 269

For Mark

COUSIN

FRIEND

RACONTEUR

WELLSPRING OF SMILES, LAUGHTER AND MEMORIES

1950-2011

Acknowledgements

No one writes in a vacuum. OK, maybe the Hoover technical writer does. He probably spends his life revising the owner's manual as he's living inside the latest upright or canister vacuum cleaner. But I didn't write in a vacuum (or a closet). Here is the list of people who helped me in so many ways.

My wife Kimberly has been my editor, proof reader, and most importantly, my go-to source when it comes to content and flow of the stories. Nothing helps me more than hearing phrases like "Did you really talk like that?" "Did that really happen?" And "I've no idea what you mean." Kimberly has encouraged me in this endeavor with her keen eye towards proper English, composition, and story format. I've ignored most of what she's suggested, except when she was right, which was almost always. She suffered through every story (more than once), corrected my mistakes, asked probing questions so I wouldn't sound like the eight year old I was writing about, encouraged me to write better (or betterer; or maybe it was bestest), and endured some of the most lame personal inside jokes I've written that only a Calf Lick from Bawlmer in the late 1950's could understand. God bless you, Anam Cara.

My daughters, Corrine and Jessica, always inspire me to be the best that I can, whether it be as a dad, a writer, or just a person.

Letter "3"(or maybe number "C"). I want to give props to

both my sister and brother. They have given me a few ideas on some stories I've written. A few were on purpose, a few through casual conversations.

When I received the cover design and formatted stories from Bookfly Design I yelled, "OH…My…God! Look at this!" I've labored very hard trying to tell these stories like a polished professional writer, but without Bookfly Design's artistic imagination designing the cover and converting the stories into print and digital formats this book would still be sitting on my laptop and only I would find it humorous. I may not be a polished writer yet, but Bookfly Design sure made me look like it. So glad I found you.

I should offer a conditional mea culpa to the nuns and priests of The Shrine of The Little Flower in Baltimore when I attended the school. But if Garrison Keillor can poke fun at the Lutherans in the spirit of humor, satire and parody, I can do the same with Catholics. Before somebody decides to bar me from Sunday mass, I will confess that I got an excellent education at the Shrine. I just didn't want it at the time.

What inspired me to write such a collection? It began with the photo of Mark and me.

The hard-boiled detective and gangster slang found in many of the genre's novels and movies make me despair of the English language, but in a good way. Dashiell Hammett, Mickey Spillane and Raymond Chandler (where their private detectives were always fighting crime) were the building blocks for the characters' profession. P.G. Wodehouse (where no one gets hurt and everybody escapes the bonds of marriage) offered an insight into written humor and John Waters, whose movies and stories celebrate Bawlmer's beloved quirky characters, history and life.

Thank you all.

Rookie Noir

That's a picture of me with my partner Mark, on the cover. You won't see us in photographs often since our careers as 8 year old private eyes dictate that we remain behind the scenes. It was caught in an Elliot Ness moment after we cracked a case. But we knew photos could compromise our ability to do our job in the Bawlmer City Northeast Pleese Precinct. It was an impulsive and reluctant photo op instigated by parents who thought it was cute. Crime is never cute. Oh sure, once in a while you run across some dame that you might say is cute, but most times she's a victim, not some moll. The trouble boys usually resemble knuckle dragging apes. What some of those moll dames see in those types is beyond me. Maybe it's that feminine instinct to teach a monkey to behave, eat with a fork and talk politely. As far as I can tell, the road to civilization for those palookas is a dead end, no matter how hard the dames try to pave the way.

I know what you're saying. I'm using words and phrases that belong to my dad's generation. Yeah, sure, I might be throwing around "dame" and "palooka" a lot. I watch a lot of TV and read a bunch of hard-boiled detective paper backs by Raymond Chandler, Mickey Spillane and Dashiell Hammett that my dad had stashed away. I watch a lot of movies with Humphrey Bogart as a tough-talking detective and silver screen toughs like James Cagney, Edward G. Robinson and

George Raft. If I had a walkie-talkie, I'd be barking "21-50"and "10-4" into it all day thanks to "Highway Patrol." I started to carry a comb because Ed "Kookie" Burns flashed it around on "77 Sunset Strip." Yeah, the words may be from my dad's time, but I used them because it made me sound about six inches taller than I was. And since I was one of the smallest kids in the class, I needed every advantage I could get.

Mark and I studied at a local school called Shrine of The Large Flower. There were three groups of students who attended the Shrine: those who thought this institution would be an inside track to heaven by becoming a priest or nun, those who were jockeying for an extended vacation at the "Hotel Hoosegow" before all the best cells with a view were booked, and those who were trying to stop the first two groups from making life altering decisions they would come to regret.

Mark and I were in that third group. I used to carry a badge. It was shiny, tin, had a pin about two inches long so I could put it on my jacket. I thought it gave me authority. It did, that is, until a Calf Lick Franciscan nun revoked it because I stabbed a classmate, Steven, in the leg during class and she put it in a desk drawer, along with a bunch of assorted contraband, where I'd never see it again.

I had to venture into the darkest chamber of life on earth. It was at least the darkest spot in a Calf Lick church. It was called confession and I was about to plead my case to a priest in a last ditch effort to retrieve my badge. As I knelt in the inky blackness which always seemed to reek of incense, I tried to keep my voice low so I wouldn't distract the horde of other third grade sinners waiting their turn to confess their crimes against humanity which they had committed during the previous week. Within the darkest confines of confession we would promise to never commit another sin of any kind, receive penance and salvation, exit the confession box, kneel in a church pew with folded hands and pray for salvation. And then usually return to our sinning lives. For some of the repentant sinners it took an hour after confession to condemn their souls to the fires of hell once again. For most it happened within minutes. Confession was every Friday. You only had to survive a week to do soul laundry and be assured passage past Saint Peter and the pearly gates.

The little window slid back and I began with my best impression of the boys I saw in the movie, "Boys Town" hoping that the priest who was on the other side of the window would be Spencer Tracy.

"Bless me, Fadda, for I have sinned, I had angry toughts about my brudda and my sista. I had impure toughts twenty times. Oh, yeah, I stabbed Steven in the leg. It was only once. Can I get my badge back?" I had no idea what impure thoughts were, except the nuns were keen on telling all of us we had them, so I figured I'd had at least twenty a week.

"Why did you stab Steven, my son?" Came a voice from the shadows that didn't sound anything like Spencer Tracy. In fact it sounded like Vincent Price which meant one thing: I was in confession with Father Duck. I decided to press on anyway.

"He made me mad, Fadda. He was hounding me for my candy money during class."

"What do you think Jesus would have done?" He asked. I had a fleeting thought about the story of Jesus losing his temper with money changers in the temple and throwing the furniture every which way this side of Tuesday, but I didn't think it was going to help my case.

"Oltno." Was all I could mutter.

"Who took your badge?"

"Sister Mary."

"You mean Sister Knuckles?" It was said in a voice that was part chuckle and the rest pure terror. Her name was Sister Mary Breaker, but since she was so quick with a yardstick across a student's hands, she earned the nickname "Sister Mary Knuckles Breaker," "Knuckles" for short. I thought it was a secret name known only to the unfortunate masses who were assigned to her class.

"So can you help me, Fadda?" I asked.

"I'm not going to ask her. Are you serious?" Obviously the parish priests were well acquainted with her wrath, and they weren't about to tangle with her. I made a mental note to keep my eyes on the hands of the priests for any unusual swelling or deformity as they handed out communion.

I sighed. Nope, no chance, no matter how many "Hail Mary's" I said. Father Duck wasn't about to put his own life in peril by challenging Sister Knuckles' idea that a couple of 8 year old gumshoes were interfering in pleesing the unruly masses at recess. From then on I knew I'd have to operate on my own without any formal Calf Lick blessings.

Mark and I got a tip that someone was dealing baseball cards at recess a week later. This was not just your normal array of baseball cards of players on different teams, but rookie cards. A Major League Baseball player is only a rookie once in their career and having a bunch of rookie cards in your possession meant you could dictate a "deal" where you could trade a player's rookie card for five or six known players' cards. It was an ugly way to acquire wealth. We decided to investigate. The best place to start the investigation was in the recess yard of the Shrine.

Mark and I spent a lot of time in the yard of the Shrine at what was called recess. Why it resembled an exercise yard at a maximum security federal prison is just coincidence. There was a chain link fence around the perimeter that insured we wouldn't breach the confines and escape to who knows where. I tried escaping three times when I was six. Even without bloodhounds and a search party of heat-toting vigilantes I was always caught within an hour. Maybe it was the uniform that always gave me away. It usually resulted in a task of "I will not run away from school" that I had to write 500 times.

The yard had a jet black macadam surface which lent itself to sliding more than twenty feet once us boys had glazed the soles of our shoes with the remains of the little wax bottles that contained some concoction of sugar and colored water. Those little bottles of sugar laced juice could be purchased at the candy store that coincidently was just 250 feet from the yard. Once you downed the shot, and the sugar took effect, you waxed the soles of your shoes and then would run, slide, and imitate a skier on some downhill race, with the leather soles of your shoes burned off within minutes. That activity insured that the local cobbler (whose establishment was next to the candy store) would survive another week. It never occurred to us that they were in cahoots. The boys in the yard kept the local economy thriving.

The stone aggregate embedded in that hard surface could take out the knee of your pants in a matter of seconds if you lost your balance, not to mention taking the skin of your knee with it. It wasn't unusual to see more than a few gimpy, limping students every day in the yard. I always thought the yard's surface was the result of a conspiracy. I heard through the grape vine that the parking lots and recess yards of Calf Lick schools were all paved and paid for by the only uniform company in Bawlmer that supplied the mandated uniforms.

A kid I knew told me his father, who was German, and an Italian friend of his, who would puke at anything that contained tomato sauce, used to eat lunch at a Jewish deli on a street called "Corned Beef Row." The Jewish owner had a neighbor, a Polish lady, who knew how to operate a sewing machine and moon lighted at the uniform company sewing pants, was told by the Bohemian secretary about invoices for paving a parking lot. Since all of his informants were still learning the Merican language I questioned the kid's credibility. But since he was Calf Lick, I knew he wouldn't lie. It wasn't just a run-of-the-mill rumor. I don't pay much attention to rumors. If I wanted to hear rumors, I would listen to my sister and her friends. Eighth grade dames love sifting through rumors.

The school's yard had a myriad of circles used for dodge ball, as well as straight lines for parking cars on Sundays, but during the week the white lined expanse of black top was used for jump rope, hopscotch and secret high level meetings of dames. Those white painted lines of demarcation assisted the school aged dames in staking out their territory during the week as they traded stories and rumors of the comings and goings of everybody in school. Other parking spaces were used by boys to hone their skills at pitching baseball cards. The area outside any of those lines was akin to a "No Man's Land." The pious penguins patrolled every corner of the yard among the 250 inmates to make sure none of us were breaking any commandments. The Shrine yard was part open air market and part hallowed ground. The bazaars of Morocco had nothing on this place. It was a crush of people where deals were made behind the backs of the nuns who strongly discouraged gambling and sinning of any sort. It was the perfect place for wheeling and dealing, a soft underbelly of life where you folded your hands in contrite posture while the sisters were near, but then acted like nomadic camel traders without morals amid all the chaos.

It was the last week in April, 1959 and the Orioles had just beaten the Yankees in a double header, 5 to 4 and 3 to 2. Baseball card collecting (and pitching) became a contagious fever as we all caught the major league virus. The virus couldn't be cured, but you could treat the symptoms by chewing the bubble gum that came in every pack of cards. If you were badly infected, you learned how to spit like a first baseman.

Mark and I patrolled the yard looking for signs of rookie dealing. We strolled about the perimeter of the yard, watching the card pitching, listening to pitchers' exclamations that ran the gamut from the triumphant yells of a "leaner" (against the fence) to the angst from poor tosses that were sure to be covered and thus losing their cards. We asked questions.

"You know somebody with a lot of rookies?"

"No."

"You traded four cards for a rookie Milt Pappas lately"

"No."

"How about a Brooks Robinson rookie card? You give up a few too many in your stack?"

"No. Leave me alone!"

We decided we had to go deeper into the darker nether world where ginks with a stack of baseball cards were dealing willy-nilly.

"Mark, how many cards do you have?" I asked.

"I have five. My mom found my stash and this is all I could smuggle out." My mom had confiscated my stack of cards during the ritual frisking she performed every morning, so I was broke.

"Let me have 'em. If I lose, I'll replace 'em."

I found a spot along the fence and struck up a conversation with two pigeons who couldn't pitch cards to save their third semester spelling grades, trying to discover who was dealing the rookies.

"You hear of anybody dealing in rookies?" I asked as I deftly tossed a card to the fence where it could never be covered. One has to be aware of wind speed, direction, and barometric pressure to make the card float to a precise spot.

"No. I ain't got no rookie cards." Came the agitated answer. With that language he's not only going to fail spelling, but English as well.

"I didn't ask you that. You hear of somebody who has a bunch of rookies?" I covered a Boston Red Sox player with my borrowed Cleveland Indian card that took a hard left three inches above the ground, spun for a second in a breeze then landed exactly where I wanted. In less than five minutes I had twenty cards and a lead.

"Maybe you need to talk to Steve," A frustrated tosser said in an effort to stop me from cleaning him out.

Of course! Steven was the guy I stabbed in the leg with the pin of my badge which caused me to lose it! He knew everything that happened at the yard. Steven was a favorite with the nuns and privy to the dark side of dealing.

Mark and I found Steven leaning against the chain link perimeter fence as far away from the Shrine as Earth is from the Sun. I should describe Steven, even though some might say he defied description. It was obvious that once Steven was born, his parents made him ride a hobby horse every day, which is why his legs were bowed. His ginger and red hair looked like a nasty argument because every hair decided it wanted to grow in a different direction. You couldn't look Steven in the eye because you never knew which eye was looking at you. I heard my mom talk about something called a "lazy eye" but at any point in time one of Steven's eyes looked like it'd had taken an extended vacation. And his head was almost as big as his body. My mom used to tell me "You'll grow into it." But she was talking about a coat or a sweater. As for Steven's head; growing "into it" could take a long time.

Sometimes at recess you could look at a kid and get an idea if he was going to be wearing a halo or carrying a pitchfork. I could never tell with Steven, though. He could easily grow up to be a professional rodeo rider or the main attraction at some seaside boardwalk side show. But Steven had moxie, he had chutzpah, and he was not only smart but quick with answers. I asked my dad about Steven and described him in detail: the large head, the eyes that never looked directly at you, his out of control hair, and his wheeling and dealing at recess and then asked him what he'd probably be when he grew up. My dad's one word answer: politician. I'm not sure if I was given an insight or a warning.

He had a couple of guys on either side who were obviously his goons. We could tell they were goons because their shirt tails were out of their pants and that would never pass muster with the pious penguins.

"Steven, we need to talk." I said.

Just then the Angelus tolled. It was high noon and the bells of the church rang out and everything, I mean EVERY-THING, stopped. The Saracens prayer regimen had nothing on Calf Licks' Angelus prayer devotion. Dodge balls hung in midair as did the leaping and cavorting of children. Spoken words evaporated into the ether so that they would not inter-fere with the prayers that were ascending. The most savvy card pitchers would time their toss so that their card would not be caught in the heavenly currents. We were expected to pray during the Angelus. My only thought was, "Please, God, let's get this over with." And, "I am so glad this isn't a Monday, since we'd have to endure an air raid drill, too." In the meantime, as the bells rang, Steven and I stared at each other.

At the stroke of the twelfth bell the Angelus ended. A few kids hit the ground, being suspended in midair for so long during the Angelus that they forgot how to land on their feet (no doubt tearing out a knee on their pants). Dodge balls sailed over heads because one can get so easily distracted between hitting an opponent in a game of dodge ball and going to heaven. It's all a question of priorities.

Steven was our priority right now.

As we approached, his goons parted like the Red Sea and Steven had that Moses (or was it Charlton Heston?) look in his eyes that betrayed his coveted knowledge. I'm not sure, but coveted knowledge may be a mortal sin (at the least it's a venial sin).

"You carrying?" (Meaning my badge), Steven inquired.

"No, Steven, I'm clean." I answered. Man, this guy won't let go of getting stuck in the leg. It only went two inches deep and it was only one time. It's not like he had to stay home from school or get a tetanus shot.

"We need information." I announced.

"What kind of information? You want to know what's on tomorrow's history test? It's gonna cost you." He answered. I could almost see his fingers clutching all of those precious nickels he received in exchange for test answers which one day would be the down payment on his huge house. Along with that Charlton Heston look (I decided it was Heston and not Moses) and his twirling fingers I thought; maybe I should have stabbed him twice.

"There's somebody dealing in rookie cards. You know anything about that?"

"Maybe….what's it to you?" He answered. Did I mention I never liked that Charlton Heston as Moses look? This guy needs to go to confession.

"Whoever is dealing in rookies is taking advantage of a lot of people. Soon, maybe not tomorrow, but soon, he could corner the market in cards. Today it's only four or five cards for a rookie. Soon it could be cards and money. One day it could be just cash, a lot of cash. That means everybody will have less to spend. No more coughing up dough for candy in the afternoons, no more paying you for test answers. They're going to spend it on buying cards."

I knew I hit a nerve. Steven was a master at manipulating his friends out of candy money for a variety of reasons. Steven always seemed to have candy money, either his own or what he was able to fleece from classmates, and when candy time came he would run the gauntlet down a classroom aisle while so many poor, sugar deficient and unfortunate hands were outstretched for a piece of candy bestowed by a confident and candy laden bearer. It resembled Jesus and the apostles trying to distribute loaves and fishes to a desperate crowd. And neither of those scenes was pretty. Selling test answers was a major source of income for Steven. I can't comment on Jesus's motivation in pitching salvation while trying to feed the hungry masses. Who's really listening to an important message while you're trying to get some tartar sauce?

"There is a guy…he's spending a lot of money on packs of baseball cards. His name is Mike. You know him? His parents give him an allowance." Steven finally said.

Mark and I looked at each other. Yeah, we knew Mike. We could count on one hand the people we knew who got an allowance. A parent of an eight year old who gave him an allowance might as well buy their kid a car right now. And he was dirty. I mean he always looked like he had taken a head first slide into third base. Yeah, "dirty Mike" was probably our guy.

"Where can we find him?" Mark asked.

"Not sure…maybe you need to hunt him down yourselves."

"Any ideas? I asked.

"I know he goes to Kiper's Grocery and Doc's Pharmacy on Saturdays. They get their deliveries on Friday afternoons." We were getting somewhere. I felt better about only stabbing Steven once.

"Thanks, Steven." I said.

"You owe me." He replied. OK, maybe I should have stabbed him twice.

Mark and I decided to stake out Kipers Grocery on Saturday. It was a corner grocery store at the edge of a residential street that saw frequent shoppers. Besides the usual grocery offerings of canned pasta, chicken noodle soup, bread and milk, their main business was custom cut meats. You could tell he was a butcher since sawdust covered the old unvarnished wooden floor in front of the meat counter. Between local butchers and the constant use of sawdust at the Shrine and other schools to soak up sick kids' puke, I figured this little corner of the world probably used two tons of sawdust a week. If I ever give up being a gumshoe I thought becoming a sawdust monger might be a good living. Mr. Kiper also had an array of candy, gum, "Pinkie" balls, kites, comics, balsa wood planes and most importantly, baseball cards.

We staked it out, wandering up and down the aisles appearing to be interested in what the shelves had to offer. Mr. Kiper recognized us even though we were clad in plain clothes.

"You boys looking for something?" He asked, as we heard the familiar sound of butcher paper being torn by a metal blade.

"We're looking, Mr. Kiper." Mark and I answered. This guy had no idea what was at stake. I'm not even sure he cared.

In order to distract him and not appear so conspicuous, I

bought a "Pinkie." Everybody needs a good "Pinkie" in order to play curb ball on a not-so-busy Bawlmer city intersection.

"Is that all, boys?"

"Did you get a baseball card delivery yesterday?"

"Yeah, some kid came in here and bought 10 packs. Why do you ask?"

We were too late. We raced the three blocks down to Doc's Pharmacy hoping to catch "dirty" Mike.

We calmly walked into Doc's Pharmacy even though we were breathless from our run. On the right was the soda fountain where hungry patrons, sitting on red vinyl stools at the white marble counter with their feet dangling just above the black and white checkered floor tiles, enjoyed a phosphate and a hot dog. A phosphate is an addition of lemon or lime or other flavor to carbonated water and some other secret ingredient. I admit my favorite was a vanilla phosphate. But we didn't have time for phosphates. There was a more important "phate" looming. Mark and I split up and wandered the aisles wondering what most of the potions and elixirs were used for.

As I perused the candy aisle I heard a female voice.

"Fust I want dat."

She was obviously foreign. I cocked my head to one side to see if I could hear better. I've seen dogs do that and I knew they could hear stuff people couldn't. Didn't help me, though. I just looked like my grandmother trying to get a crick out of her neck.

"Can I have one of dem?" Came the same voice from an aisle beyond.

Maybe Eastern European….possibly Mediterranean… definitely worth looking at, I thought.

As I rounded the corner, I spied this small dame. No bigger than I, holding onto the hand of a much taller and, dare I say, older woman. The little dame had long straight brown hair the color of that special brown crayon you only get in a box of ninety-six Crayola's. Her eyes were brown, too, comes from the same box, just a different shade. I would say her skin was flesh colored, but I would beat the crayon analogy into the ground. Besides, the crayons belonged to our sketch artist. I guessed she had nice gams, but I had no clue what gams were, except that my dad used to tell my mom that she had them.

"Hi, you come here often?" I asked, in my best relaxed voice, as I noticed her open gray tweed coat that revealed a blue blouse and green skirt. Maybe she was Irish.

"Yeth, every Thaturday"

She was obviously from some exotic place.

"Where are you from?" I asked, expecting to hear a place like Paris, London or Annapolis.

"I live on Brehms Lane."

She lived a block away! Then I noticed her two front teeth were missing. I had lost mine just months before and while I looked like a budding buck-toothed beaver, she wore the look very well. So much for falling for an exotic voice, I thought.

"You boys going to buy anything?" Came a voice that bounced off the ceiling.

"We're still looking." Mark always had a quick answer. It may have been because he had read every "Hardy Boys" case ever recorded. Mark was a devoted student of mysterious cases and always had a quick retort handy.

We headed toward the candy counter. Obviously the trays of baseball cards had been rifled through.

"Did somebody already buy some cards?" We knew the answer, but needed confirmation.

"Yeah, some kid came in this morning and bought 10 packs."

"Which way did he go?"

"Out the door."

Mark and I decided to split up to cover more ground to find "dirty" Mike. Mark would cover the Herring Run area while I scoured the Belair/Edison corridor. The world of baseball card collecting hung in the balance. Maybe not today, but sometime in the future the value of rookie cards could go through the roof.

We finally found Mike practicing his slide into second base at a baseball diamond in Herring Run Park that wouldn't be used until the next weekend. He had so much dirt on him from sliding that there was a depression in the lane leading to second base. Another few slides and he could have touched second from beneath the base. Yep, that's "dirty" Mike, alright.

Mark and I took positions on the empty infield; Mark at shortstop, me at second base, waiting for "dirty" Mike's latest practice slide. We had cut off his base running routes. He had to go through one of us. One of us could easily tag him out. We figured being tagged out was the last thing he wanted. When you're flirting with the law, or stealing a base, the last thing you want is to be called out.

Mike jumped up after touching second, dusted his shirt and pants off, and looked at us both. Clearly he was wearing most of the dirt from the diamond. His foot never left second, as if second base was a Christian sanctuary that protected him from eternal damnation. We weren't buying it.

"Heard you get an allowance, Mike. You want to come clean about all those cards you've been buying? Heard you got quite a stash of rookies." I began.

"Hey, I get lucky."

"Lucky or not, we hear you're dealing."

"You're not my mother! What law says I can't deal a few rookie cards to my advantage?" He shouted at us.

"No, but a five to one deal in cards just seems like you're fleecing the common man, Mike."

"Ain't no law against it. You're not the boss of me!" He said angrily. Then his voice changed. "Hey! I got an extra Brooks Robinson rookie card, you guys want to deal?"

Mark's hero was Brooks Robinson. He could imitate his every move at third base and make the throw to first every time. Mark was also holding the extra twenty cards that I had won in the yard. I know it isn't possible to hear someone's eyes grow bigger, but I heard sounds. I put my hand on Mark's arm as the sound grew from a clicking to something that resembled a squeaky door opening. Mark quickly regained his composure, but I imagined I still heard the quick clicking of eyelids.

"You're messing up the balance of nature, Mike. We may not have legal precedent, but we do have jurisdiction. I want you to think of your fellow human beings." I said in a calm voice.

"Do I have to?" He asked angrily.

"You Calf Lick?" Was my retort.

"Yeah." He answered. He knew he had to come clean. Maybe not his clothes, though.

"Then you have to." I said with authority.

"Dirty" Mike's shoulders slumped forward. He was caught between a rock and a hard place and he knew it. If he kept dealing rookies like he'd had, his time in purgatory could go on forever. You just can't trade rookie baseball cards for "Hail Mary's" and expect purgatory to be a short vacation on your way to heaven. Rookie cards are not indulgences where you get a pass card straight to heaven, no matter how you slice it.

I almost said, "If you don't, I'm tellin!" Telling who, I wasn't sure. I know it sounds petty, but a perpetually angry nun has my badge.

We couldn't bring Mike to justice. But we obviously put the fear of God in him and he seemed to curb his ways. Mark continued to work on sorting out local mysteries based on the "Hardy Boys" books and articles in "Boys Life." I stopped thinking that a few missing teeth and a lisp had anything to do with an exotic foreign accent. And I asked my dad what gams were: LEGS. He thought my mom had nice legs.

Two Timing the Comics

I'm not sure why the Franciscan nuns of the Shrine forced us to read "Hans Brinker, or The Silver Skates" and "Black Beauty." Blah, blah, some kid loans out his ice skates for a race and his dad has his head drilled by a quack and everybody lives happily ever after. Blah, blah, blah, a talking horse tells his life story of dragging a coach around London. They told us these books were literature. I thought they were a waste of time. They can't compare to the latest "Superman" and can't hold a candle to "Sergeant Rock and Easy Company" comics. Do those other stories have any relevance in today's world? I mean, none of the characters in the books we had to read could fly, deflect bullets, hold a 50 caliber machine gun in one hand while digging a fox hole with the other, and defeat the bad guy.

I want realism in what I read!

A dame wandered into our office holding a huge stack of "Archie" comics. Mark and I don't maintain a traditional office. It was a spot in the corner of the Shrine recess yard. No desks, no file cabinets, no bottle of scotch in the lower right drawer (I did have butterscotch candy in my pockets, though). It was just an open area with plenty of sunshine, a breeze, and an eye on the comings and goings of misdirected and misinformed humanity bent on who knows what.

"I have a bunch of 'Archies.' Want to buy some? Just a nickel a piece." Came the female voice.

She looked quite smart in her brown uniform jumper as she held them out. She had an innocent look about her, much like the paintings and portrayals of female martyrs we learned about in religion class. She, like all those martyrs, was a blonde hair, blue-eyed angel, except without a halo. But she had that look: "I-didn't-do-anything-wrong-but-I'm-still-going-to-look-good-as-I'm-burned-at-the-stake." Not a look one sees every day.

"Archie" comics were not our forte. "Easy Company" and "Batman" would be up our alley, but she held a huge stack and it piqued our interest. Either she was enthralled with Archie and Veronica, or she had just been given some comic book keys to some comic book castle.

I slowly unwrapped a piece of butterscotch candy, eyed her warily, popped it in my mouth and decided to ask some questions and look over the evidence.

"Lemme take a look." I said.

I wasn't about to tip my hand that I wasn't interested in "Archie" but a comic book for a nickel was pretty cheap. Either she needed quick dough for something (like a choir robe) or she didn't know what she was holding.

As she dumped the load in my lap, I immediately noticed something amiss. Sure, they were "Archie" comics, but the top part of the cover page was missing. If that wasn't enough, a few had greasy stains in the lower corners of the pages.

"Mark, what do you make of this?" I handed over most of the tomes.

"Looks and smells like mayo. I've read about this MO. Think the Hardy Boys had a similar mystery, can't remember the exact case, but I've seen this before. We have a two timing case, I'm sure of it."

"Where did you get these, doll? I asked.

"I didn't do nothing wrong, I thought it was a good buy!" She had a panicked look like she was about to get fingered for a crime she didn't commit and then had to go to confession to set her soul right.

"Calm down, sister, I'm just asking questions. Where did you get so many copies?"

"From a guy. He said I could triple my money,"

"You know this guy's name?"

"He said his name was Johnny."

Oh, great! Half of Bawlmer's male population is named Johnny. The rest go by Vinnie, whether that was their name or not. Somebody is digging out of date comics from the trash and selling them to the ignorant masses promising them big profits. All I have is a name. I might as well be trying to track down Santa Claus, but at least I know where he lives and how to find him.

There were ten copies of the same "Archie" comic with a few other copies of some other pulp mags that would only appeal to the softer gender. Each one was missing the top half of the cover page. Most had the telltale stains of mayonnaise and a few had a hint of egg salad.

"You guys going to buy any? If not, I'm going someplace else. I need to recover my twenty-five cents." She was regaining her confidence and some hustle after being rattled by my question.

"Slow down, lady." I unwrapped another butterscotch and offered her one, but she refused. It was probably too early in the day for her to indulge.

"You know what you have here?" I asked.

"Yeah, a bunch of mags that Johnny told me that I could triple my money on." I could tell she was good at her multiplications tables. A smart dame in some ways, not so bright in the ways of shady dealing.

"Look," I said. "The comic book industry sells a lot of comics every month. Many are on what's called a guaranteed sale. If the store doesn't sell all of them, all the store has to do is cut off the top of the cover, return it, and they get credit. They throw the rest of the pulp fiction in the trash."

"How do you know that?" she interrupted.

"My dad told me about it. He knows everything."

"Yeah, so does my dad." She answered softly.

"You ask your dad about this gambit?"

"No."

"Too bad. Anyway," I continued. "Your Johnny went digging to recover them and sold them to you for a fraction of the sale price and now it's up to you to peddle them off. You really think you can sell these with mayo and egg salad stains?"

"Johnny said that the stains and the smell would fade."

"Yeah, sure, and one day my Keds will be white again." I replied. I felt sorry for her, up to a point. She looked down at the pile of comics and her shoulders slumped. Once again I offered her a butterscotch and she took it. I popped another with her. At this rate I'll be wired out on sugar by two o'clock. I need to slow down on this stuff. One day I may, but today just didn't seem like the right day.

"So tell me about this Johnny."

"I see him in the neighborhood. He's about your size, has his hair slicked back like Elvis, wears a black jacket, always chewing gum." Now we're getting somewhere. From what she described, every boy in Bawlmer is now a suspect, pardon my sarcasm.

"Anything else?"

"He rides a black Schwinn."

"What size?"

"I dunno. A twenty-four, I guess." She narrowed it down to half of Bawlmer. I kept pressing.

"Anything unusual about the bike?"

"He always seemed to have baseball cards hitting the spokes. You know what I mean? He must have had twenty cards held with clothes pins on the fenders, and when he rode away, it sounded like a car or something taking off. Vroom!" She said as she made a motion with her hands going off towards the clouds.

He was obviously a suspect of means. Baseball cards don't last long against the spinning spokes of a Schwinn. The cards wear out and require constant replacement. It takes serious scratch to keep up the sound of vroom. We needed an area to focus on.

"Where you from, doll?" I asked.

"Parkside Drive."

Parkside Drive was on the other side of Herring Run Park. It was like living on the wrong side of the tracks, but only if you lived on this side of Herring Run. I suspect their citizens felt the same way about us. But someone could cover a lot of ground on a Schwinn and it wasn't unusual to see an invasion of hoods traversing the boundaries between the two sides of "The Run." We had narrowed down the area, but a black Schwinn sporting baseball card sound effects, pedaled by a gum chewing, slick haired suspect still wasn't much help.

"Anything else?" I pressed.

"Oh, yeah, he carries a transistor radio."

A transistor radio! Talk about well heeled! This goon is probably lousy with lettuce! I would give up my lifetime supply of chocolate Tastykakes to have one! I could listen to Orioles games during the sweltering summer nights, listen to WCAO's music as I pedaled my own Schwinn to Mark's barracks, and listen to Colts games in the fall. OK, I not only want to pinch this guy, I'm jealous.

"Look around the yard. Is he here?" I asked.

"No, I know he doesn't go here. "

"You think he's a Calf Lick?

"I don't think so. I think he's a publican."

"Bawlmer, Merlin" was founded as a haven of Calf Licks in the long ago past. I remembered that from history class. That's probably the only thing I remembered. As a short hand, of sorts, we just divided ourselves into Calf Licks and publicans. No need to get confused with all those religious denominations. We were taught all of those in history, but I decided it wasn't important to remember.

"Can I see those mags again?"

She handed them over and I took a piece of yellow paper (the kind with the small wood chips and wide spaced lines to practice your Palmer method of cursive writing) and started an evidence inventory using my sharpest #2 pencil. I noted that there were ten copies of the same "Archie's" comics, all with mayo stains on the bottom. Five copies of "Casper the Friendly Ghost" had egg salad stains, all the same issue, and five single copies of other mags. I noted which ones were torn at the edges as well as the stains. Two of the single mags had mustard on them. If you could eat paper this collection could have made a pretty filling lunch. I handed them back to our jumper clad client.

"We'll get back to you." I said.

"So you're not going to buy any?"

"No, sister, but we appreciate the offer. Want one for the road?" I asked, offering her yet another butterscotch.

"No thanks, I have to study."

I popped another butterscotch in my mouth as she walked away. That last candy may have been one too many, as I felt the sugar rush to my head. I'd probably get a task from Sister Knuckles of "I shall not disrupt the class" that I'd have to write five hundred times and turn in the next morning, because I was so wired. The pious penguins always told us we were all sinners in situations of excess of one sort or another. I think I could make the Olympic team, if sinning and writing a task in record time ever became a sport.

"Mark, look this over and tell me what you make of it." I handed him the yellow page of evidence inventory.

"I think you need to practice your cursive. Your hand-writing is horrible."

"That's the butterscotch. I write better when I'm sober. No, look over the entries."

"Well, I think we need to look at possibilities. Obviously, the mayo, mustard and egg salad stains came from a place that serves lunch. We can rule out Kiper's and the Manna-sota Market. They don't serve lunch. Doc's Pharmacy may be possible, but I don't think they carry that many comics. Same with High's on the other side of "The Run." Personally, I think this all comes from Belair Road. There's a Read's Drug that serves lunch and next to Read's is a five and dime. And there's the bowling alley underneath Read's. I think they share a dumpster. That dumpster sits out back in a huge parking lot and hardly anybody parks behind the stores. Somebody who knows the ins and outs of comic redemption and trash pickup could easily make a score."

"Know anything about comic book deliveries and pickups?"

"Last week of the month, usually. It's a matter of timing. Those comics didn't spend a lot of time swimming in mayo and egg salad by the look of the stains."

"You think our suspect has an inside track?"

"Likely."

"So we're looking for somebody who knows who works in one of the two stores?"

"Maybe, but it could be somebody that has just learned the routine. It looks like an inside job but it might not be."

What an opportunist! This aspiring jailbird may know somebody who works in a place that sells comics, or knows the routine, waits for his chance (while listening to his transistor radio), digs out the comics from the trash, then pedals them off to dames like we just met, and pockets a tidy sum. If I wasn't Calf Lick, and constantly fearful of a lightning bolt striking me dead for my sins, I might have joined him in this escapade.

I checked my calendar. Spelling test on Thursday, arithmetic quiz on Friday morning, confession on Friday afternoon. And it's the last week of the month. We could do a stake out Friday afternoon and Saturday morning.

"You up for a stake out Friday and Saturday?" I asked Mark.

"Yeah, we can do that. But I have to be home by noon Saturday. My parents are having dinner with my grandmother in Canton. I can't miss it. My Uncle Met will be there."

I knew what he meant. Sure, Mark might have to endure Mitch Miller and Lawrence Welk on TV, but he adored his Uncle Met, especially since he took Mark to Colt's games. Everybody liked Uncle Met. I thought he was great, and he never took me to a Colt's game. In fact, Uncle Met made me wish I was Polish instead of Bohemian.

"Meet me behind the Vilma Movies at 6PM." I said.

"Where we gonna hide our bikes?"

"We'll worry about that later."

On Friday afternoon I was released on my own recognizance from the Shrine and went home for dinner. It was tuna noodle casserole with carrots and peas in a sauce that resembled old Elmer's glue. And I hate peas. Little orbs of soft mush that can't be disguised in any dish known to man. Did I mention that I hate peas? I've been known to initiate a standoff when it comes to certain vegetables. I've wasted hours sitting at the dinner table alone trying to invoke my will in a standoff against my parent's best intentions to make me healthy by forcing me to eat vegetables in some form. My parents always won the standoff, by the way. Boy, I hate peas! Broccoli was a close second on my "do not eat" list. Spinach rounded out the top three.

I looked at the plate laden with tuna, noodles and the dreaded peas all stuck together with a sauce, then I looked to my dad. "Put some salt on it." He said. Salt was his answer to anything that was suspect in the food department. He must have picked up this culinary tip in the army.

I was on a deadline, though. I had less than an hour to pedal back to the Vilma Movies, and it was fifteen minutes away. I decided to hold my nose, chew sparingly, and get back to the case. Actually, dinner wasn't bad. It must have been the salt.

"I'm supposed to meet Mark on Belair Road. Can I go now?" I asked.

"Why are you meeting Mark on Belair Road?" My mom asked.

Think, boy, think! You can't divulge the real reason. Come up with a story. You can confess the lie next Friday, say a few "Hail Mary's" and be done with it, I told myself.

"There's a Colt's rally at the bowling alley. I'll be home before dark." I blurted out. I silently thanked whoever the patron saint was in charge of daylight saving time. An extra hour of daylight could make a big difference.

"OK, but watch yourself." My mom declared.

I'm not sure if my mom meant watch myself while dodging traffic, watch myself when it comes to rabid Colts fans, or just pay attention to life.

"I will." I answered.

My sister, who was sitting at the table listened intently to the exchange, and spoke up.

"Are you going to be near Mayfield Music and Cards?"

"I dunno." I lied.

"I need you to do me a favor. Go to Mayfield and pick up the top 40's lists."

"What? I'm gonna be near the bowling alley. Mayfield is like a block away!"

"It's only a few doors down. Can you pick up the top 40's lists? WCAO, WFBR, WWIN, WITH and Buddy Deane's list?"

"What?" I exclaimed in exasperation.

"Look, you walk into Mayfield, down the right side, next to the sheet music, and pick up each list. Won't take but a few seconds." She said in her breezy I'm your older sister, do as I say, tone of voice.

I looked at my mom. I looked at my sister. I finished my peas, what more could they want? I'm trying to crack a case, and all my mom and sister want is to make sure I don't get run over by a truck and bring back scraps of paper that catalog this week's most popular music. They'll never understand.

"Fine." I said, resigned to running the errand.

It was 5:45 PM when I pedaled up to Mayfield Music. I had to find these stupid lists in a hurry, scout out a place to hide our bikes, and get into position. Top 40 music lists seemed to be a rage among teens. Some teens, like my sister, watched the ups and downs of popular music like stock traders watch companies on Wall Street. You could be on cloud nine one week when your favorite tune was at number one, and then ready to throw yourself off the front porch when the song fell down the charts, but always on the prowl for the next big thing. Phrases like "Number 10 with a bullet" that local radio disc jockeys would exclaim over the air usually sent my sister to Mayfield Music in a frenzy, money in hand, clamoring to buy the new rising 45 rpm rock and roll record. I resented having to pick up these lists, especially since the Buddy Deane Show was on TV for two and a half hours every day and it seriously cut into my Mickey Mouse Club viewing. I didn't need to endure watching older kids dancing while I was deprived of picking up investigative tips from the "The Adventures of Clint and Mac" and "The Hardy Boys" serials. To make matters worse, my sister insisted that she try to teach me to dance during the Buddy Deane Show. It wasn't as bad as having to eat peas for supper, but it was near the top of my "do not do" list.

I nonchalantly walked into Mayfield Music, knowing that I had only seconds to spare since I neglected to lock up my bike. On the left side of the store was a long aisle of cards, neatly arranged by category, all created by Hallmark. Besides the usual "Happy Birthday," "Get Well Soon", and "Congratulation on Your First Communion" cards, they seemed to have cards for every conceivable occasion, except cards like "Enjoy Your Jail Time" and "Sorry You Were Convicted." If they sold those types of cards I probably would be a regular customer. On the right, beyond the cash register, held trays of the latest 45 rpm records separated by artists; above them was the sheet music needed by boys my sister's age so they could learn how to play the music of the 45 rpm grooves so dames like my sister would swoon at the sounds. On the shelf below held those priceless but useless scraps of paper that my sister told me to get. I picked up a few of each, lest she get on my case for not picking up enough for her friends, too. It felt like I was carrying the Bawlmer phone book.

I walked past the elderly female cashier, holding the top 40 tomes from local radio stations like I was carrying the Merican flag. I barely got a glance as I bolted out the door.

I pedaled down the alley between the Vilma Movies and the ladies dress shop and waited for Mark to arrive. The dumpster in the parking lot, between the five and dime and Read's Drug, sat like an abandoned Liberty ship in dry dock, it was that big. If you were going to dive into something that big and that deep, you might need some kind of diving gear. All this for some comics? I wondered. The profits must be huge.

The sun was beginning its descent and cast a long line of shadows from the buildings on Belair Road onto the parking lot. While the lights in the parking lot hadn't come on yet, lights over the exit signs from the Vilma were bright. Within a few hours all of the lights would form a wall of "V's" that left some parts of the parking lot in darkness while illuminating other areas in man-made sunshine. I spied an area forty feet away, against a steel barrier that could stop a tank from careening into the back of the houses below it. The shadows would be the perfect spot to park our bikes.

Exactly at 6PM Mark arrived. "Glad you made it, Mark. Park your bike down there with mine." I motioned towards the barrier where I had parked my Schwinn.

"Why are you carrying half of the phone book?"

"It's not. It's the top 40 songs for the week from the radio stations. You should be glad you don't have an older sister. She'd want to teach you to dance, too." I wasn't in the mood to elaborate on the arm-twisting inflicted by an older sister on her aspiring gumshoe younger brother. It would be just too embarrassing.

"Have you investigated the dumpster, yet?" Mark asked.

"Not yet. Look how big it is!"

Mark let out a whistle. "Looks almost as big as an aircraft carrier. There has to be a side entrance."

Mark did his military inspired zigzag to the side of the dumpster, walked around, inspecting every wall. Obviously he was looking for prints, or maybe just an easy access to the cavernous interior. As he slid the side door back, he motioned me over.

"You smell that?" He asked.

"Smells like garbage." I said.

"That's tuna salad. And I smell coddies, too. See those traces of mustard and crackers? Even if we don't catch this guy tonight, we can trace him and his comics to this dumpster if that stuff shows up in another load of comics. Look down there. You see that?"

"What am I looking at?" I peered into the bowels of the dumpster.

"Pierogies. Potato and onion, if I'm not mistaken."

"That makes a difference?"

"Sure. Other diner dumpsters in the area are probably throwing out hunks of beef or hot dogs. It's Friday. The smell of horseradish alone on a batch of comics will tell us we're watching the wrong dumpster if they're saturated with that perfume. Only publicans would be eating beef with horse-radish on Friday." I have to admit, Mark had a knack for fine details. But I was in no mood to stake out every dumpster in the Belair/Edison corridor. I just can't eat that many vegetables and make up that many stories to cover my tracks.

"Got a suggestion?" I asked.

"I'll go up on Belair Road and watch the front of Read's and the bowling alley. You stay here and watch the back."

Mark skulked up the alley next to the Vilma. He disappeared from view as he made the right turn towards Read's, the five and dime and the bowling alley. I turned my attention to the parking lot, the rear doors of the stores and the dumpster. It was now a waiting game.

The sun continued falling towards the horizon as I watched the parking lot and waited to hear a sound of approaching vroom.

A black 1955 Chevy, with glass pack mufflers wandered onto the lot, idled for a bit, then parked near the back of the buildings, and the occupants, a guy and a girl, appeared to be in some sort of wrestling match. They never got out of the car. It was the wrong kind of vroom, anyway.

Suddenly the back door of one of the stores opened and a young lug hauled a barrel and some boxes toward the dumpster. It must have been heavy, since I heard a loud grunt as he heaved all of the contents into the dumpster. He stopped, looked around, returned to the open door of the store, and disappeared. A few minutes later the '55 Chevy started up, growling a deep vroom, backed up, and slowly moved out of the parking lot. Obviously they didn't want a referee for their wrestling match, or whatever they were doing.

Mark walked back to join me. "Some kid just take out the trash?" He asked as he tapped me on the shoulder.

"Yeah, how did you know?"

"I was in Read's Drug. Saw the pile of trash in the back and heard the boss tell some flunky to get rid of it."

"Did you get a look at what he was tossing?"

"Yeah," he chuckled. "You won't believe this, but the boxes

must have had thirty comics in them along with other magazines like our moms would read. The barrel he dragged out was almost full of fish sticks, French fries, ketchup and tartar sauce. What did he throw in first, the boxes or the barrel?

I had to think a minute. I should know better. I wasn't paying attention to what went in first, but I knew now that the order of the tossed trash would make a big difference. Unsold comics with tartar sauce and ketchup stains (if the boxes went in first) could be traced easily, while a reverse order of disposal would make the mags almost pristine and resemble stolen federal bearer bonds: untraceable.

"We need to get to that dumpster before someone else does." I said.

Mark and I ran to the dumpster. Mark knew where the side door was, and went directly to it. As he pulled on the door it made a screeching sound that would make a great sound effect for some monster movie.

We scanned the cavernous contents of the bulk trash receptacle. We lucked out. The kid used this door to throw everything he hauled out of Read's. He must have been lazy in that he threw the boxes of comics and magazines in first, saving his strength to lift the barrel and pour its contents in over them. Ketchup and tartar sauce were draining down among French fries and half eaten fish sticks onto the cardboard boxes and the mags within. In a few minutes inked panels of graphic art would come to mingle with questionable edibles.

"By the looks of things, if our suspect doesn't show up in ten minutes to fish his treasure out, it won't be a treasure anymore." I observed.

"That's funny. Fish his treasure out. Fish sticks…treasure…I get it." Mark understood irony. I couldn't spell the word, though. I remember losing a spelling bee on that very word last year.

"We need to get back in position." I said.

Just as we returned to our darkened corner in the alley between the Vilma and the back of the ladies dress shop, we heard the unique sounds of baseball cards on Schwinn spokes. It was a vroom sound, no doubt about it and it was loud in the quiet expanse of the parking lot. Our suspect must have added a few more cards. He obviously was feeling pretty bold.

He pedaled right up to the dumpster, right to the side door. We heard the screech as he pulled the door back. I had a momentary vision of some prehistoric monster, head moving about in triumph as it held some unfortunate actor in its razor sharp teeth and biting him in half. I shook my head to clear away the vision.

"Mark, go back to Read's and grab the manager and tell him what's going on. Drag him out back. I'll take care of the suspect." Mark took off running. I had to stall the suspect long enough so he would be caught with the goods. I sauntered up to the dumpster's side door. Johnny's legs were all that poked out.

"You that hungry, Johnny?"

His legs stiffened and with a shove he was back on solid ground, looking at me like I was a ghost that protected dumpsters.

"You know my name?"

"Sure. How many Johnny's in Balwmer deal in unsold rejected stained comics?"

"You tryin to be a smart ass?"

"I am, but that's why I go to school every day."

Our jumper clad client was off the mark when it came to size between me and Johnny. This kid was three inches taller than me and weighed twenty pounds more than I did. This take down wasn't going to be easy. I hope Mark was spinning his best argument with the Read's manager to get him here quickly.

Johnny looked at me with a menacing look.

"You think you're funny?" He asked.

"Well, I am working on a comedy routine, but I'm saving it for later in my career."

"Look, little man, I don't have time for you. I need to get these comics out before they're ruined."

"Johnny, the jig is up. My partner and I will alert everybody to what you're up to. Unless you're willing to pedal to Arbutus or Catonsville, you won't sell any of these tainted comics around here. Give it up. Besides, I doubt the guys in West Bawlmer will appreciate you invading their turf."

He reached in his black leather jacket, most likely to flash a pair of brass knuckles to serenade me with some chin music. If he did, how was I going to explain the blood and bruises to my mom? Hey, mom, the Colt's fans were really excited. I doubt that explanation would fly far.

The cavalry arrived just in time, with Mark and the Read's manager, dressed in a long white coat, bursting through the back door.

"What's going on here?" The manager shouted.

"Johnny, here, wanted to dig out your returned and rejected comics from the dumpster." Mark didn't miss a beat, which was good since my heart had as I stared at a very angry Johnny.

"Boy, get out of here! Don't ever come near this dumpster again. If I even see you near it, you'll end up in it."

Johnny pedaled off in a loud vroom, screaming words that I only heard from my dad and uncles; and only when they were really mad.

"How did you get the manager out here so fast, Mark?"

"Just told him the truth. Every comic he threw out was one less comic he would sell at full price."

I pedaled back home as the sun was setting. I parked my bike in the back yard, knowing that Mark and I had just foiled yet another major crime spree. I walked into the kitchen, dropped the song lists on the table and innocently asked my mom what was for supper tomorrow night.

"Ham, diced potatoes and asparagus." She almost sang it; as if music would make it taste better.

Asparagus? I hate asparagus! It's my number four on the "do not eat" list.

Third Grade Airforce

There always seems to be some conflict going on in life. If it isn't some fighting going on in the world between countries' armies, then it's a couple of ginks in the Shrine school yard doing their best to punch each other out. If it isn't a surprise air raid drill across Bawlmer, then it's a couple of dames in a cat fight. If it isn't a ground war in dodge ball at recess, then it's an air war in class with spit balls. Where's the President of the USA with all this going on?

And then somebody comes to school with the plans for paper airplanes. Technology always finds a way to trickle down to the common man. Maybe it's because all of our dads had a subscription to "Mechanics Illustrated." And eight year old boys always pounce on the newest innovations in class disruption.

There are a lot of things that an eight year old boy would love to have. Even when you were sitting on his knee, Santa always had an excuse why he couldn't deliver a broadsword, a catapult to storm a castle, a 50 caliber air cooled machine gun from World War II, a Patton tank, or a jet fighter on Christmas morning. Since none of our dads brought these back from the war and none of those gems showed up under the Christmas tree, we had to make do with what we had at hand. What we had were pen knives, piles of sticks and tree branches, a lot of paper and a huge imagination.

Some big sticks and branches could be improvised to make broadswords and maybe we could whittle the right stick to resemble a kind of machine gun. A catapult was scaled down to a sling shot. None of Mark's troop of friends could figure out how to make a tank, even though they had tried many times. We were able to build an air force by learning how to fold paper into a delta winged fighter. Unfortunately, too many palookas, hoods and ginks also figured out how to wage a paper air war. And they carried their new found knowledge into class.

I was sitting at my desk just before class began, copying a kid's homework that I didn't complete myself because I was too busy the night before writing out a 500 line task. Sister Knuckles was late for roll call, probably because of last minute instructions on the newest and latest techniques in discipline utilizing common classroom items in crowd control. No doubt, there were lessons on sharpshooting with chalk and erasers, refinement of where to hit a kid on his body so it wouldn't leave a mark, and the art of assigning written tasks to inflict the worst hand cramps while still avoiding long term damage to the nerves in a kid's wrist.

A sleek yellow delta winged paper fighter landed on my desk just as I was copying the last arithmetic answer. It didn't have any markings on its wings like a white star in a blue circle, so I wasn't sure if what I was looking at was friend or foe. I looked around the class for a clue. All I saw were blank faces, but that was par for the course. I looked for a smile, a nod; even a smirk would help tip me off as to who launched the plane. Seems nobody was owning up to an early morning sortie.

Paper communication was rampant in third grade. The dames were the worst offenders in passing notes back and forth. I could only imagine that the volume got worse as one went up each grade. My uncle, who was a mailman, could probably double his pay from the US post office if note passing required a stamp. But a delta winged paper airplane rarely carried a message like "Meet me at recess" or "Have you seen the dreamy boy in the fourth row?" or "I have to tell ya what happened last night."

A second plane glided onto my desk just as I was handing back the homework to Benjamin. Ben was one of those types who always had his work ready and offered it to anybody who whined about a dog eating theirs. I used that "my dog ate it" excuse so many times that I was worried that Ben and Knuckles might think that my pet pooch was made out of paper mache.

I took note of the two delta wing fighters now sitting at rest on my desk. They had no markings like the P40's used by the "Flying Tigers" or the P51 Mustangs that were used in World War II. They didn't even have any nose art like the B17 "Flying Fortresses" used to display as they went on bombing missions over Berlin. I still couldn't figure out if I was being attacked or my desk was the closest thing to the deck of an aircraft carrier.

Sister Knuckles walked into class and air traffic control was halted, at least for the time being. I put the twin fighters in my desk, thinking that I'd soon understand what was going on. I'd consult with Mark at recess to see if he knew what might be going on in the confines of the skies within class.

"You see a few delta wings in class this morning?" I asked Mark at our office during recess.

"Yeah, before you walked in, there musta been a squadron in the air. I'm tellin' ya, if those planes were launched by four guys, I bet it would have been in formation, ya know? But what was flyin' was done by one gink, Ted. You know who he is?"

"Ain't he the one who wears that green Navy flight deck jacket?"

"You mean the one from Sunny Surplus?"

"Yeah, that one. Doesn't he have some drawing on the back of it?"

"Yep." Mark laughed. "It's Woody Woodpecker, goes from the collar all the way down to the bottom of the jacket. Looks really neat, too!"

I knew that jacket. Actually, I wanted a jacket like that so I could draw and paint something on the back, like Charlie Brown. Even the smallest size jacket would be big on me, but there was some kind of badge that went with the jacket and decorating the back of it. While we all wore a uniform at the Shrine, a deck jacket with a cartoon on the back said, "I may be part of the flock, but my wool looks better."

"So, you know what Ted's up to?" I asked.

"There's a rumor going around. Seems he's recruiting. Now, let's not jump to conclusions, but what I'm hearin' is Ted wants to start an air war…in class…while Knuckles is teaching. The group that gets caught tossing airplanes loses."

"Is he crazy?" I exclaimed.

"Well, he does have Woody Woodpecker on the back of his flight jacket. And besides, hasn't he always acted a bit…strange?"

"Well, yeah, but it sounds like he wants all of us expelled."

"So, you got any ideas?" Mark asked.

"How many sheets of paper do you have?"

"I dunno. I brought the usual 100 sheets with me, but I have another 300 at home. What're you thinking?"

"Not sure, but somehow we have to stop it, or at the least make sure that the entire class doesn't end up at Brehms Lane Elementary."

"Is that the sound of wheels I hear?"

"No, that's me fiddling with the change in my pocket."

"You have money, today?"

"Yeah, I had a pretty good day in bottle returns on Saturday. But the way this air war idea is shaping up, I may have to buy a box of butterscotch instead of my usual stash of candy."

"Butterscotch probably isn't the answer." Mark mused.

"I'm sorry, what was the question." I asked. Obviously my sugar level was dropping below the level of the over active kids in the yard....I was usually number one on the nun's "out-of-control" list.

"Never mind. You were thinking...?" Mark continued.

"I can't get involved in this air war." I answered. "Knuckles is just itching for a reason to get me expelled. I know it's because my mom never went through with Sister Monica's direction to make sure that I got a beating every day. But I can't just let this war happen. Any paper airplane in my direction, or on my desk and she'll be parading around at recess singing ding, dong, David's gone."

"Would she be singing that with a bunch of first graders dancing around her?" Mark laughed as he mimicked the lollipop guild in the "Wizard of Oz."

"Oh, shut up! We have to come up with the perfect diversion." I continued.

"You mean division? Didn't we learn that in arithmetic last week?"

"How do I know? You pay attention, I don't!" I answered. "We need to find out how many ginks want this war and where they sit in class."

"What we need is a clueless stoolie." Mark observed.

"I'm not so sure. You're right, we need a stoolie, but we can't have someone who doesn't have a clue."

"Well, you just whittled the possibilities down to about…" as Mark counted off on his fingers, "Maybe 3."

"Maybe we need to get Ben on our side to help us out." I said.

"Ben? Are you serious? That kid asks for help putting on his knapsack in the afternoon!"

I laughed. "That's what he wants everybody to think. Poor Ben. Poor kid. Hah! My patootie!

"You know something I don't?"

"Maybe. Listen, you know any other kid in class who always has his homework ready? Every day?"

Mark thought for a minute. "No." He answered.

"You ever hear Ben miss a spelling quiz or an arithmetic flash test?"

"Well, no, but…."

"No buts…he's sharp in class. He's faking it at recess!" I declared.

"How do you know?" Mark asked. He was wondering what I picked up on that was still a mystery to the rest of the class.

"You and I kinda know what stupid is, right?" I asked.

"Yeah." Mark answered as he was trying to furrow his brows. Furrowing brows would become easier as we grew older.

"You just can't be stupid…some of the time. If you're stupid at recess, you're gonna be stupid in class. Ben is putting on an act in the yard. I'm not sure why and I don't care, but I think we can use his stupid act to find out what's about to go on. Let's go find him."

It wasn't hard to find Ben in the school yard. His act at recess made most kids avoid him like he had the chickenpox. We found Ben, clutching the chain link fence, pulling and shoving it back and forth while he whistled to the stray dogs across the street. He acted like a prisoner of war from some old World War II movie I'd seen at the Vilma. He would have looked the part, too, except his brown uniform was freshly starched.

"You sure he's ok in the head?" Mark asked.

"Not exactly, but I'm gonna go with my gut."

"Is that near your craw?"

"How should I know? Just follow my lead, ok?"

I tapped Ben on the shoulder. "Hey, Ben, how's things going?"

Ben turned to us with a look of amazement, like we'd interrupted an elaborate escape plan that involved a diversion by a pack of stray animals. Ben reminded me of Peter Lorre in many ways. He was on the small side with a look of desperation in his large bulging eyes. He even had that same almost apologetic sounding, breathless high pitched voice I'd heard in so many of Peter Lorre's movies. It made sense that many students avoided him. A few dames I knew described him as "creepy."

"Hey, Dave! Hey, Mark! How're you guys doin?"

"We're fine, Ben. You making some new friends on the other side of the fence?"

"Yeah, maybe, I guess." He answered. "Funny about dogs and cats. Ever think about it? You can coax a dog over to the fence if you talk a certain way, but cats...they kinda know that they don't want any part of being near a pen, ya know? Cats won't even get near the fence, but dogs...that's a different story. They'll come over and lick your hand and let you pet 'em, but even they know they don't want any part of coming inside. Sometimes I'm not sure if I'd want to be a dog... or a cat. Ever think about that?"

"No, Ben." I answered. "Never thought about it." I'd heard that all dogs go to heaven, but nobody in the Calf Lick church ever said anything about where cats would end up.

Mark was standing to the side, his finger pointing to his head and twirling it while he rolled his eyes. I jabbed Mark in the side with my elbow as I tried to continue the conversation.

"Ben, Mark and me need your help." I began.

"Yeah? Sure. What can I do for ya?"

"We need you to find out the dope on something that we hear may happen. It may not, but we need the skinny just in case. Think you can help us?" I asked.

"Guess so." Ben answered. "What'd ya need to know?"

"The scuttlebutt is that two groups of guys want to toss paper airplanes at each other during class. The group that gets caught loses. They'll probably get expelled and end up at Brehm's Lane. You know about Brehm's Lane Elementary?"

"Really? Brehm's Lane? Their fence is like two feet taller than ours. Why would anybody want to get sent there?" Ben asked in a voice that just didn't sound quite "there."

"We're not sure, but Mark and me can't find out nuttin. We need somebody on the inside. That's where you can help us."

"OK. You want me to be a dog or a cat?" Ben blurted out.

"What?"

"A dog or a cat? Cat's don't wanna get close, dogs will. Which one you want me to be?" Ben continued.

"Be a dog, Ben. Get as close as you can. Get as much info as you can and let Mark and me know. But it all has to be on the "QT." Got it? Not a word to anybody about what we're doin." I said hoping that I'd got the message across without giving him a treat and asking him to sit up, roll over and stay.

"A blood hound or a beagle?" He asked.

"I don't care. Whatever you think is best, Ben." I finally said. I didn't have any doggie treats on me anyway.

"Blood hounds are really good at sniffing out clues. Beagles are too, but they're really loyal. A blood hound might spill the beans and let everybody know what's going on because they bark more. You said this has to be on the "QT" so maybe I'll be a beagle. That OK with you?"

"Yeah, sure, Ben. Be a beagle." I answered. I was beginning to wonder about my choice of spy.

"You don't have to worry about me. I don't have fleas or cooties, either. My mom checks me every morning."

Mark and me walked back to our corner office, all the while Mark was shaking his head.

"That lug is nuts I tell ya." Mark exclaimed.

"He ain't nuts. He's just got a different view of life, that's all." I answered.

"Yeah, sure he does. He's just like the people my parents tell me about who are patients at Spring Grove Hospital."

"Mark, Ben will come through for us. I know he will. Just wait and see."

"And when he does, how're you gonna understand him when he's whoofing and barking what he found out? Ever think of that? You ever been to Brehm's Lane? I mean, is it a nice school? I wanna know before we all get sent there."

"We ain't all gonna end up at Brehm's Lane." I declared.

"And this is coming from the guy who just hired a kid who's gonna find out about a classroom air war acting like a dog. Oh, I feel so much better, now." Mark answered in a sarcastic tone.

Mark had a point, even though I wasn't about to confess to it. Ben did act weird and I might not understand him if he came to the office wagging his tail and wanting me to scratch his belly, before he told us what we needed to know. But without any other inside info to go on, he was our best bet.

Three days later Ben ran into our office, breathless. He seemed excited to see both of us and as I was unwrapping a butterscotch, Ben grabbed my hand and began to lick it.

"Ah, Ben, you don't need to lick my hand. You can save that for the archbishop when you get confirmed. Stop! Did you find out anything?"

"Oh, yeah!" Ben said, as he stood up and began to resemble a human being. "The air war is set to happen this Thursday at 2:45 pm. It's just a few minutes before we get set free. There's five guys on each side. They've been folding airplanes like crazy!" Ben panted, which made me uncomfortable, not the size of the air force that could hit the skies in class, but Ben's panting.

"Thanks, Ben. You've been a big help." I said.

"Oh, and one more thing. Two of the guys are aiming for you." Ben said, pointing at me.

Great, I thought. I was going to be a target even though I wouldn't toss a delta wing in this paper dog fight. Knuckles would assume I was in on it just because I'd have planes hitting me in the head and landing on my desk. I had to stop this air war before it started. Ben scampered off back to his place at the fence, no doubt to tell his four-legged friends about his adventure inside the yard.

"Don't you think you owe the kid a milk bone, or something?" Mark asked.

"No! I'll give him one of my Tastykakes tomorrow, smart aleck."

"You sure Ben should have sugar? I hear it ain't good for a dog to have sugar." Mark replied, laughing.

"Very funny. Very… funny."

"So you have a plan to stop the bombing of class?"

"Yeah, matter of fact I do. At 2:45 when Knuckles' back is turned and every gink is ready to launch a plane, I'm going to drop every book in my desk on the floor. That ought to get her attention and stop whoever is involved to rethink what they're doing."

"You do know that Knuckles is gonna pick you out and give you a task, right?"

"Yeah, but it's better than going to Brehm's Lane Elementary for the rest of the year. And besides, I have a plan for the task, too."

I picked up a tip from a seventh grade hood that my sister knew. He told me that since he knew he'd get more than a few 500 line tasks in a school year, he used to write out the most likely sentences during summer vacation. Every week he'd write lines like "I will not disturb the class." and "I will not talk in class." about 50 times. By September he'd have enough tasks written that when he did get one in class, he'd just go to his file, pull out the required number of papers and hand them in the next day. It was not only a time saving strategy; he told me that it was turning into a profitable part time job selling the task papers to other students. I began the practice about a month ago. Every night, after my homework was finished, I'd write "I will not disturb the class" about 50 times. I had enough lines finished so even if Knuckles gave me a task, I already had it, ready to hand in.

It was 2:43 pm on Thursday and Knuckles was giving us the lesson on…I wasn't even paying attention. She could have been reciting some life of a saint, teaching us about rectangles and squares, or how George Washington crossed the Delaware River guided by a saint to defeat the Redcoats. I was focused on the clock above her. I heard the faint rustling of paper all around me, as half the boys in class were bringing up their paper air force and preparing them for flight. The clock continued to tick and Knuckles kept blabbing about…something.

Sister Knuckles was busy writing notes on the blackboard as I looked over my shoulder to see a few arms, planes in hand, practicing the inevitable toss. I looked at the clock and there was less than ten seconds left before ten boys would put the Wright brothers' first flight to shame.

WHAM!!

My seven text books hit the floor all at once. The notes in English on the blackboard immediately resembled Chinese letters as Knuckles lost her concentration and composure. Between her surprised scream and the screech of chalk across slate, came the simultaneous thump of hands stuffing something in books and returning to desktops. The US army would have been proud at such combined precision.

"Who did that?" Knuckles roared.

I raised my hand. "Sorry, 'Ster." I said.

"David! David! What is the matter with you?"

I'd been asked that question many times by my parents, aunts, uncles, grandparents, priests, and nuns. I rarely had an answer. Even when I did have an answer, it just seemed better to shake my head and be quiet. I shrugged my shoulders at Knuckles. I knew what was coming.

"You, young man, have a task."

I know, I thought. I already have it finished.

"I want you to write out both the Latin and English mass from your missal five times. I want it tomorrow morning."

"But," I stammered. My jaw dropped to the desk. I thought I was prepared.

"You want it to be ten times?"

"No,' Ster."

"If I hear one more peep out of you, you'll write it backward! You understand?"

"Yes, 'Ster."

My dad had a very large, some called it a "salty," vocabulary. Some people have a kitchen cabinet filled with exotic spices. You used some spices more than others, but just in case, you always had other spices to substitute in case of emergency. One of my dad's most used spicy cuss words began with an "s" and I'd heard him use it shouted in triumph and uttered softly under his breath, much like a chef would use something like cayenne pepper in a recipe.

Sitting at my desk, out-foxed by a pious penguin, it was the first time I ever cussed like my dad.

That Dame

I try my best to keep a low profile. I'm not some flashy palooka trying to get my mug in "Life Magazine." I'm just an 8 year old gumshoe running around like a rookie outfielder doing my best to catch the foul balls that the Franciscan nuns decided were going into the cheap seat bleachers (and then to hell). They may think that some kid has no hope for the future, but my job isn't to make that decision. I'm trying to make sure some gink is not doing so much damage to the world that we all end up paying for his extended vacation in stir where both the screws and hatchet men in the big house are telling him that they're his new best friends.

But, like I said, I try to keep a low profile. Somehow, though, some dame ends up having you on their radar as a catch and she won't take no for an answer. She may be drawn to the idea of being romantically involved with a gumshoe, maybe thinks you have ruddy good looks like Rowdy Yates in TV's "Rawhide." I'm too young to be ruddy. I've seen the cowboys on TV. There's nothing romantic about a cowhand in a cattle drive or being a private eye. But that doesn't stop some dames.

I was doing my best not to fall asleep in history class when Kevin nudged my arm. I thought he was trying to save me from an "I will not fall asleep in class" task, when he motioned to my right. I looked over an aisle. Batting eyelashes so long they could launch a small plane in their breeze, sat Veronica.

She was looking straight at me and smiling, so I knew she wasn't suffering from a nervous tick. She lifted her right hand just above the desktop and coyly waved her fingers at me. Stupid me, I waved back. What was I thinking? I might as well be a rockfish in the Chesapeake Bay taking a piece of bait on a hook. And just like a hooked rockfish I knew I would have to fight for my life.

Mark and I met in our outdoor office at recess to review the day's crime files. So many goons headed to purgatory, and even more were blazing a trail to hell; we weren't sure where to begin. So many were headed in the wrong direction that I doubted Mark and I could redirect all of the southbound traffic.

I was scratching my head when Veronica strode up. This was a dame who had a hard exterior, but you just knew she was soft on the inside. She reminded me of a candy. I just couldn't think of which one at that moment.

"Hi, guys!" She said with an off-hand greeting that implied she wasn't interested in our work, but knew how to solve what we were facing. How come dames act like that? Even if they're right, why shove it in our face?

"Hi, Veronica." I answered as I tried to keep my cool while my blood was boiling. I wasn't sure why, though. Oh, yeah, now I remember. My dad told me to never let a dame know what you're up to. If you do, they'll either tell you to stop, do it differently, or tell you how to do it better. As cool as she was coming off, that's how hot my blood was going.

"Call me Ronnie, Dave." She answered. Oh great, now we're into nicknames. That's like two steps away from going steady, and luckily I didn't have a school sweater.

"What can I do for you, Veronica?" I asked, while trying not to sound defensive.

"Ronnie" she corrected.

"OK, what can I do for you," I paused. " Ronnie?"

"Oh, nothing." She replied. I've heard that line from so many dames, I knew she wanted something. I remember last holiday season when my sister's boyfriend asked her what she wanted for Christmas. "Oh, nothing" my sister said. The dumb sap believed her! He showed up without a Christmas present! He wasn't her boyfriend on December 26th.

"Watcha doin?" Ronnie asked in that kind of bird song voice so many dames use when they're trying to pump information out of a guy. She definitely wanted something no matter how many sweet "nothings" came out of her mouth.

"Mark and I are looking over cases and deciding which one to investigate first."

"You know what you need?" Ronnie answered with so much confidence dripping onto the recess yard I prolly would have slipped on it if I was walking.

Besides an "A" in arithmetic, a couple of dumb finders so we can break a case or two, and butterscotch, I couldn't think of anything.

"No, what do I need, Ronnie?" I answered.

"You need a girl Friday."

It was Tuesday.

I couldn't figure out why I would need some girl on Friday. My look probably resembled the one I usually wore in multiplication drills in class. And just like the nuns could see that I didn't know what 8 times 7 equaled, Ronnie read my mug as well as those all-seeing nuns. Ronnie, though, seemed to be able to read my mind. She reached into her jumper pocket and pulled out a butterscotch and tossed it to me.

"Thanks." I said. I needed a sugar shock to my noggin to help me wade through this pile of crime reports and evidence sheets. Somehow, this dame knew what I needed.

"A girl Friday would help you sort through all that paper. Maybe, if she was really good, she'd even help you on some cases by asking questions of the girls in the yard. She may even be willing to work undercover. At the very least, she'd make sure you always had a supply of butterscotch."

"And where would I find such a dame, if she even existed?" I asked.

Ronnie was swaying back and forth, batting those long eyelashes, toying with the hem on her jumper. It was all bait on a hook and I was that hungry rockfish. It didn't matter that I knew this. I took the bait anyway, accompanied by a piercing feeling in my lip. I fought the urge to stand up and throw my head from side to side, though. She was smooth. She must have relatives living on the Chesapeake Bay who make a living fishing and crabbing.

"I can be your girl Friday." She answered. I thought I heard the ratcheting of a fishing reel and felt a sharp tug on my mouth as she said this.

"You? What makes you think you can handle this dirty work, doll?"

"First, my dad is a Bawlmer City flatfoot and I listen to him tell my mom about every case he's working on. Second, I can talk to the broads in the yard and I know you both are too shy to do that. Third, I've earned an "A" for best organized notes in all my classes. Fourth, you won't get a lead out of the pious penguins around here because they know you're going to hell in the fast lane and they won't talk to you. And, fifth, I know you're addicted to butterscotch and my uncle owns a candy store. Oh, and one more thing, don't call me doll!"

"Sorry, sister." I answered.

"Don't call me that, either!"

Mark and I looked at each other with a stunned look on our

faces. It was like looking in a mirror, except I knew I was better looking than him. This dame had chutzpah. She had moxie.

"We can't pay you anything." I said, trying to feign a head move to the right as I worked to dislodge this baited hook held by Ronnie.

"I'm not looking for scratch." She said.

"What are you looking for?"

"Experience. Working under cover, if that's what it takes. I want to learn the ropes. My dad talks about his cases, but never goes into the dirty details. I want to learn the details."

I took a second look at this tomato. I never really looked her up and down. While it was true her lashes could keep a kite flying at 500 feet above us, beneath those lashes were gray eyes that resembled concrete; and a look that told you she could be just as hard. The kind of dame that can scream at the mistakes you make with just a look on her face. Her short wavy dark brown hair just added to her appearance that told you she was a girl, but you just didn't want to get on her bad side. Her pouty mouth, though, gave her away as a softie. The scary part was she seemed to know all of this and she had no reservations about using what my dad called "feminine wiles." Even though Mark was by my side, I felt we were outnumbered.

"Lemme take a look at those papers." She said curtly.

Mark and I handed them over without even a mumbled protest of "but you're a girl!"

Ronnie rifled through the yellow pages we had collected, quickly examining each one. She quickly sorted them out in piles, tossing a few in the air.

"What's this?" she asked, as she held up a picture of two stick figures exchanging a square of some sort.

"We caught this a few weeks ago at recess." I answered defensively.

"Really?" It was the first time I heard sarcasm cascade like a water fall. And my shirt suddenly felt damp.

"Look, our sketch artist has the mumps. It was the best we could do under the circumstances." I replied.

"And you're going to finger some lug based on this? It might hold up…if we were in first grade!" Ronnie crumpled the paper and threw it to the ground.

Organization seemed to come with a hard-nose attitude. I looked at Ronnie's nose and it didn't look very hard, but I didn't dare reach out and touch it because I was afraid she would sock me in the jaw.

In less than five minutes, she had sorted out the papers into three piles.

"We have a klepto who is bent on stealing pencils and fountain pens." She declared.

"WE?" I thought. Since when did Mark and I suddenly become "we" that included a girl?

"We also have someone who likes to collect stray jacks."

There's that "we" again.

"Lemme see those papers!" I said impatiently. I was sure we were dealing with at least fifty crimes of theft, until I looked over the piles she had organized. Ronnie was right. The disappearance of so many pencils and fountain pens had all occurred within a three week period. The reports of fountain pen ink refills disappearing happened within the last two weeks. With so many ginks wearing pocket protectors, I knew we couldn't look for shirt stains. Whoever it was, these massive thefts were well thought out and planned, otherwise we would see a blue ink streak on a suspect's shirt as long as Bawlmer's Gay Street.

"I'm guessing you have something in your head, Ronnie." I said.

"I do. But you gotta let me work the yard."

"OK, but you have to let us know, even if you have to use the phone."

Ronnie sauntered off, jumper swaying in the spring breeze. From behind, she looked soft; I just wouldn't want to meet her face to face in an alley if she was in a certain mood.

"You dizzy with that dame?" Mark asked.

"Me? Nah, I ain't dizzy with no dame." I replied angrily.

The following week I was letting off steam playing a hotly contested game of curb ball where Lyndale Avenue alley and Brendan Avenue met. The score was tied at two in what I believed was the 18th inning. A game of curb ball only ended when someone's mom would come out of the back door and yell her son's name, telling him it was time for supper. We paid attention to the score, never the inning. A game could last five minutes or five hours. That was especially true on Saturdays in the summer when we were always interrupted by "Arabbers" peddling fruits and vegetables in horse drawn wagons, the knife sharpening guy who worked the area as well as the Good Humor Man. Our side had a man on second and I was up. Just as I was taking aim at the top of the curb and about to unleash a blazing pinky fastball on it, a black Ford Fairlane with a cherry on top and a shield on the door rolled into the center of the field. Actually it was the intersection. We played curb ball in the middle of the street.

I heard the yell, "Cheese it! It's the cops!" and turned around. My friends had disappeared like a balsa wood plane had just met a cherry bomb. The flatfoot driver motioned me over to the car. I wasn't afraid. We were on the same side of the law, except maybe he knew that I was operating without a badge. OK, maybe I was a bit nervous. I walked over to the side of the Ford and saw Ronnie sitting in the passenger seat. Great, I thought, this dame wants me to post bail for her.

"Dave, this is my dad. I have a lead. Something you need to follow up on." Ronnie said as she leaned over to the window.

"Hi, officer. Watcha got, Ronnie?" Her dad and I exchanged knowing looks, the same kind of look that cops in the murder and the robbery divisions give each other when they know there's a connection in the crimes they're working on.

Ronnie handed her dad a folded sheet of paper and he handed it to me. When I opened it, my jaw dropped. On it was a name. A name of a dame! It took me a few seconds to recover my composure. Calf Lick girls don't act this way. They all want to grow up and be housewives, nurses or secretaries. The most wayward of them want to become nuns. I couldn't believe what I was reading.

"You sure about this, Ronnie?" I finally asked.

"It's the best lead we got. I've been asking around the yard, talked to the penguins, and even watched her playing jacks at recess. She can pocket a jack faster than one bounce of a ball. And get this. I sit a row over from her in class and every morning her pencil case is almost empty. By 3 o'clock it's bulging. Been watching her for a week now. Every day, same thing. And each day she uses a different pen in cursive class."

"So what do you want me and Mark to do?"

"Tail her for a few days. Watch her when she walks into school and then when she leaves and pay attention to her book bag. I'm guessing it gets bigger between 7 and 3. Meanwhile I'll work the inside, leaning on my stool pigeons."

Ronnie's dad had this wide grin on his face that said, "That's my girl."

"We'll get on it." I said.

As the cop car drove off every boy who was playing curb ball magically reappeared out of basement doors, from behind bushes and out of garbage cans.

"You under arrest?"

"They takin you to the big house?"

"Didja kill somebody?"

"Naw," I answered. "Just Po-leese work. Bawlmer City Pleese need my help in a case." I answered with a voice of authority.

We were just about to resume the game when Mickey's mom called him for supper. Game over. We'd begin a new game on Saturday morning. I walked down the alley to our house and went straight for the blower to call Mark.

I dialed the phone. It rang. It rang 17 times before I remembered there's a family secret code. My aunt always refused to answer the phone unless a code of rings was employed.

"Mom! What's Aunt Dee's secret code for phone calls?" I yelled. I was frustrated. Why can't people just pick up the phone when it rings? Then I remembered, she had a party line and not every phone call would be for her.

"Let it ring twice, then hang up, count to twenty and dial again." Came my mom's voice from upstairs.

I did as instructed. On the fourth ring, my aunt answered.

"Hi, Aunt Dee, it's me, David. Can I talk to Mark, please?" Why my aunt wouldn't recognize my voice was a mystery, but she yelled for my partner. He was on the line in seconds.

"What's up?" Were his first words.

"We have to be at school tomorrow morning for a 7 AM stakeout and we may have to be the last to leave."

"7 AM? How am I supposed to explain that?"

"Tell your mom you have a requiem mass tomorrow."

"Did somebody die?"

"Somebody always dies! Just tell your mom you have mass. Ask her for 45 cents and I'll meet you at Pelham Bakery at 7 AM. We have a suspect that we have to tail."

"Who came up with the suspect?"

"Ronnie."

"Are you sure you ain't gettin dizzy with that dame?"

"No! I ain't dizzy with no dame! Just meet me at Pelham Bakery."

The Pelham Bakery opened at dawn and had a mindboggling array of donuts and pastries first thing in the morning for a sugar coated breakfast. I always ordered their "Bismark," a pastry which was as big as my face with honey-dipped icing oozing from every corner. With a cuppa chocet moo juice to go along with this battleship sized pastry, I was wide awake for the next three hours. Just what I needed on a stakeout, or a requiem mass; whichever came first.

I conned my mom out of 50 cents the night before, telling her I had to officiate at a requiem mass as an altar boy. Don't laugh. Undercover work demands we wear a lot of different disguises. And Mark and I had picked up many crime leads posing either as altar boys or singing in the choir. There was always a chance that between two altar boys, a priest, a choir, and a load of pious kneelers filling the pews at a Calf Lick mass; at least two had something to hide. Besides, parents don't quibble between sending one of the faithful to heaven and a couple of quarters for early morning breakfast when one of their offspring is helping the dearly departed on their way. But this was all a ruse to get a jump on tailing a suspect. If there was a mass that morning, somebody else would be reciting the prayers for whoever was taking the big sleep.

I was sitting outside the Pelham, my cuppa moo beside me with icing from my "Bismark" dripping onto every finger as well as the tips of my shoes, as Mark strode up. I should have asked for extra napkins.

"Mornin'. Jeet jet? So, who's the gink we're looking for?" He asked.

"Get your brefast first. I'll fill you in later." I responded.

Mark walked into the Pelham and in minutes he was back outside sitting beside me. He had two honey dipped donuts and a steaming cup.

"That a cuppa joe?" I asked.

"You kidding me? I won't be ready for a cuppa my own joe until I'm like….fourteen. At least that's what my dad tells me. I don't get it, though. I can drink his Natty Boh, but I'm not old enough to drink coffee." He sighed.

I understood, to a degree. Your dad would gladly share his beer, but not his coffee. Probably had to do with moving gun installations at first light during the Ruhr River crossing, and since neither Mark nor I moved canons at 5 AM, I guess they felt justified. I can only imagine what they planned six years from now. Which comes first, coffee or camouflaging cannons in the neighborhood?

"No, it's hot chocolate." He finally said. "What do we have?"

"Jeet?" I asked.

"Yeah, I'm done."

I handed him the folded sheet that Ronnie had given me the day before. Mark read the name on the paper. He folded it, then unfolded it, and read it again. The look in his eyes told me that he couldn't believe the suspect's name any more than I had. It was like being told that the pope wasn't a Calf Lick.

"No way! It's a dame! It can't be her. I've known her since first grade. Her hand is the first to go up whenever the monsignor asks who wants to be a nun. I can't believe it." Mark said in disbelief.

"Look, I have a hard time believing it too. Other than that one time she tried to kiss me in second grade after the bell rang, and that time she put a note in my lunch box telling me she wanted to marry me, I've never heard a peep out of her. Oh, and that time she was hugging me during air raid drills. And then there was that time she…." My voice trailed off as I shuddered.

"What time?" Mark asked with a glint in his eye.

"Never mind. It was a long time ago. Like last year."

"Was she getting dizzy on you?"

"Maybe, but I think she outgrew it." A whole year at the Shrine makes you grow up pretty fast.

"So, what's the plan?" Mark asked. I was happy that he decided to concentrate on the stake out and not my unfortunate run-in from last year.

"I'm not sure which way she walks to school. We have to split up and cover both avenues. Pay attention to her book bag. Ronnie said that she walks into school with an almost empty bag but at the end of the day, it's pretty big. We're also going to have to watch her during class."

"Doesn't give us much to go on. What about tailing her before and after recess? The way I see it, she has to have opportunity, not just motive. I'll bet her pencil case swells right after lunch."

"You're right. But how are we gonna finger her?" I wondered.

"The coat room!" Mark exclaimed. "We hide in there when we take our lunchboxes back there and pick up our jackets for recess. We can be the last to leave, or at least maybe one of the last to leave."

The coat room in a Calf Lick school was a dark alley at the back of the classroom. This is where you hung your jacket, your snow covered boots, and put your lunch box when you reported for duty first thing in the morning. There was only enough room for a single file procession to navigate its dark interior. More than one person squeezing into the room, and God forbid it was a dame vying for space within the confines, and you would be getting too chummy with classmates. It was yet another reason for confessing your sins. But, since there were openings on either side that opened to the room, we had a view of the empty desks abandoned by kids who were clamoring for the fresh air of the recess yard. We decided to wait a bit in the hidden coat room when the bell rang for recess and see if our suspect was casing the joint and picking up pens.

I finished my bologna sandwich, (the third one this week) and was ready to polish off my Tastykakes, when Knuckles announced that it was time to go outside. The frenzied crush of students rushing towards the door looked like a stampede except without the "mooing"' sounds made by cattle in a similar situation. Mark and I casually walked towards the coat room, empty Davey Crocket lunch boxes in tow, and waited in the darkness. Hopefully, Knuckles wouldn't patrol the empty room.

Sister Knuckles had left with all the other misdirected kids, no doubt to herd them into a group so they wouldn't stray. Some Calf Lick religious dames take that whole shepherding thing way too seriously. Mark and I waited at the corner of the coat room. The classroom was empty and we thought we may have missed an opportunity. Almost every desk had a pencil, a fountain pen or both just waiting to be snatched, but we were the only ones in the room.

We were about to join everyone else and patrol the yard when the door quietly opened. We froze. It might be some kid who forgot a secret toy he wanted to show off to his friends, or maybe a dame who was sent back by Knuckles to get something from the room. It wasn't. It was Christine, the name of the dame Ronnie wrote on the paper and handed to us. If she gets caught I doubt the pious penguins would allow her to enter the convent since we all knew that nuns never committed a sin in their lives. An arrest record for theft, even in the third grade, would probably leave her out of the eligible pool of sales clerks at Hutzler's Department Stores. Some people just don't think ahead; or if they do, just not further than the next morning. If we didn't short circuit her crimes and show her the error of her waves, who knows what kind of life she'd end up leading. She'd probably wind up marrying Steven and become a moll housewife.

We watched her every move as she strolled up and down the aisles of desks. She seemed pretty particular in her choices of what she would lift and what she let lay. Christine was interested in sharp #2 pencils with good erasers, leaving the worn ones, the kind I carried, on the desks. She was drawn to the best Parker Fountain Pens, unscrewing a few to see how much ink was in the cartridge. She put a few down, no doubt because they were low on ink, or she didn't like the color. In less than five minutes, Christine had collected fifteen pencils and ten Parker Pens. She walked to her desk, reached underneath for her pencil bag, put in the stash, and left the room.

"Did you see that?" I asked Mark.

"No, I was taking a nap. Of course I saw it. Now what do we do?"

"I'm not sure, but we can't let this go on. Let's get out to the yard. We have to figure out our next move." Mark and I raced out of the room, down the hall and into the yard, hoping that we wouldn't be questioned by the nuns if we were caught in the building.

Once in the yard, Mark and I walked over to our casual open air office. Ronnie was already there, waiting for us.

"Well? Did you catch Christine?" She asked.

"We saw her lift a lot of pens and pencils."

"And you didn't collar her? Are you two dopes? You saw her, red handed, taking pens and pencils and you didn't even arrest her?" Ronnie threw her hands in the air with a look of "I give up" frustration.

"It's just not that cut and dried, Ronnie." I answered.

"Cut and dry? How much more cut and dried do you need? You should have put the cuffs on her right then and there!"

"We aren't allowed to have handcuffs, yet." I answered. Actually, I don't think you were given cuffs until you got on the safety patrol as crossing guards. I think they were issued along with the bright yellow sash you had to wear at street crossings. Besides, you had to be at least ten years old to get on that squad.

"You know what I meant!" She said, angrily.

"Calm down, Ronnie. Mark and I need to talk to somebody about this first. We'll keep you informed about what our next move is."

"You better! I didn't do all this undercover work, just to see that stealin' broad go free." Ronnie walked away in a huff. It wasn't so much of a huff as it was a cloud of dust, as she kicked up pebbles and small stones on the yard.

Mark looked at me with a questioning look. "Who we gonna talk to?"

"Father Duck."

Father Duck's real name wasn't Duck, but he waddled when he walked and when he spoke he sounded like Vincent Price would sound as a duck with a nasal condition. A Latin mass was always a challenge to follow when he was on the altar since even the old folks would look at each other and whisper, "What'd he say?" Without a missal to help us follow along nobody would know when to sit, stand or kneel, let alone know when to go get communion. But Father Duck was a thoughtful man, slow to condemn us for our sins, and always offered good advice.

Occasionally the parish priests would wander the recess yard. They had already said mass, or gone fishing or golfing, and the recess yard with so many souls wandering about, gave them a chance to practice their Papal wave to the crowd, just in case one of them got the call out of the blue to become Pope.

Luckily, Father Duck was waddling among the throng of wandering kids, waving, sometimes in a papal way, laying his hands on some kid's head and quietly doing whatever parish priests do when you can't hear their voice but they're mouthing something. We all liked to think that this laying of hands and silent mouthing was a prayer, but I suspected it was more on the lines of "Go away, kid, you bother me."

"There he is, Mark." I pointed in Father Duck's direction.

"I don't think I can do this." Mark answered.

"Why?"

"I have a hard time not laughing when he talks. All I hear is…quack quack…quack, quack, quack."

"What do you hear at mass?" I asked.

"Quackus, quackitcus…quackis, quackus, quack." Mark laughed.

"Then get a grip on yourself. I have a serious question to ask him. If you feel like you're gonna laugh, turn around." I said.

"How many times?" Mark laughed.

"What?"

"How many times can I turn around if I feel like I'm gonna laugh?" Mark was already laughing.

"I dunno. As many times as it takes."

"I think I'll get dizzy, then."

I walked up to Father Duck and tapped him on the shoulder and accidently interrupted one of the best papal wave imitations I'd seen in years.

"S'cuse me, Fadda, can I talk to ya for a sec?" I said in my best Bowery Boys voice.

"Of course. It's David, right?" He answered as he looked down at me, but kept his right hand waving. This wasn't going to be easy. Obviously he knew my name since I had drawn his confessional so many times. He's a guy who knew every sin I ever committed. This could be uncomfortable and for once I didn't do anything wrong, yet... today.

"Yeah, Fadda." I answered.

"Mark and me," I began. "We have this friend, actually we only know her, er him. And this person is doing something that's pretty bad and it's costing other people we know. We don't want to rat her, excuse me, him out, but what they're doing could be...how do I put this?"

"Sinful?" Father Duck offered.

"Yeah, yeah, sinful. Mark and me ain't sure if we should turn her, sorry, him, in to the 'sters , or do something else."

" A fronte praecipitium a tergo lupi" He quacked. Mark was beginning to twirl.

"Sorry, Fadda, what?" I asked. This chant wasn't in the missal so I had no idea what he was saying.

"It means between a rock and a hard place, loosely translated. That's what you feel you're in, right?" He said to me.

"Yeah, yeah, that's it." I answered even though I still had no idea what he had said in Latin, but, heck, I would go with it for the time being.

"So give me a few more details." He said.

"We don't want to ruin this moll's, sorry, gink's life forever, ya know. Maybe we can do sumpin to head them off at the pass." I was getting a bit nervous talking to Father Duck because I thought he might bring up my own sins in the conversation.

"So you want to intervene before things get out of hand." Father Duck said as one hand stroked his chin and the other continued to wave at the crowds.

"Yeah, yeah, that's us. Mark and me. We want to do dat."

" Malum consilium quod mutari non potest" Father Duck proclaimed as he looked upward. Mark was now spinning, almost doubled over. If I kept this cryptic conversation up much longer, I was sure Mark would puke from laughing.

"Sorry, Fadda, what?" I said.

"It's a bad plan that can't be changed. Don't you two pay attention in Latin class?" He asked in frustration, as if Latin wasn't frustrating enough to those of us who spoke fluent Merican.

"And that means what to our friend, Fadda? More important, what do you think we should do?" I was trying to get to the heart of his advice before he wandered off into Latin that was so obscure that even the Romans would be scratching their heads.

"So, whaddya think, Fadda? Do we rat them out, or what?" I asked.

"Veni, Vedi, Oriole Veci." He answered. Now I was really confused. Not only is he speaking in Latin, but there's a baseball team involved.

"I'm sorry, Fadda. What's that mean?"

"Did you listen to the Orioles game last night?"

"Yeah, but…" I began.

"Do you remember what the last play of the game was?"

"Yeah, it was a fielder's choice, but I don't get…" I began again.

"There's your answer." He said with a triumphant grin on his face. I'm not sure what my face looked like, but Mark's face was almost beet red and he was beginning to gasp for air.

Father Duck looked at us, raised his hands, gave a few papal waves to those kids who were gathering around, and with his best priest-instructed gaze said, "Semper idem." Wait a minute! Even I knew that one! "Always the same thing." That's the best Latin wisdom he could come up with? Confused didn't even begin to describe what I was feeling.

Mark looked at me after he stopped turning around, not to mention his laughing, as Father Duck wandered into a crowd of children who just knew he held the keys to salvation.

"Well, that went pretty good, dontcha think?" He laughed.

"Shut up! He was sayin' sumpin. I'm just not sure what it was….yet. You heard him, what did you get out of it?"

"Quack, quackus, quacktilius….quack, quack, quack" Mark answered, almost doubled over in laughter.

"Thanks. Thanks a heap."

I tried to get my noggin to work on what Father Duck had said, but all I heard was quack, quack, quack. The Latin phrases didn't help, nor did last night's Orioles game, as I sat on the ground in our corner office in the yard. It was obvious that I needed to become holy in order to understand Father Duck, but I didn't see anything holy coming my way in the near, or even distant, future. I was at a loss for what to do about Christine and the stolen pens and pencils.

"You figure out what Father Duck told you?" Mark said as he strode up to me.

"No. Have you?"

"When in doubt, just…quack." Mark was again in the grips of laughing.

"You're not helping me. You know that, dontcha?"

"Sure I am. Kinda. Sorta. The way I see it, once we throw out all the quacking Latin, we can concentrate on the other stuff." Mark said as his laughter turned down to a chuckle.

"Like what?"

"The Orioles game. What was the last play, again?" Mark asked me.

"A ground ball up the middle to the shortstop. It was ruled a fielder's choice."

"There ya go." Mark said, as if he understood all the Latin quacking.

"There I go, where?"

"Fielder's choice. That's what Father Duck was saying. It's your choice." Mark finally said.

"How did you get that idea? I thought I'd have to pick you up off the ground you were laughing so hard."

"I was listening. It didn't look like it, but I was."

"So now I have to make a decision. Do we trot Christine off to the wayward girls' hoosegow and give her a record or do we offer her the chance to make amends and repent?" I asked as I looked up to heaven in hopes that a bolt of lightning would make me smart.

"That's how I see it."

"Still doesn't make the decision any easier. And Ronnie is so mad that if we don't put the collar on Christine, she'll probably beat me up some afternoon after school. She'll beat me up because she knows I won't hit a dame, not even in a fist fight, even if she started it." I stammered.

"What did Jesus say?" I asked in frustration and still trying to understand.

"Which time?" Mark answered. "I remember he bought everybody drinks at a wedding. He probably said something like, "Is everybody hungry?" after some long sermon when he only had some fish sticks and some bread. There was that camel through a needle in a haystack, thing. Not sure what you mean."

"It's OK, I'm not sure I do, either." I had a decision to make and it just didn't look very popular whichever way I went.

It's pretty easy to put the cuffs on some gink who was a mile south of the law and speeding in the wrong direction. But, this was a dame. I felt we should at least try to stop her criminal ways before things got out of hand and she joined the "Moll Housewife Club" and married Steven.

"OK." I finally sighed. "We'll try the repentance and salvation avenue first. If that don't work, we'll cuff her."

"You worried what Ronnie is gonna say?" Mark asked me because I was sure he was looking at my attempt at furrowed brows.

"Yeah, but I think I have an angle on that." I finally answered as an idea came into my head. Sometimes a few butterscotch candies helped.

"It's your funeral." Mark said.

My first move was to talk to Ronnie and explain what I was doing. I knew that she would be mad, but before she socked me in the jaw, I thought it would be a good idea to get her to talk to her flatfoot dad and explain it all and ask for his advice. I was hoping that he would tell her that my idea was better than just throwing Christine in the slammer and tossing the keys. If her dad thought I was wrong, well, I guess I'd get socked.

I found Ronnie at recess, working her stoolies, and asked her if I could talk to her in private. Talking in private among

250 chaotic, sugar drenched, and excited kids, was like asking for privacy in a war zone.

"So, are you gonna put the collar on Christine today?" She asked.

"No. You, me and Mark are gonna talk to her first." I answered.

"What?" She almost screamed. Her hands knotted into a fist and I braced myself to duck a roundhouse punch.

"You gonna let that stealin' conniving, underhanded broad walk?" Ronnie's knuckles were turning white with anger but I stood my ground.

"I want to give her one last chance."

"Chance? Chance! She's had so many chances that she's stolen almost everybody's pens and pencils! How many chances are ya gonna hand out?" Ronnie yelled.

"Look, Ronnie, I know you're upset…"

"Upset? Me? Not me! I just spent weeks putting the finger on this broad. And you want to give her a pass. Me? Upset?" Ronnie went into a pose that resembled a pitcher about to hurl a fastball, and it was headed right for me.

"You look like you're upset." I said as I stalled for some time

"Look," I said. "Before you sock me in the jaw, talk to your dad. Tell him what's been going on. Ask him what he would do."

"He'd tell me to sock you in the jaw!" She said to me.

"He might, but ask him first. I'm not saying Christine didn't do something wrong, I'm only sayin' we should give her a chance to make things right, given her lack of a criminal record."

"He'll still tell me to sock you in the jaw." She repeated.

"Just talk to him, Ronnie." I finally said as I had backed up a few feet.

"OK."

Ronnie walked off in another cloud of dust along with a generous helping of huff. I had to wait for her to calm down, talk to her dad, and tell me if I was right or not, or try and explain to my mom why I had a shiner.

"Well, gee, that went according to plan, didn't it?" Mark said over my shoulder.

"Oh yeah. Sure. Just as I planned." I answered. But any plan had ragged edges and stuff you can't predict. It seemed like a plan, but I wasn't so sure it was a good plan.

The next day at recess, Ronnie walked to our office. She had changed, somehow, but I wasn't sure how. She still reminded me of a candy that was hard on the outside, yet soft on the inside. One of these days I'll think of which candy it was.

"I talked to my dad last night." Ronnie began.

"And what did he tell you?"

"He told me to sock you in the jaw." She continued.

Oh, Great. I thought. I was already starting to look over my penciled list of excuses of what to tell moms what had happened to faces and limbs while at school, when she continued.

"He said you were right."

"Me?" I asked. I was more surprised at the answer than she was.

"Yeah, he said just because I fingered somebody, I can't be the judge, jury and executioner. He said sometimes you have to make decisions in the field that might make a difference in somebody's life. Sometimes, some people deserve a second chance."

"What else did he say?"

"He told me to sock you in the jaw." Ronnie smiled.

"Yeah, I know. I got that part."

"No, he told me twice to sock you in the jaw."

"So?" I asked.

"So, what?"

"Are you gonna sock me in the jaw?" I had to ask, just in case a roundhouse was coming special delivery

"Not today. One day I might. Just not today."

I felt pretty good about my gamble. Not only did Ronnie's dad back me up, but I was going to get to keep both eyes open, or at least be able to continue chewing my dinner. We now had to find and confront Christine. This wasn't going to be pretty, considering that we'd probably be met with denial, tears and another threat of getting socked in the jaw.

Ronnie found Christine sitting along the perimeter fence playing jacks with a few other dames. I never got the game of jacks, so I wasn't good at it, but these four dames could bounce a ball in the air and snatch a handful of jacks spread out over a few feet and catch the ball before it bounced a second time, all with the same hand. It obviously took a quick hand and I wondered if old West gunslingers ever played the game to perfect their quick draw, just in case they were standing in the middle of a Western town at high noon facing down a bad guy.

"You see how fast Christine is?" Ronnie nudged my side, whispering.

"Yeah."

"You ain't seen nothing yet. Watch her right hand and then where it goes to her left. She's gonna pocket a jack. Just watch." She whispered again.

Holy cow! If Ronnie hadn't told me what and where to watch, I never would have seen the move. It was so subtle and so smooth that three dames sitting just two feet away from her didn't even see Christine do it. But stealing a jack was still a mystery to me.

"So why pocket a jack, Ronnie?" I asked.

"I asked my dad the same question. He called it practice.

He thinks that Christine will eventually do it in card games. He called it palming."

"So what's the big deal? We only play "Go Fish" and "Old Maids." I said.

"My dad told me there's a game called poker. People play it all the time for money. If you can cheat at poker, you can make some serious dough."

"So that's the card game I always see cowpokes playin' in saloons. Somebody always gets shot because some cowboy wearing a black hat is called a cheat. I always wondered what they were playing." I said as if some mysterious passage in the bible finally became clear.

"Yep."

"Get her attention, Ronnie. Tell her we need to talk to her. But be nice about it, ok?" I said as I watched a second jack vanish without a trace.

Ronnie walked over to Christine and tapped her shoulder and motioned towards Mark and me. Christine wore innocence like some dames wear makeup. You know it's there, but if it's done right you aren't supposed to notice it. Then again, some dames don't do such a good job and their red lipstick is all over their front teeth when they smile and then you notice all of the makeup they plastered on. I wasn't sure about Christine, yet. I needed a closer look.

"Christine, this is David and Mark. We need to talk to you." Ronnie began.

"What about?" she asked. She said it so nice that I was sure I wouldn't see lipstick smeared on her teeth. This was not a sloppy tomato. But we knew that she wasn't innocent, either.

"First, Christine," I began. "Take the two jacks out of your pocket."

She reached in her jumper pocket and searched around.

"OH, these? I wonder how they got there." She said in an innocent voice.

"We know how they ended up in your jumper. We watched you pocket them." Mark pointed out.

"Really? I had no idea. It's no big deal, ya know. I woulda given them back, anyway."

"We're not here about jacks, Christine. We want to talk to you about vanishing pencils and pens." I said as I tried to keep from being distracted about a few stupid jacks and looking for lipstick on front teeth.

"I heard about that. I lost some pencils and a pen, too. You wanna ask me who I think it is?" Christine asked in an innocent voice.

"We already know!" Ronnie said in a very menacing voice.

"Really? Who is it?" Christine was playing a very good game of "I'm sure it wasn't me."

"You!" Ronnie's voice rose and she took a step towards Christine.

"Me? You're kidding, right?" Christine said. I'd heard that same voice and the same line last night on "Dragnet" so I wasn't buying it.

"Yeah, Christine! You're a stealin' cheatin' broad and we're about to put you in stir!" Ronnie said loudly. The heat of the moment was about to go beyond boiling as Ronnie started to stoke her inner fire. This was supposed to be a confrontation, not a blood bath. I tried to calm Ronnie down.

"Simmer down, sister."

"I told you never to call me that!" Ronnie said as she spun around to confront me. Boy was she mad. Somehow, in the heat of the moment, she forgot what her dad had told her, except maybe to sock me in the jaw.

"Christine," Mark began. "We've been watching you for

weeks. We know how big your pencil case gets at the end of the day. David and me, we even watched you walk back into class two days ago and lift a bunch of pencils and pens off of desks. We were hiding in the coatroom. We know what you're doing. We saw you."

Christine's look changed from innocence to defiance in an instant. And then it went right to unbridled anger. I kept telling myself that this was all going according to plan, but it sure didn't feel like it.

"You three were spying on me? If the penguins weren't so close I'd knock you all to the ground!"

"Take your best shot, lady!" Ronnie barked. Oh, yeah, this was going exactly like I thought it would. Except it wasn't going well.

"Take it easy, Ronnie. " I said.

"You and me, after school! Anytime, ya hear?"" Shouted Ronnie. Yep, just like I planned. Except now it was going downhill and picking up speed.

My mom had told me a story about herself when she was 9 years old. She was coming home from school and accidently walked between two cats who were about to go at it. And then they did, with my mom caught in the middle. She told me how painful it was as they clawed at her legs, trying to tear each other apart. Then she told me how painful rabies shots were. I didn't want to get in the middle of these two dames, who had unleashed their own claws, and were ready to try and tear each other apart. My mom was pretty graphic about how much rabies shots hurt, and I wasn't prepared to end up in an emergency room with a sawbones looking me over, dressing my wounds, and discussing whether I needed rabies shots. "Got caught between two girls who had a fight? You look pretty torn up. Do ya know if they ever had rabies shots? No? Sorry, kid, pull up your shirt. This is gonna hurt….a lot."

But I had to get between them. I'm not sure of the reason, I just knew I did. As I faced Ronnie I tried to get a hold on her wrists. I paid attention to her nails that suddenly resembled daggers, and tried not to get scratched. Mark took my move as his cue and did the same with Christine. Both of us were now standing in the center of a dame storm as they swore, clawed and hissed at each other. All I heard in my head was: rabies shots hurt a lot.

"Calm down, both of you!" I said, still holding Ronnie's hands at an angle so I wouldn't get shredded. Mark seemed to have a good hold on Christine, but I'm sure he was looking at her ten deadly weapons.

"We can solve this, OK? Just calm down." I yelled.

I made a big mistake as I said this. I relaxed my grip on Ronnie. In an instant, she had broken my grip, almost jumping over me towards Christine. As I tried to grab her arm, I felt a searing pain on my right hand. Four sharp fingernails dug into me and blood was already oozing out. Great! Somehow I didn't remember this as part of the plan, but a voice in my head said that all of this should have been included, along with rabies shots.

I recovered and got another grip on Ronnie who was still hissing and showing what I thought were fangs. Funny, I didn't remember her as having fangs. Mark was still between Christine and Ronnie, holding off a two dame riot.

"Would you two just stop?" I shouted. I almost said, "if not for your own sake, think about me. I may have to get rabies shots later today. I'm bleeding."

Both dames seemed to relax a little, but Mark and me stood between them. I went for the evidence part of the investigation, hoping that Christine would understand that we had the goods on her, and Ronnie would remember that she couldn't be the executioner.

"OK, Christine." I began. "We got so many reports about missing pencils and pens that Mark and I had to investigate. Ronnie, here, has helped us out. She's watched you for weeks, especially how you are able to palm a jack without any other dame catching on. Ronnie fingered you as a suspect, but Mark and me, we did the tail. We watched you, girl, we watched you lift half the pens and pencils in class."

I wasn't sure what I was seeing in Christine's posture. While she still stood straight, which the Franciscans demanded, she seemed to relax but not in a military "at ease" way.

"Christine?" I asked. I wanted to know if she had heard me.

"If my dad finds out, he's gonna be really mad." She said.

"Why would your dad be mad? Because you stole so many pens?" I asked.

"No, that I got caught doing it."

I realized that none of what she just said was part of my grand plan, which went to hell in a hand basket fifteen minutes ago. The deeper I went into this case, the less sense it made to me.

"Excuse me, your dad is gonna be mad that you got caught?" This idea never was part of my plan, and now I'm not sure I even had a plan.

"Yes."

"You wanna come clean, Christine?" I asked her.

"Clean, Christine! You're a poet and don't know it." Mark said, in an obvious attempt to diffuse an already tense situation with a bit of humor. Mark realized what he said, looked down, and kept quiet.

"You ever heard of the Romany?" Christine asked us.

"Yeah, there's like ten restaurants in Little Italy that have it in their name." Mark said.

"NO! You dunce! The people of Roma heritage." Christine answered in frustration.

"Sorry, Christine, doesn't ring a bell." I said.

"You guys call us gypsies. My family has wandered for generations trying to find a place to live. We've had to live by our wits even before you were born. Anyway, we settled here in Bawlmer, but the livelihood of my parents and grandparents are still taught to me. My dad learned certain tricks and skills as he tried to make a living for my mom, me, and my brothers. I just picked up on them."

"He taught you how to steal?" I asked. Wow, what a dad, I thought. All my dad had taught me so far was how to lay brick, saw a 2 by 4 the right way and the best glass jug to take to the local tavern for some fresh Natty Boh.

"No! Not steal! That's a bad reputation that some Roma get, but it isn't true. I've been taught magic tricks. Making a jack disappear is kinda like making the ace of spades rise to the top of a deck of cards. Getting people confused and wondering if what they saw, or didn't see, is a part of being a magician."

"But your dad never told you to steal, did he?" I said.

"No! Look, I always put the jacks back, OK? I got carried away with the pens and pencils. It all became so…easy. I told him every night about how I was able to palm the jacks, and he seemed pleased that I was catching on to the magic tricks he was teaching me. But I never told him about the pens and pencils."

"You know we can put the collar on you, right?" Mark said.

"Yeah, I know," she sighed.

"We ain't gonna do that, though." I said.

"You ain't?" Christine looked at the three of us in amazement.

"No, but you gotta do two things. If you don't, I'm sure Ronnie will be very happy to rat you out. Won't you, Ronnie?" I said as I relaxed my grip on her wrists.

"Yeah, I will." Ronnie's voice sounded pretty disappointed. She probably wanted to go home and excitedly tell her dad that she had collared a thievin' dame: about as much as Christine wanted to go home and not tell her own dad that she'd been caught. It's the same coin, just a different side.

"OK, first, I want you to promise that you won't palm another jack at recess. Second, I want you to return all of the pens and pencils you took." I said.

"How am I gonna do that?"

"Promise us you won't palm another jack." I forgot to include the powerful "cross my heart and hope to die" part, but I didn't want to get into the fine print right now.

"I promise." Christine finally said.

"Next, you have to give back all the pens and pencils."

"If I do that, everybody is gonna know who took 'em. I'll still get a reputation as a thief." Christine's voice was close to breaking.

"I have a plan for that." I answered. Great, I thought, another plan, since this one worked out so well. I was hoping that this plan would be better than the first one.

"Tomorrow, I want you to bring back every pen and pencil you lifted. As good as you were lifting 'em when everybody went to recess, I want you to dump all of them on Sister Knuckle's desk after everybody leaves to go to the yard. You can leave a printed note, something like, "these belong to the class," or something like that. We'll let Knuckles sort out whose pen belongs to who. Everybody gets their pens and pencils back and we won't tell….will we, Ronnie?"

"No, I won't tell." Ronnie said in a dejected voice.

"OK, I can do that." Christine's voice had brightened. She knew we were giving her a second chance at redemption and she wasn't going to be fingered. But she also understood that we three had the goods on her and if she tried to scam us, the nuns, her dad, and all the saints would come down on her like a plague of locusts. And nobody wants to be swatting at grasshoppers while you're pretending everything is okey dokey.

As Christine walked away, Ronnie gave me a puzzled look. Then she looked at my right hand and saw the blood almost creeping onto my fingers. Her puzzled look gave way to alarm, much like my mom's look when I was late for dinner, or when she noticed I was bleeding from a game of mumbley-peg.

"You're hurt!" She exclaimed.

"Naw, it's just a scratch."

"You're bleeding!"

"Really? I hadn't noticed." I lied.

Ronnie picked up my right hand. "Did I do this?"

"Maybe, it was the heat of the moment. Ain't nothing. Forget about it." I said.

"I am so sorry, David."

"It's alright. Can I ask you something?"

"Yeah, sure." She said as she pulled a handkerchief from her jumper to clean the wound.

"You get a rabies shot?" I asked since my mom's voice was ringing in my head.

"What?"

"Never mind, it ain't important." I finally said, and walked away.

The next day, after recess, Knuckles was greeted with a small mountain of pens and pencils that sat on her desk. I watched her pick up a small note, pocket it, and then declare to the class that if any of us had misplaced our pens and pencils, this was the chance to reclaim the mislaid instruments. A small, yet controllable, stampede rushed towards her. Mark, me, Ronnie and Christine were the only ones who remained seated.

I sat there and thought….case closed. I looked over at Mark, and he had that gleam in his eye. I knew that gleam. He was gonna wait till the end of the frenzy of reclaimed pens and then walk up and take what was left. Mark always walked a fine line between pious and truthful, and enjoyed the thrill of crossing over to a place where the ginks, the hoods, and jailbirds took up residence. It's what made him such a great gumshoe.

I had just shed the band-aids on my right hand in late May and school was about to end for the summer in just a few days. The recess yard was warm in many different ways. The frenzy of trading baseball cards had subsided. The rampage of dodge ball games had become a bit more sporty, the clicking of the cricket by Sister Salvatore wasn't so frequent. I had no reports about missing jacks from the dames in the yard. It was a good time to be eight years old. I was looking forward to summer vacation and a break in crime fighting.

"David?" I spun around to see Ronnie in front of me. She still wore that hard-on-the-outside-soft-on-the-inside candy look. One of these days, I'm gonna remember which candy she reminded me of.

"Hi, Ronnie. How're ya doin?"

"Fine. I have to tell ya sumpin." Ronnie had a solemn look on her face that I couldn't quite read.

"What is it?"

"Well," she began, "My dad got transferred. He's gonna be working the Catonsville precinct. My mom and dad sold our house and we're gonna be moving to the other side of town. I won't be at the Shrine next year. I'm going to Saint Agnes. "

"Oh?" I said, so casually that I'm sure it sounded like I didn't care, but I started to feel my heartbeat in my stomach. While part of my noggin told me that she was just a dame, another part was telling me that she was special. Hard-on-the-outside-soft-on-the-inside. Now I'd never figure out which candy she resembled.

"Thank you for all you and Mark did. I learned a lot. "

"It's OK. " I answered. What else was I going to say? I came up with an answer.

"I'm gonna miss you, Ronnie." I finally stammered. Boy! That was smooth. But it didn't feel smooth.

Ronnie took my face in her two hands and looked at me like the pious penguins did when I had done something really wrong and needed to go to confession in the next ten minutes. But, Ronnie's gaze was telling me something different.

"We'll always have recess." She said, as she kissed me on the cheek and then walked slowly away and blended into the crowd at recess. I watched her disappear, and couldn't make sense of myself and what I was feeling

"You dizzy with that dame?" Mark asked over my shoulder as Ronnie walked away.

"Me? I ain't dizzy with no dame, Mark! You hear?" I shouted.

I looked into the crowd again and muttered, "I ain't dizzy with no dame."

Busted Downey Oshun

Everybody needs a vacation at least once a year. I wasn't sure our parents needed one, but I knew Mark and I earned one. After a school year of preventing so many potential jailbirds from trading in their names for prison numbers, we needed a break. We had just finished working a bunko case involving a fixed "Three Card Monte" game at the Shrine recess yard. The loss of so many nickels by unsuspecting pigeons that took the bait and bet on the game was so large that I heard the US Mint had to make an emergency run of nickels so the economy wouldn't collapse. I knew that the game was fixed when I watched my dad and my three uncles play pinochle one day. Within minutes of the cards being dealt, they all knew what cards each of them was holding. Obviously, playing cards wasn't a game of chance, unless you played "War." Playing cards was a game of skill. It took Mark and me more than a month to crack it, but that was partly due to the end of semester exams we had to study for. Going to Ocean City for a couple of weeks was just what the captain of the Bawlmer Pleese Department would have commanded, if the captain actually knew about us.

Preparations for a two week escape to the Merlin ocean resort began in April, even though we wouldn't be there until July. Mark and I prepared to leave our detective gear behind, such as evidence pads, pencils, and case files. We left it all with our sketch artist who already was carrying the huge box of ninety-six Crayola's and construction paper. He had a lot of room in his old Army knapsack that he got from Sunny Surplus. All he had to do was keep it out of the sun so the crayons wouldn't melt and ruin our files. We decided to take our pen knives and magnifying glasses, since you never know when you may need to dig evidence out of a crucial wooden pylon that supports the Ocean City boardwalk or burn up an invading army of ants by using the sun's rays to focus its heat and stop their intent on carrying off our food. Other than the usual reference books we referred to for detective work, like the latest "Batman," "Superman," and "Easy Company," we left the packing to our moms. We learned that delegating those mundane details was to our advantage. Besides, it didn't help to argue with superiors.

In late June I walked out on the concrete front porch of the brick end of group row house we called home to soak up some early morning sun. The notes to Cloverland Dairy and Rice's Bakery delivery drivers informing them that the family was going on vacation had been stuffed in the empty milk bottles and the plastic crates. It was a quiet morning; even the REA Express truck barely made a sound as it drove down the street.

And then Miss Marie, our next door neighbor, came out of her door. I'm not sure why she was out so early; the neighborhood steps were concrete, not marble. Marble steps required a ritual morning scrubbing in Bawlmer and not doing so religiously probably required confession and penance. No need to scrub concrete steps, unless she was out early to ask my mom about some phantom emergency concerning her daughter, Sharon. Why this early in the morning? She usually just wrapped on the common wall with a rolling pin to get my mom's attention, as if the phone was still an unreliable form of communication. She waved at me in a way that resembled someone leaving on the Queen Mary for an around the world voyage, never mind that we were only fifteen feet apart.

"Goin downey oshun, Hon?"

"Yes ma'am." I answered. I watched "Dragnet" on TV the night before and liked how Joe Friday was quick and to the point when talking to witnesses. No need to get chummy, just give short answers, ask direct questions, and focus on the facts.

"We went once, but Mr. Ted didn't like it. Sharon did, though." She said.

"Yes ma'am." I didn't need to know the details. Asking for details would open a can of words.

"Tell your mother I need to talk to her."

"Yes ma'am." I think Joe Friday was onto something with his short clipped banter. I wasn't bludgeoned with boring details about their vacation, even if it was miserable for some reason. "Just the facts" was what Sergeant Friday said. I need to remember that.

Throughout June I was assaulted with the same question from neighbors – Goin' downey oshun? If word leaked out that Mark and I were off patrol for two weeks I wondered what havoc and crimes we would have to face when we returned. I had summer book reports to write, and trying to clean up the mess of unsolved crimes would make the long hot and humid summer months even hotter and more humid.

I retreated through the front door, bounded down the basement stairs, and opened the basement door to our back yard. I was one story down and thirty feet away from interrogation by neighbors. Safe at last, I thought. Not quite.

To my right, just beyond the chain link fence that declared "this is my yard, that's yours" was my neighbor's daughter,

Sharon, and her friend Vicky playing 45 rpm records, undressing and redressing their dolls. How dirty can a doll get that it needs that many costume changes? I'll never understand dames. My dad always told me that it was a lost cause to try and understand women anyway. I think he bet on the horses at Pimlico Race Course to remind himself that he had a handle on odds. The odds of predicting my mom's reactions to anything we did was worse than rolling a pair of loaded dice that you never knew were loaded.

Sharon waved at me with the same enthusiasm as her mother as I walked out the basement door, except this time I was six feet away and I was sure I wasn't boarding a ship.

"Goin downey oshun?" She asked, as so many had repeated.

"Yes."

Seems like word about our family's intention to go on vacation required constant reinforcement by the entire neighborhood. Maybe my dad should have alerted the news desk at "The Bawlmer Sun" and "The Noosemerican" except that I'm glad that he didn't. Criminals read the newspapers, too. An announcement that we left for two weeks could unleash a crime spree. Only a few more weeks of constant interrogation by neighbors to endure, then I could relax.

It was still dark as my dad woke me at 5:30 AM on the Saturday that we were to leave.

"Time to go." Was all he said as I tried to sit up in bed and wipe the sleep from my eyes. I walked into the front bedroom to the window to look at the street below.

He had the '54 Buick almost loaded with everything we would need, including the TV. He probably left the kitchen sink because it was too much trouble to unhook. The Buick was as long as a Bawlmer row house is wide and with so much stuff tied to the roof, it looked like we were taking the second story of the house, except there weren't any bricks on the car's roof. The rope that held all the cargo in place was a spider web of perfect knots that even a hurricane couldn't blow away. I figured my dad had used a half mile of rope to tie everything down, which left another half mile of unused rope tucked somewhere inside the passenger compartment. I was sure it would be under my feet for the entire trip.

As I walked out the front door, clad in the clothes my mom had laid out, Miss Marie was standing on her front porch making sure that life was as it was supposed to be.

"Enjoy da oshun, hon!" As she waved to all of us and my dad tried to position another suitcase in the cavern of the trunk of the dark green Buick. It's a vacation; we're not going to another country, unless you think the Eastern Shore of Merlin was that. I heard stories that my granddad and his brother had a big fight about my great uncle moving to the Eastern Shore back in the 1940's. OK, maybe it was a foreign country for some people.

I heard a grunting and rustling over my left shoulder and spun around. There was Paula, one of my sister's best friends, struggling with a suitcase. She'd obviously packed her entire bedroom in the fashionable puke green Samsonite suitcase. I figured the walk of a half block, dragging that bag which probably weighed 200 pounds, took her an hour. But how come my sister got to invite a friend on vacation? I looked at my dad. He read my expression like some people read tea leaves.

"Look, she'll keep your sister out of your hair for the next two weeks." He said.

I felt grateful, but a bit confused since my parents decided that I needed a buzz haircut and I looked like an eight year old on his first day at Army basic training. They said my short hair would keep me cooler. I didn't have hair that they could get into, but I suspected that both my sister and her friend would end up getting under my skin. Cooler? I wasn't so sure.

My mom sauntered out the front storm door with a wicker basket in her arms. I knew there was lunch for all of us, but the way she carried it, my guess was there was enough rations for the 84th division where my dad served during World War II. Probably fried chicken and potato salad, along with all the plates, napkins and eating utensils required to feed an army embarking on maneuvers. She returned to the house, only to reappear with my little brother in tow. This was going to be a long trip.

We waited for the other car in our convoy to arrive which would carry my aunt and uncle, Mark and his baby brother, along with our grandparents. This could end up being a long vacation, too.

As the black Dodge rolled down the street, my dad announced, "OK, we're burning daylight." That was our cue to pile into the back of the Buick and get settled for the trip "downey oshun." Obviously my dad had been reading Zane Grey or Louis L'Amour novels since "burning daylight" was a phrase in their books used by cowboys during a cattle drive. I think my dad always wanted to be a cowboy, but the closest he could get to a cattle drive was peddling hamburger to local supermarkets. Ground hamburger doesn't wander far from the truck. He likely hummed the theme to "Rawhide" as he made deliveries.

The rear seat in a 54 Buick was as spacious as a pew in a Calf Lick church, except without the kneelers. But just like a Calf Lick church, you could get scrunched into uncomfortable situations. With a half mile of rope under my feet and my sister yakking to Paula, I felt confined. Maybe not confined, claustrophobic might be a better word. I rolled the window down so I could breathe.

It took six hours to drive the 150 miles from Bawlmer to Ocean City on the two lane road which is Route 50. Between the nonstop jibber jabber of my sister and Paula sitting next to me, my mom constantly watching our speed and oncoming traffic and telling my dad to drive carefully, and my brother asking "Are we there, yet?," every few minutes, I think I understood why dogs put their heads out car windows. It wasn't until I saw the billboard that said "Welcome to Ocean City" that I started to smell the salt air. Then there was that magical sound of tires rolling over the steel portion of the Route 50 drawbridge that told me that we had finally arrived.

The Buick made a left turn onto Ocean Highway. Actually my dad turned the car left instructed by my navigator mom, who, by the way, never learned how to drive. Those who can, do. Those who can't, tell everybody else how to do it correctly. In my mom's case, do it safely and at a low rate of speed. We made another left at Melvin's Steak House on First Street and pulled up in front of the first white house behind the restaurant.

It was a two story frame house that had two doors, one in front and the other facing the back of Melvin's. Sinepuxent Bay was half a block away to the left and "da oshun" two blocks away to the right. Once our convoy parked, army training kicked in as my dad and uncle untied the ropes from the cars' roofs, opened the trunks, and began instructing all of us in the art of military bivouac. Within minutes both cars were unloaded, cargo stowed in the correct rooms, and Mark and I were ready to enjoy a real vacation.

It was 3 PM when Mark and I finally walked out of our temporary quarters and walked towards the bay. The sun was shining on the calm waters of the bay as we watched the pleasure boats returning from a day of "oshun fishin" and we listened to the unique tire sounds coming from the drawbridge portion of the Route 50 Bridge. No crimes to investigate, no misguided humanity to save. I could get used to this, I thought.

After dinner and a walking tour of the commercial fishing boats at their docks and inspecting their catch from that day to make sure they had caught the biggest fish swimming in "da oshun," we returned to the house. It was almost time to bed down for the night. While it was a vacation, it was not the time to leave lifes routine behind. We would all be up at sunrise (or earlier if we went crabbing) and ready to soak up the relaxation of vacation at a frantic break-neck pace.

"Mom, where am I sleeping?" I asked.

She led me to a spot in the second story hall and opened the door. "Here." She pointed.

"Here" was not a bedroom. It was a walk-in closet and my dad had erected a cot (obviously brought back from the Army) that spanned the interior.

"Here?" I asked. I neglected to count the bedrooms when we first arrived. While the house appeared large, there were only four bedrooms. Counting adults and my sister and her friend, they had confiscated the real bedrooms while our little brothers would sleep in parents' rooms, leaving me and Mark to find a place to bed down. Two weeks sleeping in a closet was not my idea of a vacation. The area was smaller than a prison cell, but at least there was a window facing me as long as I kept the door open. I was beginning to know how the other half (the criminal element) lives.

We all attended the early Sunday mass the next morning. You might be on vacation, but God doesn't seem to take a day off, especially that 7th day we were told that He rested. It must be tough being God. Never get a day off, not since that first seventh day of rest.

Once back at the house, Mark and I raced up the steps shedding our clothes like they hurt. In seconds we were ready to invade the beach and the waves that glistened in the early morning sun. As we each clung to a towel, we looked at our mothers.

"Can we go now?" we both asked.

"OK, but watch yourselves." Came the response in perfect harmony from my mom and my aunt. I don't think they had rehearsed it, but it almost sounded like a song. I wasn't sure if they were cautioning us to make sure we didn't get hit by traffic crossing the streets, watch ourselves when it came to the ocean's undertow, or just stay away from ravenous sharks that may be lurking in the breaking waves.

"Go straight from the street to the beach. We don't want to hunt you two down when we get there." My mom said. Since we hadn't learned the finer points of Lewis and Clark's surveying techniques in third grade history class, we did the best we could to maintain a straight line of sight.

By 11 o'clock the rest of the family wandered onto the beach. My dad and uncle looked like pack mules under the weight of blankets, chairs, and picnic baskets. Both my brother and my young cousin appeared to be trying to escape the firm grip of my mom and my aunt. Our grandparents wore wide grins, no doubt because neither one was carrying nor dragging some sort of cargo. My sister and Paula meandered onto the beach, turning left, then right, pointing, and giggling. A temporary camp was set just yards from the waves, as my dad retreated to find the local beach bum who rented chairs and umbrellas. He returned minutes later with a blonde haired lug, umbrella on his shoulder, and looked like he needed assistance getting dressed in the morning. As the guy planted the umbrella, rocking it back and forth to bury it in the sand, I noticed that my sister and Paula were also rocking back and forth. Dames were just strange, but even more so on a beach. Maybe it had something to do with sun tan lotion, since both were applying it to each other in huge quantities.

Meanwhile, Mark and I had built a sand castle, complete with a moat, where the waves broke onto the beach. We knew it was a losing cause as the ocean continued to wash away our best efforts. But we figured we might have to take engineering in the fourth grade, and testing our abilities at questionable construction may come in handy during the lessons. We got bored with battling the elements, though, and went back to the shade of the rented umbrella.

"We're bored." I said. Isn't vacation supposed to be boring? I wasn't prepared to be bored.

My dad took out two dollars from his pocket, as did my uncle, and handed it to Mark and me.

"Why don't you two go on the boardwalk?" My dad said.

Holy Cow! Two dollars! I haven't seen this much cash since Steven emptied his pockets during recess. Armed with two bucks each, Mark and I raced towards the boardwalk.

The Ocean City boardwalk is a sea of humanity in the summer, complete with currents and crashing waves. If you weren't careful you could get carried away by crowds of meandering people only to finally escape their wandering feet three streets away from where you wanted to go in the first place. You had to time your crossing against the sea of people like you timed yourself with the waves on the beach. We knew we had to be quick. We waited for our chance when we spied an elderly couple lazily walking by and obviously holding back an impatient throng. We ran across the boardwalk and headed south, timing our run across the boardwalk so that we would blend into the south bound current of people who were going no place in particular.

The stores on the boardwalk are a paradise of temptation. Not since the Garden of Eden were there so many temptations in one place. I wasn't paying attention at the sermon at the morning mass, but I imagine it had something to do with buying stuff you didn't need and instead giving the money to the poor. But here, on the boardwalk, you prolly forgot all about what you heard about the poor and their daily needs. Here, if you didn't need it, it was here telling you that you did, and who cared about the poor anyway. Every shop seemed to be telling Mark and me that we needed to spend our two bucks right now. Between the aromas of pizza, caramel popcorn, and the sound of the machines that made soft ice cream cones coated in hard plaster chocolate, all the signs told us that this place on the boardwalk had the best salt water taffy in the world, or the best popcorn, or the bestest fries known to man. We could have been parted from our money within two minutes, but we had a mission. We were headed to Marty's Play Land farther down the boardwalk and their games of skill, notably Skeeball.

"Hey! You twos!" Came a voice.

Mark and I looked at each other then looked around. Everybody else on the boardwalk around us seemed to be travelling in packs of twenty or thirty. We looked to where the voice had come. Behind a three foot wall was a guy waving in our direction. His hair looked like he used an old leaky axle for a pillow, and the way his hair looked he probably tossed and turned the entire night. He had teeth that looked like the pearly gates. That's to say that there were two of them in his less than toothy grin. He was tall, skinny, and his worn blue shirt hung from his shoulders like he had borrowed it from his bigger, older and well fed brother.

"Yeah, youse two. Come here." He was waving at us with that "around the world cruise" wave I'd seen before.

The stall he was working was the rifle shooting gallery complete with different size targets and moving ducks and other animals. There were a dozen weapons tied securely to the top of the counter in case some shooter decided to find similar targets away from the gallery. If you were a marksman you could win a prize, but only after you had shelled out twice the dough it would have taken to buy one of the stuffed animals.

"How would youse two gentlemen like to make a dime a piece?" He said. From twenty feet away, this carny looked scary; close up, he looked even worse, like a refugee from a bad horror movie.

"What do you want?" Obviously Mark had watched "Dragnet" too, and used Joe Friday's short clipped questions.

"Bizness ain't doin too good, unnerstand? I need to get more marks, er, customers here. Pick up a rifle, shoot a few off, and I'll hand youse a big bear. Walk down da boardwalk ta Thrashers, wait a few minutes, den walk back. If anybody asks ya where ya got da bear, tell'em ya won it here. When ya come back, I'll give ya a dime. When youse two come back, your friend can do da same thing."

I looked at Mark. He was usually the one who wouldn't be afraid to bend the rules if it meant learning how the criminal mind worked, even if it meant pretending to be a criminal.

"OK" Mark said, as he picked up a rifle. He had squeezed off only four rounds when the carny yelled.

"Another winner!"

This carny obviously had a stage voice that carried, which was why he was hired in the first place, as he handed Mark a huge stuffed bear and ten guys stopped walking and turned towards the shooting gallery, girlfriends in tow. I'll never understand what it takes to impress a dame.

Mark and I walked north towards Thrashers French Fries, wrestling the huge bear the whole time. The sixty foot long snake of patrons waiting for French fries from Thrashers seemed more intent on buying fries than a couple of kids with a bear and where we got it from. We waited a few minutes, navigated our way to the other side of the boardwalk and returned to the shooting gallery.

"Youse guys done good. Thanks." As he handed Mark two nickels and Mark returned the huge bear.

"Your friend wanna try?" He asked.

I picked up a rifle and shot five times.

"Another winner!" He yelled.

I hadn't hit a thing on the back wall, but like magic he handed me the same bear. Another bunch of guys stopped, turned and approached the shooting gallery. What a racket! What a scam! And now I was part of this criminal scheme. I'll have to wait two whole weeks for confession, probably have to pray the rosary for penance, and hope I'm not dragged out to sea by a shark instructed by God to drown me before I got absolution, lest I meet this carny's relatives and be forced to mingle with them in hell for eternity. I kept telling myself I was doing this for criminal research but I got a dime for the risk of eternal damnation. What were the odds? I'd ask my dad but I doubt stuff like this shows up on the betting boards at Pimlico Race Course.

The fear of burning in hell forever was lost in my mind when Mark and I walked into Marty's. The sights and sounds drowned out any idea I may have had concerning eternal fires as we looked for open Skeeball lanes. We exchanged our dollars for coins. It was time to test our skills. Exactly what skills we were about to test, I wasn't sure, but it certainly beat anything we had encountered on the boardwalk.

After two hours of Skeeball we had a ribbon of tickets that would surely net us something spectacular from the prize case. Armed with advanced math skills, we determined we could get a pencil and a funny eraser. Not my idea of a productive afternoon, but we could keep coming back every day to accumulate more tickets. If my skills improved, I might be able to redeem my tickets for the transistor radio in the prize case that I coveted. I already had 2,000 points and only needed another 230,000 to get it. At least playing Skeeball at Marty's wasn't a scam.

Before we returned to Marty's each afternoon to increase our bounty of tickets, we spent our mornings on the beach. We discovered strange creatures that were washed on shore by the waves, only to frantically dig themselves back into the sand. We called them sand crabs, some called them sand fleas, but their activity to avoid capture was mesmerizing. During the days that followed, we had dug up at least a hundred of them, letting them loose and watching them dig furiously into the sand at the wave's highest point on the beach.

Mark and I had deftly manipulated our parents into buying us buckets and shovels during the first week. We may have used the argument that we needed them to hone our skills in sand castle construction, but at any rate, they bought us each a set. Our sand castle construction drastically improved, but we had something else in mind.

There were as many dogs and cats in our neighborhoods as there were families back in Bawlmer. In addition to canaries, parakeets, fish and those little turtles that most kids had, along with an occasional duck, the animal kingdom as pets were well represented. But no one kept sand crabs. We could be the true animal tamers of Herring Run Park and Belair/

Edison. If we could tame the common hoods destined for incarceration we encountered every school year, we could tame the wild kingdom, we thought.

After a few days of capturing and releasing the sand crabs, we decided to capture them like so many "Walt Disney Presents" TV shows that showed the wild animals of Africa being caught and sent to a better life in a zoo somewhere. It helped that we weren't trying to corral a cheetah, a rhino, or any other animal that could kill us. As far as we could understand, all the sand crabs required was ocean sand and salt water. We could do this. We shoveled a pile of wet sand into a bucket, and using the other bucket we dumped sea water over it, making sure that there was at least two inches of water from the waves above the sand in the bucket. We then proceeded to find a suitable array of sand crabs. We dug, we inspected, we graded by size and color, we tossed a few that we thought weren't perfect specimens. By the end of the afternoon we had nearly fifty sand crabs in a gallon bucket. We walked away from the crashing ocean waves and the beach, water sloshing around the bucket as we struggled to carry the heavy load back to the house behind Melvin's Steak House.

Mark and I knew that bringing wild life into the house would be too risky. Adults don't seem to understand the needs of keeping wild creatures in captivity. We decided to put our capture under the steps of the side door; the one closest to Melvin's Steak House. They should be safe there, since Melvin's never offered a sand crab special on their dinner menu and the steps were always in the shadows.

It was three hot July days later that everyone in the house was walking around, nose in the air, sniffing the wind, and trying to determine the origin of a smell. It smelled like something was dead and rotting. Everyone believed that it was coming from the back of Melvin's. After all, they cooked and served dead beef parts, seafood and shrimp. It was probably coming from their dumpster.

On the afternoon of the fourth day the odor was so bad in the house that every adult went on a frantic search to find where the deadly fumes were coming from. Our grandfather compared it to a gas attack he endured in World War I. When Mark and I returned from an inspection tour of the bay we were surrounded and confronted. As the adults discovered, the smell that resembled rotting flesh was our captive sand crabs which were stowed under the porch. They were all dead in spite of our best efforts to take them back alive.

No adult was playing "good cop" in the old "good cop, bad cop" interrogation process. The only thing missing from this scene was the single bare burning light bulb over our heads as we were subjected to every degree of questioning including the third one. The questioning was rapid fire and relentless, mostly focused on our sanity, common sense and what was going on in our heads before, during and after bringing back our catch. My uncle even implied that we were not real members of the family since no one in the family would do something so stupid.

We were charged, under parental law, with human endangerment, animal cruelty, possessing wild animals without regard for living conditions, and the worst charge, stupidity. We were ordered to dispose of the creatures immediately and turn in our buckets.

As we walked to the bay, bucket in hand, and gagging all the way, I said to my partner, Mark,

"Guess we've discovered what it feels like to be a criminal, huh?"

"Guess so." He answered between dry heaves.

The Cricket Clicker Caper

The Franciscan nuns always seem to be armed with the latest weapons in crowd control. Besides the usual long arms, like a yard stick, and a side arm in the guise of a ruler, plus the airborne weapons such as chalk and erasers which have been used with uncanny accuracy, there is one special device that is only handled by the nun in charge: the cricket. Obviously only the principal has the carry and conceal permit for something this deadly. Crickets came in several sizes, but they all had the same construction. It was a metal shell, shaped like an insect with a piece of spring steel underneath. Depressing a side of the sprung metal made a sound that echoed off the outer shell. The smaller crickets made a chirping sound and were harmless, but the larger caliber crickets evoked fear in anyone who heard it. The principal of the Shrine carried at least a 50 caliber cricket. Possibly, it was even larger.

Maybe I need to explain the power of the cricket. It all begins in first grade. There are a number of sounds in Calf Lick schools that demand that you freeze in place: the Angelus at noon, the ringing of the bells at recess, and the clicking sound of a cricket at any time. We were trained to stop and freeze in place at any of these sounds. It's like training a dog, except without the treats. When the church bells rang out for the twelfth time for the Angelus, life returned to normal at recess. With the ringing of the bell at recess, we would freeze and wait for the second bell that would signal an orderly return to class.

The clicking of the cricket was a different matter. If that loud 50 caliber click was aimed at you, and you'd know it because it would make your ears ring, you froze. And you'd stay in that position until a second click was triggered. I've seen friends in some strange positions, never moving a muscle, until the cricket was fired a second time. To move before the second click was an invitation to a very long written task. You could be trading a leg cramp for a wrist cramp. With a homework load of three hours a night, a leg cramp seemed to be the better trade off, so nobody ever moved.

You were trained in the first few grades to freeze under "fire"(standing, running or jumping), and life as you knew it, stopped. What may have been seconds, felt like days. What you were thinking vanished. What you were going to say, you forgot. You waited for the second click. No "atta boys." No pats on the back. No treats. I read somewhere that this tactic is similar to training a wild animal like an elephant.

I walked into class on a chilly fall morning and was met with a shakedown by Sister Knuckles. I've been known to bring a lot of stuff to school that could be confiscated if Knuckles ever caught me. And, occasionally, she did. My full infantry division of green plastic army men was now just a company of men in various poses, and I've had to scrape lettuce together to replace so many confiscated yo-yo's that I've lost count. But this morning was different. Knuckles was searching for something specific.

"Empty your pockets, David." She said. I did as I was told and revealed a stack of baseball cards along with a handkerchief and ten cents in change.

"Open your book bag." I opened my Army issued knapsack from Sunny Surplus. In it was nothing more than forty pounds of text books and my homework.

"Open your lunch box." I opened my Davy Crockett lunch box, to reveal a bag of potato chips, some butterscotch Tastykakes, a thermos of milk and the third cheese sandwich I'd had in a week. Rations at home must be running low.

"OK. Go hang your coat up and take your seat." Was all Knuckles said as the next one in line stepped up for a pat down.

As I took my seat in class, I looked around. The eyes of the eternally confused ginks and dames looked even more confused than I was, and tongues were wagging like forty dogs left out in the yard in Bawlmer's August heat. Something big was going on and the nuns weren't letting on.

"I hear every class is getting the same treatment." Someone said.

"They must be looking for an atomic bomb." Came another voice.

"Yeah, I heard that those new watches that glow in the dark are radioactive." I heard that, too.

"I heard that some kid in sixth grade is from Russia and he wears a watch." It must have been a birthday present, I thought.

"I think somebody wants to blow up the school because we're Calf Lick and commies hate Calf Licks." Wait a second, blow up this school?

"Yeah, and you remember what Knuckles said. The commies hate children, especially Calf Lick children."

All of this jawing was getting out of hand. If order wasn't restored quickly, some sixth grade kid with a watch and an accent was about to get a bashing at recess.

"Ahh, excuse me. Has anybody asked Knuckles what this is all about?" I interjected in the frenzied back and forth conversation that looked like it was heading to a very bad end.

"I did. Knuckles just said it was nothing to be concerned about." Came a reply.

Nothing to be concerned about was something the pious penguins said when there was something big to be concerned about. But the nuns were a tight-lipped group. We were even told history stories about some of their own who went down in a blaze of martyrdom because they wouldn't rat out someone.

Something big was going on and they weren't talking. At least they weren't talking to us. Whatever it was, it was big, and only the inner circle of the Franciscans knew what it was. While most of the dames and a few mugs were waiting for the atom bomb to drop on the Shrine, I tried to figure out what all the body and possession searches were about. It couldn't be stolen money. Only one kid in a classroom usually had a wad of dough, snookered out of the rest of the class. I doubt it was jewelry, since as Calf Licks, we didn't wear jewelry. The reason we didn't was because there were so many jewelry deficient and starving children in China. A real weapon, like a knife, was out of the question. We knew better than to come to school armed. A penknife was a supersonic one-way ticket to public school. I couldn't think of a thing that caused such a school wide shakedown and frisking.

Just when most of us were released to the recess yard, two official black Bawlmer City Fords parked at the Brendan Avenue entrance to the Shrine. I expected to see a couple of flatfoots get out, but they were dressed in suits. Detectives! My kind of guys! Oh, this was even bigger than I thought.

They walked into the school where Mark and I couldn't go, since we were required to play outside. I wanted to go into the Shrine's hallways and listen in on the reports that were being taken from the nuns by the plain clothes dicks. I knew Mark and I could help break this case, but I also knew we'd get a 500 sentence task entitled "I will not bother the pleese." and we'd probably have to stay after school to do it. Mark and I would have to muscle every pigeon in the yard to get some kind of lead. I tracked Mark down in the corner of the yard. He was giving the third to some gink about a missing rosary, or maybe it was a Saint Christopher medal. I wasn't sure which, and I didn't care.

"Mark, can you leave that hood alone for a minute?" I asked.

Mark strolled over, with a parting shot to the suspect. "We're gonna keep our eyes on you."

"You ain't my mother! And you and an army ain't gonna do anything about it!" Came the response. Ginks and hoods get this idea, and then a big mouth, when they know they're getting let off. It's all big talk from a small mind.

"Didja get a gander at the two pleese cars out front?" I asked.

"I saw 'em. I figured you were inside helping 'em."

"You know I can't. I've spent so many days after school writing tasks that my mom thinks the school day has been extended."

"You see anything?"

"I saw three plain clothes dicks walk in. That's all I know."

"Three?" Mark whistled. "You absolutely sure that the commies ain't gonna blow up the school?"

"I'm sure. Well mostly. If we have an air raid drill after recess, I may have to rethink the atom bomb thing."

I continued, "You need to work the yard. Lean on whoever you have to. "

"Pretty big, huh?"

"Oh yeah, it's big. I know it." Actually I didn't know it, but you can't shuck off a shakedown of the entire school.

Mark and I walked off in different directions in the yard. We had to work every gink, every hood, every dame and moll that we thought might hold some inside info.

I met up with Mark in class after recess.

"You get any leads?"

"Nope. You?"

"Not a thing." I answered.

"Didja notice sumpin strange today at recess?" Mark asked.

"No. I mean, not anything more than the usual hoods and jailbirds tryin to get the best of everybody else. Was I supposed to notice sumpin?"

"It was quiet." Mark said.

"Quiet? It sounded like Paris during the revolution! We have all the noise without all the blood. Where do you get this quiet idea from?"

"Something was missing. A sound. Something. I'm not sure, but there was sumpin missing."

"If ya think of it, let me know."

"I will." Mark replied.

The pleese had left, obviously with a lot of notes stuffed in their pocket protectors and coat pockets, which left Mark and me to figure out what was going on because we were working the inside. A detective who shaves would never be able to work undercover in this school, unless you were in the eighth grade and you got held back about four times. Unfortunately, I'd seen at least two of those types at the Shrine.

Mark caught up with me as I walked home from school in a steady rain, trading a dismal cell of learning for a dismal barracks of overcooked food, homework and chores.

"I think I figured it out!" He declared.

"Good. Now would you like to tell me what you think you figured out?"

"The quiet. I knew there was a sound missing." Mark said.

"Oh, and what sound was missing?"

"The cricket!" Mark sounded like he had just gotten a 100 on every test that the nuns could inflict on the class in a month.

I stopped walking and looked at him. It was beginning to rain harder and my army knapsack was getting soaked. But I knew he was right. I was so used to the sound, so familiar with so many classmates suspended in mid-air when the "click, click" was deployed towards them, always looking over my shoulder waiting for that cricket to be aimed at me, that the sounds almost became part of my life. But I hadn't heard them today in the recess yard, and the halls of the Shrine were silent. Could this be the reason for a school wide frisking?

"You may be onto something. We gotta look into this. Lets' see if the cricket shows up tomorrow." I said.

Mark and I parted ways, he towards his home and me towards mine. I expected to be greeted with shouts of "don't bring your soaked clothes into my living room, I just vacuumed! Take them off, now." It's no fun peeling your duds off down to your underwear, running upstairs to put on dry clothes while your older sister is snickering at your half-dressed escape. I walked in the front door and heard exactly what I thought I would hear, complete with a giggling older sister.

I was thinking about the lack of the sound of the cricket throughout dinner. I was thinking about it so much that I even ate the asparagus on my plate, and didn't even protest why my mom had given me such a crappy vegetable. At any rate, I'm sure she thought she'd finally triumphed in the "get David to eat vegetables" department.

After a watery dessert of strawberry Junket, I went to my room to do my homework, except that English and arithmetic weren't on my mind. Something big was going on. The Shrine nuns had called the coppers to investigate. The cricket's terrifying sounds were not heard at recess. And for all I knew, we would all face another day of a shakedown. I tried to picture what was going on at the Shrine convent.

I imagined a gathering of the Franciscan pious penguins in their convent; sitting around a great table with large sheets of white paper and more than a few handy drinks, all of it illuminated by brightly lit candles, and the smoke from burning incense turning the room into a flickering, smoky cloud. The Irish nuns would, of course, have a healthy cup of Irish coffee, while others would be drinking from mugs spiked with their own ancestral grog. They would be trading notes and suggestions, all the while looking over an extensive list of students-turned-suspects. They were doing their own investigation. As they looked over the wide sheets of paper that I'm sure contained a monthly schedule of reprimands, beatings, tasks and possibly even grades, they searched for likely suspects.

"When was the last time you whacked Michael?" asks Sister Bernie of Sister Monica.

"Lemme see. Aahh…it was two weeks ago." Sister Monica would answer, as she looked over her secret chart.

"Whack him again tomorrow, then." Sister Bernie would say.

"Has John's bruises on his hand faded yet, Sister Mary?" Asked Sister Agatha.

"Yes, he can even hold a pencil, now." Would be Sister Mary's response.

"Good. I think a sharp wrap to his palm might open up his soul to confession."

"But he seems like such a good boy, Sister." Would come the protest from Sister Mary.

"There is no such thing as a good boy, Sister. 'Good' and 'boy' don't belong together."

"Do we know of anyone else who might help us locate the cricket?" most of the pious penguins would muse out loud.

"Richard might know something. He's friends with every other boy in class. But he gives me no trouble during class." Would be offered up by Sister Regina.

"He's a boy, isn't he?" It would be almost a chorus of nuns singing the same question.

"Well, yes, but…"

"Then he hasn't given you trouble… yet. Give him a 5,000 line task tomorrow. Something like, 'I will not talk in class'… or something like that." Coming from Sister Bernie.

"But Richard never talks in class!" Protested Sister Regina.

"Make him! And then offer him a plea deal. You'll cut the task down to 500 times if he finds who stole the cricket." Sister Bernie should have been a Vatican investigator, she was that good.

"So, have we narrowed down the vile, unclean, sinning group of boys who could have committed such a crime against us?" This would come from Sister Salvatore's nails-on-a-chalkboard voice as she entered the hall floating just above the floor as she always did. You never knew when she was near, she moved so silently. That's why we all figured she floated above the ground like a ghost. We would tell ourselves that the resemblance between her and a ghost was just coincidence, but we weren't 100% sure.

"Not quite yet, Sister." Would come the reply.

"I want this resolved tomorrow! You understand? I don't care how many bruises you inflict! Find my cricket! Have any one of you asked Father Duck if he's had a boy in confession who told him that they stole my cricket?"

"Ahh, Sister, you know that priests are forbidden to reveal what was said in confession."

"Lean on him, anyway!" Sister Salvatore would roar.

And so it might have went; deep into the night, with notes and suggestions offered back and forth between the nuns in that smoky candle lit room. It became a to-do list of likely suspects, sprinkled with a group of boys who were overdue for correction of some sort.

I walked back to school the next morning fully expecting to be frisked once again. I wondered how quiet school would be without a cricket. But it may not be a cricket. Something was missing in the chaos of recess and the school's halls. Mark had zeroed in on it, though. I decided to focus in on that sound.

I walked into class and events (or a lack of them) had grown larger. Instead of being a full body and knapsack frisking, the nuns resorted to strong arming. As I walked up to Sister Knuckles, she grabbed my tie and slightly lifted her hand. The Shrine's tie for boys had a "SLF" embroidered near the bottom. While we knew it reflected the school's name, Shrine of the Large Flower, most of us referred to the initials as "Salvatore's Little Feet." But all of us knew that Sister Salvatore probably didn't have any feet since she had learned to levitate. The boys' tie was a woven hangman's noose or at least a soft garrote that the nuns could use to extract information. It's the reason none of us ever wore our tie straight.

"Tell me what you know, David." Knuckles said to me as her hand slowly twisted.

"I don't know anything 'ster." I gasped.

"You sure? You aren't keeping anything from me, are you?"

Knuckles voice almost approached a whisper as her hand continued to twist my tie. I could only answer her in a whisper as I was seeing stars and gasping for air.

"No, 'ster."

She abruptly let go of my tie, dropped her hands and sternly said, "Next!"

As I tried to remember how to breathe, I looked around the class. Seems most of the boys were also trying to do what I was doing. Amid the gasping, choking, wheezing and red faces, we all knew the nuns were searching for something.

"Open your religion book to page 5." Knuckles demanded. "Today we're going to focus on the Ten Commandments. Marsha, please read the eighth commandment."

"Thou shall not steal"

And so the morning class began. We not only got an in-depth lesson about the sins of stealing, we also got into the finer points of not coveting stuff. I knew what the method was. Instill guilt. Guilt usually worked on Calf Licks of almost any age. But by the time lunch rolled around, nobody had fessed up to stealing or coveting a cricket.

I met Mark in the recess yard to see if he had heard anything. Mark had already started questioning some of the older kids.

"Find us a lead?" I asked.

"Not really. But it seems that everybody in school got the same lesson in religion class today. Some kid got a 5,000 line task in sixth grade and he's already working on it because he has to turn it in tomorrow."

"Well, there goes his recess time, huh."

We both scanned the yard for a possible suspect. We were looking for some hood who was wearing a smirk that matched a stupid look.

"Mark, I think we should talk to Steven."

"Good idea." He answered as we walked off to the farthest corner of the yard.

"Hi, Steven." I said as Mark and I walked through his group of goons. Steven usually wore a smirk but rarely had a stupid look. Today, he must have left his smirk at home, but brought a worried look instead.

"You carrying?" Steven asked me.

"Steven you always ask me that. No, I'm clean." Even Steven should know that I never got my badge back.

"Look, I don't know nothin' bout no cricket!" He stammered.

"Did I say anything about a cricket?"

"No, but you were gonna."

He was right. I was going to ask if he knew about a missing cricket, but I didn't want to tip my hand. If I let on, he'd probably clam up.

"What are you talking about, Steven? What cricket?"

"The principal's cricket! You ain't noticed how quiet it's been the last few days?"

"Gee," I answered. "I hadn't noticed. But you look a bit nervous, Steven. You need to come clean about anything?"

"Look," he answered. "I didn't have nothin' to do with no cricket getting pinched, see? Sure, Johnny here has spent the last two days not stuck in midair, but I didn't take Salvatore's cricket."

"Then why are ya shakin' so much if you didn't do it?"

"Cuz the nuns think I did. You gotta find that cricket, Dave. You gotta help clear my name before Knuckles hands me one of those 5,000 line tasks and hangs me up by my tie. I don't have time for no tasks, I gotta bizness to run."

"We'll start working on it right away, Steven."

"Yeah, yeah, sure, good. Youse two do dat. I got a bizness to run, see."

"Yeah, you told us that already." I answered as Mark and I waded back through the sea of goons.

"You think he took it?" Mark asked.

"Naw. Steven ain't stupid. If he would have, he would have sold it on the black market by now and he'd have that smirk back on his face."

"Think he knows who did?"

"Naw. If he did he'd be workin' both sides. Extortion on the thief's side and negotiating a reward on the other."

"Got any other ideas?"

"Nope. But you were right. The nuns want that high caliber cricket back, pronto. All we can do is keep our eyes and ears open and wait for a break."

"Let's just hope the break isn't a broken neck." Mark said.

"You mean from the ginks and hoods going crazy on each other, or the nuns stringing somebody up?"

"Either one, whichever comes first." He answered.

"Let's see if we can get some skinny on the pleese coming to school yesterday from one of the penguins."

"You think any of them will talk to us?"

"Not to me, but I bet Sister Bernie would be happy to talk to you. She's Polish, too, ya know."

"What am I supposed to say to her?"

"I don't know. Use that charm of yours."

"I don't think I have any charm. Ain't dames supposed to have charm? I think I gave up charm for Lent." He laughed.

"Everybody's a comedian. I'll meet you back at the office."

In ten minutes Mark was back at the office as I was just unwrapping my second butterscotch of recess. I couldn't read his face so I wasn't sure what type of news he was bringing me.

"Well, I have good news and I have bad news." He began. "Which do you want first?"

"Give me the bad news." I said as I braced myself.

"The bad news is those plains clothes we saw yesterday? They weren't detectives. They were from the Bawlmer Far Department doing a routine inspection. Seems we're on our own tryin' to find that cricket."

"What's the good news?"

"Seems I do have charm."

"Oh, brudda." I said as I wiped my hand over my face like Bugs Bunny and imitated his voice. We really were workin' the inside of this case and with no backup. Now, more than ever, we needed a break.

Bathroom breaks at a Calf Lick school go by a strict schedule. Starting in the first grade, you learn how much to drink so you can pee at the right time. The schedule is so rigid that by the time you reach adulthood, you can fight an entire war and never have to go and later, you can skip bathroom breaks for a full eight hour work shift no matter how much "joe" you've been drinking. But it takes time to learn the schedule and it wasn't unusual that one of us would need to go at a time that was not the appointed time. Frustration and anger usually showed on the faces of the nuns if you raised your hand, but they never said no to having to go.

"'Ster, 'ster!" I was waving my outstretched hand like I was trying to get the attention of a rescue plane.

Knuckles glared at me. "What do you want, David?"

"Can I please go to the boy's room?"

I heard an exasperated sigh from Knuckles. "Yes. You have three minutes."

As I walked up the aisle, I saw the saddened look of

classmates that said, "Poor boy, you'll never be able to work a full shift at Bethlum Steel."

I ran down the dimly lit hall to the boy's room. As I entered the lavatory I heard a familiar sound. It was the sound of a high powered weapon…the cricket. There were two older boys in there; one holding the cricket, the other looked as if he had run into the tiled wall. I stood there for a few seconds and what I thought I saw, I actually did. One kid would run towards the wall, and just before he would hit it, the other pressed the cricket. The running kid collided into the wall, got up and said, "Try it again." And then they did, with the same results.

"What are you two trying to do?" I asked. I tried to remain calm as I spoke, since I finally found the cricket.

"Hey, squirt!" The kid with the cricket in his hand said with a giggle in his voice. "We're trying to get this thing to work, see. Sister Salvatore can point it at any one of us and we freeze in place, see. I found it on the second story window ledge a few days ago, and me and Les are trying to see if we can get it to work like she can."

"Any luck?" I asked, trying to sound composed.

"Nope. Les has run into that wall I don't know how many times. Hey, Les, how many times you hit that wall?"

"Bout thirty." Les answered in a groggy voice that sounded like he thought he should have been a winner in a boxing match with a heavy weight champion.

"You know the entire school is getting frisked because you have the cricket?" I asked.

"Hey! Easy, squirt. We're just messin with it. I'll put it back."

"When?" I asked. I was getting impatient and besides, I really had to use the restroom.

"When we're ready! What are you, the nun's pigeon? Look, if we get caught, I'm gonna come looking for you, see." The older kid glared at me.

"I ain't a snitch. I'm not tellin' nobody. But everybody is getting tired of being in a lineup and frisked every day." I tried to sound calm but firm. It was almost convincing, except that I still had to use the bathroom and I knew my time was running out.

"I said we'd put it back. Hey, Les, run at the wall again. This time I'll aim at your legs." I heard the sound of the cricket and the thud of Les's skull hit the wall as I did my bizness. I didn't want to get caught with these two ginks who were trying to unlock a mystery of the Calf Lick universe.

"Just so I get it, how have you been able to carry it in and out of school. I mean, one day I may want to learn how to smuggle stuff." I asked as I came out of the stall.

"That's the easy part." The gink laughed. "When I found it, I just put it in my coat pocket. But, to get it back into school? I'm a genius! Pure genius. I knew the nuns would be tearing the school apart trying to find it, see. And it's been really chilly the past few days, ya know. So I've been wearing mittens to school, see. And just when I got to class, I'd take off the mittens, put the cricket in one, and then stuff the other mitten inside the first one. They never asked me about my mittens and the cricket was all wrapped up, safe and sound-like."

"Wow! That is genius." I said. Actually, it was genius. I wasn't sure whether to file this new info under "jailbird smuggling basics" or under "ideas you can use."

As the door of the boy's room was closing when I left, I heard a painful "Ow!" and "OK, one more time, Les. Run at the wall." As I hurried up the quiet hall back to class, I wondered if anybody would notice the colored eggs on Les's forehead. I sat down at my desk with Knuckles' glare trying to drill a hole in my shirt.

Mark and I finally got a break, but only of a sort. I now knew it was the cricket that the nuns were so intense in retrieving. I also knew who had it, but I couldn't tell any of them. The older gink told me he would put it back, but I couldn't be sure if he would. It seemed like a waiting game.

After school, walking home on a frigid fall afternoon, I told Mark what I had discovered. I didn't tell him I was thinking about asking my parents for a pair of mittens for Christmas, though.

"So how many times did this Les guy run into the wall?" Mark asked.

"He said about thirty times. But that bozo hit the wall three times while I was in the lavatory. His head looked like an Easter basket. "

"Wow, looks like if you can make it past sixth grade, the sky's the limit for being stupid."

"Seems so. I doubt none of the pious penguins want to be saddled with a gink in class who has to shave before he comes to school, so I'm sure he'll pass."

"You know these hoods?" Mark asked me.

"I've seen 'em in the yard, but I don't know 'em."

"Maybe we should tail 'em, just to make sure they don't try something really dumb, like trying to freeze a first grader. Those kids are so…young." Mark said.

"Good idea. Besides, one of them said he was gonna put it back where he found it and we need to make sure he does."

Mark and I patrolled the school yard like we always do, but we were paying attention to the two older ginks who had the cricket. We finally tracked down the two older hoods in the yard and they were acting normal-like. I mention acting normal in the sense of how a prisoner of war acts in a detention camp and has an escape plan, but that was normal enough for my liking.

I tapped the cricket-holding hood on the shoulder. "You put it back yet?" I asked him.

He turned to me. "Hey, squirt. I told you I was gonna put it back, didn't I? I have to wait for the right moment, though. Besides, I think Les ain't feeling so good right now. Says he wants to go to sleep. Anyway, I can't seem to get it to work right. Fun tryin, though. I'll put it back and the nuns won't be any wiser. Hey, Les! You OK, buddy?"

"I'm really sleepy, man. When can I take a nap?" Everything above Les' eyebrows looked like somebody had painted it with bright watercolors. Put a basket on his head, add some fake grass and a chocolate egg or two hung from his ears, and he was ready for an Easter costume party dressed as a one man Easter parade. Too bad Halloween was already over.

"You have to stay awake, Les. You got the rest of the day to get through."

"Oh, yeah. Right. What day is it anyway?" Obviously Les was not going to be a contender.

Mark and I walked away shaking our heads. There was nothing either of us could do until we reported back to class in the morning and see if the nuns were still searching everybody. We needed two things to happen in the morning to make sure the cricket was returned. We needed to not be heavily frisked, not to mention threatened, and we needed to see one or two classmates frozen with that I-got-caught-somebody-please-help-me look. If we saw a few students suspended in mid-air, we didn't need to hear the heavy caliber sound of the cricket. We'd know.

As we walked the last few steps on Brendan Avenue to the Shrine entrance, the next morning, we got our answer. It looked like a forest of human trees with branches and limbs going in all directions. Students were everywhere, in all kinds of positions, all wearing the same look on their faces, and none of them moving. Mark and I had to weave our way through the mass of frozen humanity to walk through the doors. Once again we were happy that we hadn't come to school early.

"Looks like the nuns got the cricket back." Mark commented.

"Yeah, but did you see how many kids there were?"

"When they found it, they probably got it blessed by Father Duck, reloaded and decided to test it to make sure it wasn't contaminated with some mortal sin." Mark commented.

"You think so?" I asked. "Looks like somebody went on a clicking spree."

"Oh, those kids will be ok. With another click of the cricket, they'll all go back to life as normal and they won't even remember what happened."

"How do you know that?" I asked. I wanted to know. Even though I've been hit with the cricket click many times, it's all a fuzzy memory. How did Mark know?

"It's got a lot to do with breathing. It may have been a "Hardy Boys" story, can't remember which one, but I think they got frozen. They figured out that if you got zapped when you were breathing in, you lost your memory. But if you were breathing out, you could remember. OK, maybe it wasn't the "Hardy Boys;" maybe it was an article in "Boy's Life," or maybe "Mechanics Illustrated." Anyway, every time I heard the first click, I breathed out. And while the click froze me up, I kinda knew what was going on even though I couldn't move a muscle. When the nuns triggered the second, releasing click, I remembered what I had done."

"You did this in the name of science?"

"No, I did it in the name of survival. I come home from school every day and my mom asks me what went on, what I learned, and so on. If I couldn't tell her, I'd get the third degree during dinner."

"Oh." I said. Now one of life's mysteries was finally making sense to me. My mom would ask those same questions. "Oltno." Was always my answer. And now I knew why I said that. I was breathing in when I was hit with the clicks of the cricket, and I've been a favorite target of the cricket for years. It wasn't that I didn't remember, but because I'd taken so many shots at recess and in the Shrine's halls…and all the time I was breathing in when it happened. Leave it to Mark to come up with the answers to life's most confounding questions.

"Thanks, Mark." I said.

"What for?"

"Just…thanks."

There was no frisking, no shakedown, and no tie twisting when we walked into class.

Christmas Ginks 'n' Santa's Elves

The Thanksgiving holiday was just days away and Mark and I were trying to clear our case load before we had a few days of "R&R." It was a typical Bawlmer fall day. If you can see your breath at noon you just tend to slow down. The inmates…er, students… in the recess yard also seemed to feel the chill of fall. Bears go into hibernation, according to my latest issue of "Boys Life Magazine," squirrels hide their acorns in trees, every biting insect in Bawlmer has died because of the cold, the birds stop singing, and baseballs and footballs sting your hands when you try to catch them. We were all about to adjust our lives to the slower pace dictated by late fall and winter.

And then…

We weren't expecting interruptions at our outdoor office in the recess yard on such a cold afternoon. Mark and I were trying to shuffle both papers and our feet to keep warm on such a sunny, but chilly, day. A skinny kid with a cap that covered his ears barged into our office. A brown curly lock of hair was doing its best to escape from each side of his cap, and he looked like an escapee from the North Pole. OK, that makes it sound like we had a door on our corner of the yard, and with the frosty air and breeze, I wish we had but we didn't, which means anybody from the North Pole could invade our space and ask us to solve a case. It's the price you pay to be accessible to every Tom, Dick, Harry, and sometimes a dame called Lola.

"You Mark and Dave?"

"Yeah, that's…"

"Youse guys gotta help me now, see."

"What seems to be…" I began.

"Somebody done stole my Duncan Tournament. I need it back….like now."

"When was the last ti…." I tried again to speak a full sentence.

"I brought it to school this morning, along with my Duncan Butterfly and Imperial. Had them in my coat pocket. I was practicing for the competition this weekend. I was gonna enter all three classes, and I was about to practice with my tournament, see, and it was gone!"

"When was the last…" I tried to interrupt, but this kid was on a roll.

"Ya know, it's pretty easy to walk the dog with the butterfly, and even easier to do the rock the cradle trick with it, but it ain't so easy with the tournament, ya know what I mean?"

"I'd heard that. So, tell me…"I tried again to ask a question.

"I reached in my pocket for it and it was gone! Somebody done stole my Duncan Tournament! Whatta ya gonna do about it, huh?" the kid asked with a look that demanded immediate results.

"You got a name, Bunky?" I asked.

"Jack, Jack Diamond."

"Does that make you a pair of Jacks?" Mark asked. I could tell Mark was in one of his mischievous moods.

"No, just one Jack."

"You got an older brother named Ace?" Mark asked.

"No, just a sister."

"She go by queen?" Mark could hardly contain himself. I was waiting for him to ask Jack if he was related to the Heart family, or if they belonged to a club and if his mother dug in her garden with a spade.

"When was the last time you saw the yo-yo in question?" I asked, trying to head Mark off from making jokes involving playing cards.

"This morning when I hung up my coat in the coatroom. It was there in my pocket when I came out to recess. Somebody pinched it, I tell ya!" Jack was on the edge of losing his cool. We were surrounded by fall air so I figured he was closer to losing something else, like his confidence.

The call to go outside for recess at the Shrine looked like a cattle stampede. Except not a cowboy alive, riding his favorite bronco, would want to tangle with hundreds of kids running to find some freedom. Cowpokes might be firing off their six shooters, cracking whips and yelling "get along little doggie" as they tried to turn the stampede towards itself so the frenzy would stop, but I doubt a third or fourth grader would be paying attention to any of it. Instead, there were the Franciscan nuns, clickers in hand, and gigantic rosaries and knotted waist ropes, standing in stairwells and halls, guiding young humanity towards recess. With a bit of imagination on my part, I figured we should all go outside and graze on the grass and say an occasional "moo." Except the recess yard never had any grass to speak of.

"Can you give me a description of your Tournament?" I asked Jack.

"You know what a Tournament looks like!" Jack said.

"Yeah, we do, but we need a description of YOURS." I was

getting impatient. I was cold and, getting a description of a missing yo-yo in this type of weather, I would have preferred it to be in writing and in the warmth of a classroom.

"Oh, yeah, right. It's red." Jack finally said.

"Look, Jack," I began, trying to hold back my cold frustration, "in this yard right now there's probably at least 15 red Duncan Tournament Yo-Yo's. How are we supposed to make sure we get yours back? Mark and me ain't got time to gather up that many yo-yo's, put them in a pile so you can pick out yours. Unless it's got some mark on it so we can ID it, I'm afraid we can't help ya."

"I have my initials on it. A "J" and a diamond in white. The "J" is on one side and the diamond on the other. That way it stays balanced, see."

"Yeah, nice touch, Jack. I'm sure your tournament spins straight." I answered.

"Yeah it does. I just got new string for it so it spins great."

"I'm sure it…" I began, trying to get this kid to stop so we could start our investigation

"Buddy Deane." Jack blurted out.

"What?"

"Buddy Deane Show. Saturday. This Saturday afternoon. Youse guys don't know about it, huh? He's gonna have a Bob-A-Loop demonstration and then a Duncan Yo-yo contest. My parents are gonna take me there so I can enter. The Duncan contest, not the Bob-A-Loop contest."

"I didn't know abo…." I began.

"You know about the Bob-A-Loop, right? Greatest skill toy ever invented in the world! You think it has anything to do with Lucy Ball shouting Bobalouie? Probably not, but you know about it, right?"

I knew about the Bob-A-Loop. I'd just seen it being played

within the last week. It was a face breaker, as far as I could tell. A large heavy wooden barrel with a hole in one end, connected with a string to a stick. You'd whip the barrel up towards the stick to try and catch it. Oh, yeah, sure, and break your nose, blacken an eye, take out a few front teeth, all in the name of skill. I suspected it was invented by a starving dentist. Thanks, but I'll stick to my knife throwing games like stretch and mumbly-peg. They're safer.

"Ok, Jack. I think we have everything we need. Mark and I will patrol the yard and see if we can find your Tournament. We'll get back to you." I said.

"When?" He asked.

"As soon as we can. Practice with your Duncan Butterfly and Imperial. We'll go to work."

Jack walked out of the office, hands in his pockets, brown hair waving in the cold breeze from under his cap. I watched the kid walk away. Jack used to own three yo-yo's and a shot at being a contender, but now he only had two yo-yos and was doubting himself in the weekend's upcoming bout. Could he win one round out of two? His odds were better in three rounds and he knew it. Maybe losing the Tournament affected his wrist flick, maybe his hands wouldn't be fast enough for the array of tricks; maybe he felt like he'd lost his edge. I watched him walk away, shoulders hunched forward, all the while quickly wiping his nose with his right hand and moving side-to-side. I noticed Jack moved a bit too much to his left, and his right hand wasn't quite high enough as he flicked his imperial yo-yo towards the ground. He seemed a bit gimpy, not quite a limp, but a bit off kilter. I turned to Mark.

"What do you make of it, Mark?"

"Kid obviously lost a yo-yo. I don't think it was pinched.

You see his coat? There's no way he could put two Duncans in one pocket. I can hardly put my hand in my coat pocket with one yo-yo. He dropped it somewhere in the crowd. "

"I agree. Let's split up and you take the North side of the yard and I'll work the South. Meet me back here in fifteen minutes. Let's see if we can turn up the Jack of Duncans."

"Diamonds." Mark corrected.

"I was making a joke."

"You were? Pretty lame, partner. "

Mark and I walked off into the recess yard looking for a red Duncan Tournament Yo-Yo. Shouldn't be too hard to find, I thought. All we had to do was look for a red yo-yo, stop and take a closer look.

But the air was chilly and just like baseballs and foot-balls stung your hands when you caught them, a yo-yo spinning at a million miles an hour and returning to your hand demanded dedication to the sport. Not many boys were throwing yo-yo's for obvious reasons in this weather, the least of which was because most of us had the Palmer method of handwriting right after recess. With cold stinging hands from recess we might as well be trying to form the cursive alphabet with a pen in our armpits once we were back at our desks. I kept looking for a yo-yo in the hands of a new-found owner.

Wandering around the yard, looking for the not-so obvious suspects, I think I found him, and maybe the yo-yo in ques-tion. Standing close to the fence, turned slightly away from the crowd stood Tony Fedora. His right hand gave away that telltale flick of the wrist, quickly turning his palm down. A red Duncan Tournament spun just a few inches above his shoe tops and an inch above the bottom of his pants. I watched his hand jerk and the yo-yo climb up the string like a spider in a panic, back to his hand. Tony had this smile on his face as if he had just discovered electricity but didn't want the world to know just yet. I stood there and watched him launch the Tournament a few more times as his smile grew wider with each throw and retrieve.

I knew Tony pretty well. A well behaved kid, one of ten, who lived in a 14 foot wide, 3 bedroom, 1 bath row home. He was quiet, always had his homework done on time; an almost "A" student and dressed like he wore hand-me-downs. He never complained about his situation, better yet, he was always the kid who stood up for other kids. I didn't want to confront him, but I knew I had to.

"Hey, Tony, how are ya?" I asked.

"Hey, Dave, I'm fine." He answered as he flicked the Tournament down, let it sleep for a few seconds and with a slight twitch, brought it back to his hand.

"You're pretty good. Wurjagitdat?"I said.

"I just found it. Think it has a new string. It's spins perfectly."

"Can I see it, Tony?"

"Sure" He said, as he handed the Tournament to me.

I looked at the yo-yo. It was a Duncan Tournament and it was red. Inside I was hoping that I wouldn't see a painted "J" on one side and a diamond on the other. I've seen balls get hit over my head to the fence for homeruns and watched a kid run for a touchdown beyond my reach, but my heart never felt so low when I looked at Tony's "found" yo-yo. The marks were there.

"You say you found it, Tony?"

"Yeah, just a while ago, just outside the school doors. Why?"

"We have a report about a Tournament with a "J" on one side and a diamond on the other side that went missing just a little while ago. Sorry, Tony, you have a Duncan that belongs to somebody else. I'm gonna have to take it and return it."

I may as well have said, Tony, we're going to take away that dog you found. The one that acts and feels like your best friend. The look in his eyes said the same thing. A best friend, a best toy, a new found something that belonged to him and wasn't a hand-me-down from an older brother or cousin. A tear welled up in his eye, but Tony was quick to wipe it away, telling me it was just the cold air that made his eyes water.

"Ain't possession nine-tenths of the law?" He asked.

"Only when the pleese hold it for 30 days and it goes unclaimed, Tony. Sorry. The Tournament belongs to a kid named Jack Diamond. I have to take it back to him. Sorry."

I walked away from Tony with the red Duncan Tournament with a new string in my hand, but carried a weight inside that made it hard to walk across the recess yard. I may have been doing the right thing, but somehow, it just didn't feel like the right thing.

As I trudged back to my recess corner office, I started thinking. I know if I had said that to Mark, he would have told me that I was never good at doing two things at the same time, like walking and thinking. But somehow the idea that one lug had three yo-yo's while another kid had to wait for the same toy to find its way to him by way of an older brother or an even older uncle, just stuck in my craw. While I had no idea where my craw was on my body, something felt stuck. Somewhere.

Mark caught up to me just as I entered our corner office.

"You've been trying to think and walk at the same, haven't ya?" He asked.

"Yeah," I answered absently, "How'd you know?"

"Cuz you look like Pop after he's had six beers. You're weaving and bobbing all over the place."

"Sorry, I didn't think anybody would notice."

"Pop never thinks so, either." Mark replied.

Pop was our grandfather, dad to both our moms, a house painter by trade. When the families would gather on Sundays, at some point in the afternoon our dads and Pop would grab their gallon pickle jars and walk towards the door and one of the cars parked at the curb. One of the lady-folk would always inquire where three grown men were going on a Sunday afternoon, carrying pickle jars. "We've got to go get some vitamins." was always Pop's reply. Of course we all knew what he meant. They were off to a local tavern to get some fresh draft beer. Since Pop was about 100 years old at the time, drinking the "nectar of the gods" as my uncle always called it, made sense if I wanted to live almost forever. I always viewed the daily vitamins my mom would hand me with suspicion.

"I see you found Jack's Tournament." Mark observed.

"Yeah, I got it back." I replied. "But something is sticking in my craw, Mark."

"You have a craw? I know that a cow chews its cud, but I'm not sure what a cud is. You think you have a cud in your craw? Hold on, what's a craw?"

"I think my craw is about here." I answered as I pointed to the middle of my chest.

"You're not gonna puke, are ya?"

"No!" I answered. "I can't quite explain it. Know who had Jack's yo-yo? Tony Fedora."

"You mean that 'I-talian' kid with a hundred brothers and sisters who live down the street from you?" Mark answered with a look of surprise. "I heard there's so many of 'em that they have to share plates for dinner. He's the one who has to wear the same uniform pants he was wearing two years ago. His family is the poorest family at the Shrine.

"He ain't got a hundred brothers and sisters. He's got nine. I been to their house, once. The only place somebody isn't sleeping is on the stairs."

"I always liked Tony. Good kid. Always happy, always looking out for the first graders." Mark replied.

"Yeah. Always happy. Always looks out for the younger kids." I answered. I think my craw was getting tighter as we discussed Tony.

"Look, Mark, we gotta do sumpin' for Tony." I blurted out.

"What? Like get his brothers and sisters adopted?"

"No! My guess is, by the look in his eyes just a little while ago, that Santa just doesn't have too much in his sack when he gets to Tony's house. See? I know he's a grateful kid, and all, but somehow Santa's bag just doesn't have very much by the time he slides down their chimley."

"Ah, Dave, you know there ain't no Santa Claus, right?"

"Yes there is! Every Christmas morning I come downstairs and there's all these presents for my sister, my brother and me. My parents don't have that kind of scratch to give us those things. That HAS to be Santa Claus!"

"The Fedora's don't have a chimley and neither do you."

"Oh yeah? Well my dad puts up the cardboard brick fireplace in the basement every year. It's Santa's secret opening to the house. So…there!"

"There ain't no Santa, Dave."

"Yes there is!" I exclaimed.

"No there ain't."

"Is too!" I hollered, as I stamped my feet, not so much for emphasis, but because my feet were cold.

"Is not!" Mark was stamping his feet, prolly for the same reason.

"Is too!" I shouted.

"NOT!" Mark answered.

"TOO!" I shouted. My feet were going numb as I answered.

"NOT!" Mark shouted. Obviously his feet were feeling the same.

"TOO, TOO, TOO!"

"NOT, NOT, NOT! You sound like a moron, Dave! There ain't no Santa!"

"Well, you sound like a gink! Because only ginks don't believe in Santa!" I shouted back.

"I ain't no gink! Take that back!" Mark shouted.

"I ain't takin it back until you take back calling me a moron."

"Fine…fine…you ain't a moron."

"You ain't a gink, either. Sorry I said it." But the debate wasn't quite over. We both had cards to play in this hand of Christmas poker.

"You ever see Santa in your house?" Mark was pressing, but I was about to press back.

"Well, no." I answered, but I had another card to play in this argument. "But have the Hardy Boys ever come to your house?" I was trying to get the upper hand in this argument.

"Well, no, but…the Hardy Boys are something different."

"SEE? SEE? You ain't never met 'em, but you think they're real…dontcha?" I exclaimed. I could almost see the words I just spoke being formed in the frosty air.

"They are real! Look at all those cases they worked on. It's all there in black and white. And besides, they have a mom and a dad." Mark sputtered.

"Well, then, if Santa ain't real, then neither are the Hardy Boys." I retorted.

"Santa ain't real, Dave." Mark replied. Obviously I was trumping him and he was going back to the original argument.

"Yes he is real!"

"No he ain't!"

"Yes, he is."

"No he ain't!"

"Is too!"

"Ain't!"

"Too!"

"Ain't!"

"Lemme ask you sumpin, Mark." I was about to throw my ace in the hole at him. "Where you going in two weeks, this Saturday?"

"The Polish Home. Why?"

"Who's gonna be there, Mark?"

"A bunch of people from Canton, along with my parents, my Busia, and my Uncle Met."

"Yeah, I know that, but who's gonna be the center of attention during this Polish Home Christmas celebration?"

Mark was hesitating in answering me. He and I both knew the answer, but he wasn't about to say it.

"Well? Who's gonna be there, Mark?" I pressed.

Mark looked down at his cold shuffling feet. "Santa." He muttered.

"And are ya gonna sit on his lap?" I was tightening the argument noose around his neck. At some point in time, he'd have to admit that he believed in Santa. Just to tighten the noose a bit more I asked. "And are ya gonna tell him what you want under the tree on Christmas morning?" I was beginning to feel good about where this was going.

"Yeah." He finally answered. But then he stammered, "Hey! I'm just tryin to cover all the bases, ya know. Just in case."

"I know that, partner. I know that." I answered. Poor kid is feeling a bit like a lost boy from "Peter Pan"... growing up and all. One year you're eight years old, and then, BANG! You're nine. It's not easy keeping up with school work and it's even harder to keep up with knowing all the answers, especially when so many grown-ups think it's fun to keep asking so many questions. I tried to change the subject and let this argument pass so he wouldn't feel so bad about himself.

"Mark, I really want to help Tony Fedora enjoy Christmas."

"I bet you have an idea about that."

"If you would have seen Tony's face when I took that Tournament out of his hand..." I began. "Well, it was pretty sad. I might as well as took his dog."

"Tony has a dog?"

"No! But the look was the same. He really loved tossing that yo-yo. It was like it was his best new toy."

"Yeah, a kid that poor, I can imagine it was not only his best new toy, but his only toy."

"Right. I want to get Tony Fedora his own Duncan Tournament...for Christmas."

"Fine, Daddy Warbucks. You got a dollar? Go buy him one."

"I ain't got two pennies to rub together. You know that. We gotta get creative."

"And this is where you get us involved in something that I'm gonna have to talk about in confession. Are we committing a mortal sin or a venial sin?"

"I ain't sure. Lemme just say that my idea involves a bit of pressure."

"Oh great! It's gonna be a mortal sin. If I die before we carry this out and I go burn in hell, I'll never forgive you."

"That's OK." I laughed. "I'll be in hell right next to ya."

Mark laughed, too. After such a heated exchange about Santa, it felt good to get back to work and the holiday season.

"Here's my plan," I began. "When Jack shows up tomorrow about his yo-yo…we're gonna charge him a five cent finder's fee. If he won't cough up a nickel, he won't get his Tournament back. And that means he won't be able to compete on Buddy Deane's Show on Saturday."

"Five cents is a long way from a dollar."

"Yeah, I know that. That's when you and I go into action. You and me…we're gonna twist every gink, every hood, every lug's arm to cough up some dough. I don't care if it's a penny or a nickel. We're gonna come up with a buck to buy Tony his own Duncan Tournament."

Mark started to walk around in circles, looking intently on the ground.

"What are you doing?" I asked.

"I'm looking for your brains, cuz I know you just lost your mind."

"Hah-hah. Very funny. So funny I forgot to laugh. What's the problem?" I asked.

"If word gets around the Shrine that Dave and Mark are using extortion to get money for a good cause, and I agree with you that it'd be nice to get Tony his own yo-yo for Christmas… we're going to go from private eyes to public charity. We could lose our reputation. Every Larry, Moe and Curly will come to us for a handout. Think about this, Dave. Easter is just five months away! You may want to play Santa, but you want to be the Easter Bunny, too? Charity is what the Knights of Columbus do and I'm in no hurry to join them. They'd have us working the tombola or the money wheel during their bull and oyster roasts by spring if they find out. No thank you!"

"I know it's a gamble. We're just going to use some gentle extortion, that's all."

"Gentle extortion? You mean tighten the screws, don't ya?"

"Well," I said. "Yeah. The big deal is that we keep our intentions on the 'QT.' Got it?"

"And you have a plan for that, too. I hope."

"Sorry, no plan yet. But while the ginks in the yard don't believe in Santa, they still have a soft spot for Christmas."

"You're sure about that, huh?"

"You think they want to be known as naughty or nice?"

"Ah…got it. Can I tell them why they're doing such a good deed?"

"No, unless you trust them to keep their mouths shut. Tell'em it's better to give than receive, good deeds never need to be known. If they spill the beans, you'll tell every nun at the Shrine. Fah-la-la-la-la, la-la-la-la."

"And we deck the halls with THEIR boughs of holly."

I laughed. "Right."

"OK, here's the deal." I began. "You got a list of the hoods and ginks that you muscle every day. You go after them. I'm gonna talk to Steven and see if I can get him and his goons to part with some scratch."

Mark walked away in one direction while I sauntered over to have a heart-to-heart with Steven.

Steven was in his usual place, surrounded by so many goons that it felt like I was hacking my way through an Amazon jungle. Steven was barking orders, pointing in every direction, all the while sucking on a Tootsie Roll Pop.

"Steven, I need to talk to you in private." I said. Talking in private in a school yard was like trying to have a conversation on a phone party line. You may or may not be able to control who was listening in on the call, but worse, anybody within five feet could hear what was being said, too.

"You carrying?" Came Steven's standard response.

"Look, Steven." I began. "You'd know before me if Sister Knuckles was gonna return my badge. Why do you keep asking me that?"

"Because I like watching your face get all screwed up. Your look makes me laugh."

"Great, Steven. Just great. Now that I know, I won't take it so personal."

"Hey, everybody needs a bright spot in their day, ya know? I just like watching your face pucker. Puts a smile on my face. See? I'm smiling right now." Steven wore a wide grin and I was about to look around for the new car I think he just bought.

"I gotta talk to ya 'bout sumpin. I don't want this to get out, so I'm counting on you to keep what I'm gonna tell you on the 'QT'. Got it?"

"Oohh…ya got the goods on one of the nuns?" Steven cooed.

"No, Steven. I need to ask for your help."

"Oohh…the nuns got the goods on you?" He answered as his hands began to twirl.

"No! it's got nuthin to do with me or the nuns. I'm…Mark and me…are tryin to help somebody's Christmas be a bit… brighter. You listenin?"

"Yeah, sure, I'm listenin." Steven replied, but I could tell from the look in his good eye that he was observing the clouds above, and he wasn't hearing me at all. I started to lose my temper.

"This is important, Steven! Stop looking for angels, they gave up on you and me a long time ago…like, in first grade.

I'm tryin to do a good thing for somebody and I'm asking for your help."

"When was the last time you knowed me to do a good deed for somebody else?" Steven asked.

"Never, but I was hoping you had a soft spot somewhere in your heart."

"OK, just for laughs, tell me what's rattling your noggin. Make it quick, cuz I got a bizness to run." Steven was getting impatient. I could tell, just like the car salesman who was sticking a pen in my dad's face and pointing to the bottom line to make the last sale of the day.

I quickly laid out the facts. Jack Diamond was saying that his Duncan Tournament was stolen, even though he actually dropped it. It was found by Tony Fedora and I had to retrieve it from him.

"So, what's the problem?" Steven asked.

"You know these two palookas, Steven?"

"Yeah, Jack is always yapping about something. The kid is good, though, with yo-yo's. I've watched him play with 'em, one in each hand. Pretty cool to watch."

"What about Tony?"

"Tony? He's the poor kid, right? He's probably wearing his older sister's underwear as a hand-me-down. He's got like fifty brothers and sisters, ain't he?

"Tony's one of ten, but other than that, yeah, he's the right kid."

"What's your point?" Steven asked. I could tell he was in a hurry to get back to bizness, so I had to make this quick.

"Mark and me want to get Tony Fedora a new Duncan Tournament for Christmas. Santa's bag is probably empty by the time he reaches their house. I'm askin you for some scratch to help us buy it."

"What's in it for me?"

"Nothin." I answered.

"What's your cut?"

"I ain't takin no cut, Steven." I answered. "I'm just tryin to make some poor lug's season bright. It's Christmas, Steven."

"You ain't takin' a cut?" Steven asked as his mouth hung open.

"No."

"You ain't never gonna be a successful biznessman, Dave. You're too soft."

"I'll worry about success when I get to high school. Right now, I'm tryin to make Tony's Christmas better. So, are ya gonna help?" I asked.

"I don't know." Steve began. "I got overhead and stuff. Christmas just cuts into my profit, ya know? The nuns are hounding us about being grateful, what with Advent and stuff, see? This time of year, it's hard on bizness. Too many kids thinking of the poor starving children in China and other places like South Bawlmer. They don't want to cough up nuttin for test answers and homework. I don't know, Dave."

I knew I had to play hardball with Steven. He wasn't about to part with a penny unless I threw down my ace in the hole.

"OK, Steven, you don't wanna give me a dime? That's fine. But tomorrow, I'm gonna tell Sister Knuckles what you been doin. Scratch for test answers, strong arming kids for candy money. Hey! I might even tell 'em you've been stealing from the poor box in church."

"That's extortion! You can't prove any of that!" Steven shouted.

"I know, but it'll make your life miserable for the holidays, won't it? Every pious penguin in the school will be grilling you. It'll be no fun. Just like Tony's Christmas. Besides, don't think of it as extortion, think of it as holiday hush money." I said.

Steven finally looked me in the eye. Well, his right eye and my right eye met. We'd come to an agreement, of sorts.

"So, Steven, you wanna spare a dime and twist a few arms of your goons to cough up a nickel or two so Tony Fedora can actually get a real Christmas present?" I asked.

"You gonna keep your yap shut?" Steven replied.

"I'll keep my yap shut as long as you and your hired ginks will keep theirs shut. I don't want Tony to know where his Tournament came from."

"You gotta a deal. Come back on Friday and I'll see what I can get. You'll get your Tournament for Tony. It may not be the whole amount, but I think we can help ya get close."

"Thanks, Steven. I knew I could count on you." I started to walk away knowing I was a few steps closer to making somebody's Christmas just a bit brighter.

"Oh, and Dave? There ain't no such person as Santa Claus!" Steven shouted.

I stopped and turned back to Steven. "There is now, Steven. There is now."

I was just unwrapping a butterscotch at our corner office, when Mark returned. Since he didn't have bruises and a cut lip, I figured his foray into the world of Santa-denying ginks went OK while he twisted a few arms here and there.

"So, how'd you make out?" I asked.

"Think I did OK. Ya know everybody wanted to know why we were doing a good deed at Christmas and, worse, they wanted to know what our cut was."

"Yeah, I got the same line from Steven. What'd ya tell 'em?" I asked.

"I told 'em that we were skimming 50% off the top."

"What?" I asked almost indignantly.

"Just kidding. I told 'em that we were trying to make somebody's Christmas bright."

"And…how'd that go?"

"I woulda done better if I'd told them we were skimming off the top. I got a few hoods to cough up a nickel each. They tell me we have'ta wait till Friday. How'd you do?"

"Bout the same as you. Friday seems to be the day we collect. I had to pull the 'I'm gonna tell the nuns' card on Steven. He wasn't happy." I answered in a matter of fact voice.

"You ever seen him happy?" Mark asked.

"Yeah, the day before a test when a bunch of pigeons cough up some dough for the answers."

"Other than that?"

"No." I answered. And it was true. Steven wore a scowl and a sour face every day like he wore the "SLF" emblazoned brown tie to school. Both the tie and a less-than-happy face were required for proper attendance and to remain Calf Licks in good standing or at least, proper looking Calf Licks.

Friday recess finally arrived and Mark and I were ready to scour the yard to collect the donations that we were promised. I popped a butterscotch to steal my nerves, and set off to see Steven and his goons. Mark went off to coax his own stable of wayward hoods to shake them down for a donation or two.

We returned to the office just after the Angelus ended, ready to compare notes and our take.

"How much were you able to get?" I asked Mark.

"Not much, 32 cents."

"Who gave you two cents?"

"Just about everybody. How'd you do?"

"Not much better. Steven twisted a few arms, but he only handed me 50 cents."

"Man, we're kinda short. How're we gonna come up with the difference?" Mark asked me.

"I have just one idea left." I answered.

"And…?" Was Mark's reply.

"You gotta talk to Mary Margaret."

"What? What? Are you crazy? She's got this Christmas-with-Mark thing in her head! One of her girlfriends handed me a note yesterday with Mary's Christmas list. You really want to see me married by fifth grade, dontcha ya? That dame is crazy, I tell ya! And you want me to ask her for money?"

"Calm down, partner, calm down. Tell her the truth. Tell her we're tryin to get a present for a needy kid. Ask her to talk to her friends. Maybe we can come up with the rest of the dough."

"OH….SURE…go the honest route! Tell her the truth…. SURE! Like that's gonna work. I tried that….remember? All she got outta of it was I was gonna marry her! There's gotta be a better way to raise some scratch. Think we could rob a bank?"

"Look, a bank robbery for 40 cents would get us both 10-20 in the big house."

"Yeah, but marriage lasts a lot longer and at least with a prison sentence you get time off for good behavior."

"Mark, listen to me. Talk to Mary Margaret. Tell her what we're tryin to do. Ask if she and her other dames can help. You want me to go with ya, when you talk to her?"

"You remember the last two times you went with me? The first time you told her you wanted to be my best man. The second time you made a comment about how she looked kind of frumpy. When she sees you she's either gonna knock your block off or she's gonna make you rent a tux. Either way, I'm gonna be in the hot seat. No thanks."

"So, you'll talk to Mary Margaret?" I asked.

Mark once again began to walk around in circles intently looking at the ground.

"You looking to see if I lost my mind?" I asked.

"No, I'm looking to see if I lost mine."

"Does that mean you'll talk to Mary Margaret?" I asked.

"Yeah, I'll talk to her. What do we need? About another 40 cents? "

"Yeah, about that." I said.

Mark walked off looking very much like Jack Diamond did: head down, a slight limp, and a look like he was staring down certain doom with one less yo-yo to carry him through. I unwrapped a butterscotch and hoped for the best.

Mark returned before recess ended with a look on his face like he'd just endured a third degree. He handed me 50 cents in nickels, dimes and pennies.

"Look," He said. "The next time you ask me to do something with those dames, just send me into hand-to-hand combat, OK? Just give me my pocket knife and point me towards the enemy. I got a better chance, ok?"

"But you got the rest of the scratch we needed. What was so terrible?"

"I did what you said. I told Mary Margaret the truth. That dame ran off like a city rat being chased by a junk yard dog. She was back before I could say 'Jack Diamond' with a herd of dames all looking in their pockeybooks and digging out change."

"Yeah, and so…?"

"They coughed up the dough, all right, but then they all wanted to hug me!"

"Is that so bad?" I asked.

"You don't get it, do ya? There musta been twenty dames all standing around. Every one of them wanted to give me a hug. And then….and then." Mark's voice trailed off. "Mary Margaret came up to me, hugged me, and said 'You're my hero.' I ain't some dame's hero! You ever heard that many dames say 'Aaww' all at once? I'd rather hear cannon fire going off. At least I'd know the direction. I was outnumbered, I tell ya! They were coming at me from every direction!"

"But you made it through, right?"

"Yeah…sure…I made it. Got the rest of the dough. Got hugged by a herd of dames. Barely escaped with my life. Tell me again why we're doing this?"

"Tony Fedora."

"One day I'm gonna tell Tony what I had to go through." Mark said with a tone of 'you owe me' in his voice.

"Tony never has to know."

"Yeah, I know." Mark said. "But he's never had to go through that many hugs from that many dames."

"Hopefully, you won't either, again."

"Just send me into combat. Just send me into battle. Man! That was horrible! Being hugged by so many dames! I think I need to go to confession." Mark was slowly shaking off his experience as he spoke.

"So we got the dough, thanks to you. Now we have to buy a Duncan Tournament and figure out a way to give it to him for Christmas without him knowing where it came from."

"Look, I'm done. I did my part. Now, it's your turn." Mark exclaimed.

"I'm thinkin." I began. "Maybe we need to talk to Sister Bernie. You and me, we'll buy the Tournament, I'll snag some wrapping paper from my mom, and we'll give it all to Bernie. Let her come up with the right way and the right time to give Tony his gift."

"You? Talk to Sister Bernie? In case you forgot…wasn't it

you that got caught munching on hosts in the sacristy with Billy between masses? That penguin believes you're evil! She won't even believe you when you say the sky is blue. And..." Mark laughed. "You want her to believe you, with a yo-yo in your hand, Christmas wrapping paper, and maybe a card, that you're doing this to help one of the poorest kids in school? If she could, she'd have you turned into dust and mixed with oil for Ash Wednesday. I can see Father Duck right now saying ....'and let this be a lesson to you' as he smears your ashes on every kid's forehead"

"OK, maybe that wasn't my best side." I countered.

"Lemme handle this. We'll buy a Tournament, you get some wrapping paper, and then we'll talk to Bernie. But lemme do all the talking. OK?"

"OK." I answered. I wasn't too keen on the idea of ending up being smeared on kids' foreheads on Ash Wednesday. Besides, I'd miss the Easter Bunny.

On Saturday Mark and I sauntered into the Murphy's 5 and Dime on Belair Road and plunked down a buck to buy a brand new red Duncan Tournament, complete with jewels. We even had a few nickels left over to buy a pack of trick yo-yo strings, just in case Tony needed them. Over the weekend, I found some Christmas wrapping paper and a tag, perfect for a gift from Santa.

Mark and I met up first thing on Monday morning. Armed with a brand new red, jeweled Duncan Tournament along with extra string as well as some wrapping paper and a gift tag, we waited for recess so we could approach Sister Bernie to help us carry out our plan.

"Lemme do the talkin, OK?" Mark said to me.

"Yeah, sure, you're in charge." I answered.

"I want you to keep your yap shut. The last time you

yammered about out-of-date choir songs and why we can't bring farm animals to mass to get blessed."

"It was the principle of the thing, Mark."

"We live in Bawlmer City! Nobody owns cows in the city!"

"So, I should just shut up?"

"Yeah, please." Mark answered.

We found Sister Bernie officiating a dodge ball competition in the middle of the yard. As much as catching a football would sting your fingers in this weather, being hit with a dodge ball on any part of you could bring tears to your eyes. Mark walked up and interrupted the play.

"'Ster…'Ster…can I talk with ya?" Mark called out as he waved his hands.

Sister Bernie excused herself from refereeing the intense dodge ball game to walk over to us.

"Hello, Mark. How are you?" She asked. Turning to me, she said "David….are you still here?" I thought, yes, and I'm not gonna be anybody's Lenten ashes if I can help it.

"'Ster…We got a favor to ask. Me and Dave, we had this case, see. A kid said his yo-yo was stolen, but it wasn't, see? And the kid who had it…he didn't know it was missing, but we had to get it back, anyway. The kid who found it is pretty poor and probably won't get nuthin…

"Anything." Sister Bernie corrected.

"Yeah, won't get anything for Christmas. So….me and Dave took up a collection in the yard to try and get this kid his own yo-yo. Anyway, we got the dough and bought him a yo-yo and string, and Dave got some wrapping paper. You think youse…"

"You." She corrected again.

"Yeah…you could wrap it up and give it to him?"

"That's very kind of you both" Sister Bernie answered,

but she was only looking at Mark. I may as well have been the ugly hunchback who rang the bells at church. Ringing bells still beat being burned at a stake and having my ashes dispensed at Ash Wednesday services, though.

"Anyways," Mark continued. "If we give ya…"

"You."

"Yeah…you…do you think you could wrap up the yo-yo and the string all nice and pretty and give it to Tony Fedora? He'd don't…"

"Doesn't"

"Yeah…doesn't….have to know who it came from. It's kinda like a general present. Like from a bunch of us in the class."

Sister Bernie was obviously moved by Mark's story. The look in her eyes said, "You can skip confession for the next two weeks." She looked at me and said, "David, it was very kind of you to get some wrapping paper."

My mouth hung open. I was glad this wasn't May otherwise I'd have eaten about a hundred flies. This was my idea! Mark was playing up to Sister Bernie like he came up with the gambit. And Sister Bernie was eating it up like chocolate covered communion hosts!

"So 'Ster, youse knows how…"

"Do you know how" Sister Bernie corrected again.

"Yeah…yeah… right….do you know how to pull this off?" Mark asked. I closed my trap just in case some flying bugs that didn't know how cold it was were flying around anyway. I also didn't want to look like a dunce.

"I'll take care of it, Mark." Sister Bernie replied, and returned to officiating her dodge ball game.

I punched Mark in the arm as we walked away. "This whole thing was my idea! How come you're taking all the credit?" I exclaimed.

"Look, you want to tangle with about a hundred dames trying to hug you, or try and convince Sister Bernie that you're jake?"

I thought for a minute. A hundred dames wanting to "oohh and aahh'"and hug me made me want to run. Trying to convince Sister Bernie that I wasn't a first cousin of Lucifer was even more challenging. There was no good way out of this.

"Ok…Ok…I get it." I finally said. "You're right. What's our next move?"

"Bring me what you got; yo-yo, string, wrapping paper and tag. I'll schmooze Sister Bernie to get her to wrap it all nice and pretty. I'll leave it up to her when it comes to the best time to give it to Tony. I'm thinking, maybe, he should find it on his desk on the last day of class before Christmas, right after recess. Whaddya think?"

"Perfect!" I said.

Friday, December 18, 1959, was cold in the recess yard as we swore our sins would be frozen out of our souls so we could skip confession. It was the last day of class before we could run home, huddle around a heat vent, get ready for Christmas, and leave the Shrine behind us for about three weeks. Only one more thing needed attention.

Word had gotten around in class that there was something special about to happen. The buzz ran the gamut from "we're all going home with a Russian orphan" to "Father Duck finally learned to speak English and not Latin." Only a few of us knew of the surprise.

Every desk top in the class was clean as we walked in, hung up our coats and shivered back into the classroom, except for one desk. Sitting in the middle of Tony Fedora's desk was a small festive, red and green box.

There were forty pairs of eyes focused on Tony as he took

his seat. Tony looked like he'd just been hit with a frozen dodge ball as he stared at the middle of his desk at a red and green cube. We all looked at Tony while Tony looked at the present.

"Tony." Sister Bernie said. "Tony, would you like to open it?"

Tony looked around as if someone would say, "… and if anyone has just cause why this present should not be opened, speak now or forever hold your peace."

We all waited. Tony slowly untied the ribbon and neatly peeled off the wrapping paper. He was, no doubt, trying to preserve it all so he could carry home the paper and ribbon so it could be reused for a younger brother or sister.

"C'mon, Tony! Open it already!" Someone shouted.

I've seen dames in movies swoon and faint when they get some sparkly piece of jewelry. Some lug hands 'em a box and the next thing you know, she's throwing her arms around him, kissing him, and saying mushy stuff. I was hoping Tony wasn't going to act like that.

As Tony opened the box and took out the Tournament, his eyes grew so big that his eyebrows vanished under his hair. He looked around the class with a look of confusion and a smile spread across his face as he gingerly handled the gift.

"Merry Christmas, Tony!" Came a shout. I didn't even need to look to see where the voice came from, I knew. It was Steven. I shook my head and thought Ginks at Christmas. What's the world coming to?

Class was dismissed early and as we were heading out the door for Christmas vacation I heard Jack Diamond say to Tony, "Look, I'll teach you a few tricks on the way home."

I walked home humming some very out-of-date Christmas carols and not minding how old they were.

The Spitball Shooter

Each Franciscan pious penguin had their peculiar method of separating the dames from the boys. I'm not sure what the logic behind it was…except to remove the angels from the demons, if only by an aisle. A few of the nuns would muster their courage and place the boys in the front of the room. A casting of holy water to drive out the well-known male's sinful ways was easier since one didn't need to aim the blessed shower at any one in particular. While most of us boys got wet, none of us cried out as our faces were supposed to melt and reveal how evil we were.

A few nuns would put the boys in the back of the class. I guess it made sense, since if you're going to teach arithmetic or religion, you'd want your most attentive students in front of you and let the unruly masses, which would be every boy in the room, fend for themselves.

Sister Mary "Knuckles" was in the latter group. As far as she was concerned, if you were male, you were a lost cause; condemned to an eternity of fire. I couldn't argue with that, since Mark and I had so many cases involving potential crimes perpetrated by boys. I noticed how many angels in paintings, with halos shining, looked like dames. I never saw a boy angel in my life. While Eve may have taken the first bite of the apple, it was the second bite that sealed our fate. Thanks, Adam. The nuns noticed.

With roughly twenty boys in the back of the room, odds were that there would be a few aspiring jailbirds trying to see how far they could push the law. It didn't take long.

I felt the sting of a spitball on the side of my face. Seconds later, Mike, the mild mannered kid who sat beside me, whipped his hand up to his neck. He had the foresight not to cry out. Me? I was used to being shot at, so I didn't flinch when I felt it. I looked over my left shoulder to see if I could ID the shooter.

There sat Robert, smug, smiling, and looking for affirming laughter from his friends. He had deftly moved the drinking straw with his right hand towards his left shirt pocket. He obviously had pocketed his weapon so as not to be caught by Sister Knuckles, as well as confuse his targets so he wouldn't be fingered.

I've got to investigate this further. I have a suspect who is obviously armed and dangerous. He's using a sawed off version of a weapon that some of us carry. I doubt it's even registered. This collar was not going to be easy.

I was grazed by another shot. Mike took two more to the side of his head. Kevin looked badly wounded as three spitballs struck him in his cheek. A glance over my shoulder told me that Robert was aiming at the choir boys. Seems it's always the pious ones who get targeted. I need to put an end to this mayhem posthaste…except I wasn't sure what posthaste meant. I guessed it meant right now. I should pay more attention in class.

I met Mark at our corner office in the Shrine recess yard.

"We have a shooter." I said in the Joe Friday "Dragnet" tone I had copied.

"Paper or plastic?" He asked in his own Joe Friday response. He knew it was important to establish the type of weapon we were dealing with.

"Looks to be paper for now, but I think he has a sawed off version." I knew where he was going. The durability of a paper straw would not last. And the hand-shortened version wasn't as accurate. But this guy seemed to have been practicing. You don't hit someone in the cheek three times with a spitball in rapid fire without practice.

"You sure it wasn't plastic?" Mark asked.

"I'm pretty sure. Plastic comes in colors and I watched him pocket it. If it was plastic it would have lit up his shirt pocket protector."

Plastic straws were a pretty new item and had just recently appeared in students' lunch boxes and were colorful. Holstering a plastic straw would be hard to conceal since they never matched the color of your Parker pen that you carried in your left shirt pocket. The plastic versions were always pink, light blue or puke green. You could saw those off to become concealed weapons, but you'd have to do it at home since none of us carried our pen knives to school. With a paper straw, it was just a matter of a quick snap on the edge of your desk.

"He's getting really bold, too. Mike, Kevin and I sit two rows over. He's not even trying to hit a kid in the next row. "

"Knuckles see him?" Mark asked.

"Are you kidding? He's so quick that she hasn't a clue. And his victims know better than to finger him during class. Nobody wants to be called a snitch. And Robert knows it." I added.

"Looks like a situation that only we can deal with. If he gets his hands on one of those plastic bendy straws, saws it down a few inches, he'll not only be able to conceal it; he'll be able to shoot spitballs around corners."

"I know! Got any ideas?" I asked.

"Two ideas…we can confiscate the weapon or we can set him up to get caught."

"Do I look like a pickpocket? That art takes practice, and I'm not sure we have the time." I exclaimed in frustration.

"Yeah, but how much ammo do you think he can make?" Mark was right. A sheet of paper could yield close to a hundred rounds and we all carried a hundred sheets of paper to school every day. Robert was a walking arms factory.

"Got a clue how we could set him up? I asked.

"Nope." Came Mark's Joe Friday-like reply.

"Thanks, that's encouraging." I said. It appeared Mark and I would have to practice the fine art of pickpocketing for the next few days in order to disarm Robert. We needed a friend to act as our mark during practice.

Mark recruited Dominic to help us out. Dominic didn't attend the Shrine, so we knew he was safe. The last thing we needed was for someone to blab about what we were trying to do during recess and it get back to Robert. We had to be cool, smooth and undetectable.

We outfitted Dominic with a Parker pen, a pocket protector, and a sawed off straw. As Mark walked up to his side, I faked a clumsy stroll to the front. The idea was for Mark's bump to be enough of a distraction that I could lift the straw out of the pocket protector.

"Nope, I felt that." As Dominic moved to the left and I reached for the weapon.

We tried again, this time Mark coming from behind as I stumbled to Dom's front left side.

"You trying to feel me up? Man! That was too obvious."

We worked on different approaches, different moves, and various reaches. Each time Dominic told us he could feel me lift the weapon. I needed a guy like Fagan from "Oliver Twist" to help me refine this type of larceny and not get caught.

As we practiced in the alley, looking like the Three Stooges, up strode some palooka to watch us. He had a smirk on his face and a knowing look. He was a teenager and had a smirk that said he had every answer to every question. Except that he didn't know the questions.

"Why don't you just kiss him?" He asked, laughing.

"I don't want to kiss him! I'm trying to lift a weapon without him knowing." I was frustrated that our rehearsals were going so badly and then to be questioned about my…. my….whatever….I'm not sure what he was implying, but it hit a nerve.

"So what are you Bozos trying to do, now?" He asked with that nonchalant James Dean look.

I reached into Dominic's pocket and pulled out the straw and waved it in front of his face.

"This! We have a spitball shooter at school and we need to get…this." I said with frustration dripping from my voice.

"So, why don't you kiss him?" He wasn't outright laughing at us, but he wore a smug expression that he probably had since birth.

"Lemme see you try and lift that from your mark's pocket. I wanna watch. Maybe I can help." Great, James Dean's younger brother is going to show us the finer points of theft.

Mark walked up behind Dominic and bumped him just as I approached him from the front.

"Nope. Sorry, I felt that." Dominic said.

"You clowns have it all wrong. You ain't never gonna lift that straw the way you're going about it. Want me to show you how it's done?"

"He's not gonna kiss me, is he?" Dominic looked more than apprehensive. He had agreed to help us, but getting kissed by another guy was unnerving, to say the least. What would his friends say about it, if it happened? And if it did, how many showers would Dominic have to take, never mind what he would say in confession.

"You ain't gonna really kiss him, are ya?" I asked.

"You, kid." He said as he pointed at Mark. "Walk up behind him like you did before." Mark played his rehearsed role and bumped into Dom's back. At the same time the teenager bumped into him from the front, his left hand grazing Dominic's hair just above his ear.

Dominic's first move was to wipe his mouth to make sure he didn't have any spit on it that wasn't his. His second move was to straighten the hair on the right side of his head.

Our teenage tutor was spinning the straw in his hand with that now familiar smug look on his face. How is somebody born with a smug look?

"Did you feel that, kid?" He asked.

"No." Dominic's hand went to his shirt pocket. He looked amazed and relieved. One, he hadn't been kissed and two, the straw was gone and he obviously hadn't felt a thing.

"You guys are too obvious. You have to work on distracting your mark. You, kid, you have to use both hands. One to distract him, the other to lift what you want. Got it?"

"I got it." I said.

"Whisper in his ear" The teenager said, still smirking after his successful lift.

"Huh? Like what?" I asked.

"Say excuse me, or sorry." He said. The James Dean/Marlon Brando look was wearing thin. Don't get me wrong, I was grateful that he taught us a technique, but did he have to look so tortured and complacent? I expected him to tell us that he used to do this move on some dame called Stella.

The kid with the DA haircut watched us for a while as we practiced what he showed us. Dominic became a bit more comfortable with our collisions because he knew I wasn't going to kiss him on the cheek. My moves became a bit more refined as I practiced the double move between hair and pocket.

"You feel that?" I asked Dominic.

"Feel what? I felt you touch my hair. Don't ever do that again!"

I held the sawed off straw in my right hand. He didn't feel a thing except embarrassment. Neat! I was getting the hang of this. Mark and Dominic traded roles to make sure I was lifting the weapon without being noticed. And while I could pick a pocket, I still had participants that knew basically what I was doing. We needed someone who didn't have a clue. We thought of Frankie.

I turned to our teenage educator, obviously free on bail, who watched our rehearsals. His smirk and his tortured gaze never left his face. In the course of helping us do wrong, he did good. I imagined his next visit to his parole officer. "I taught some kids how to pickpocket, but it was for a good cause. Can I go now?" "Sure" The PO answers. "As long as it was for troof, justice and the Merican way."

"What's your name, stranger?" I asked.

"Call me Vinnie."

"Well, thanks, Vinnie. We appreciate the education. If there's anything we can do for you, let us know."

"Naw, it's ok, unless you three want to show up at my next meeting with my PO."

I knew it! But why am I surprised? Mark and I have rubbed shoulders with so many ginks in the last year we should have a record ourselves. It's just that you don't often meet a jailbird who wants to turn a corner in life, even if that corner goes right back down the wrong street. Vinnie adjusted the collar on his black leather jacket, turned and walked away.

We turned our attention to get Frankie out of his house to help us refine our technique.

"Oh, Frankie's mother! Can Frankie come out?" We chanted from the alley.

Gregorian chants seldom get a response from anyone, even when you're doing it at the top of your lungs from the choir loft. However, a chant from an alley requesting a friend to come out and play always did. Maybe the Calf Lick church should take notice. "Oh, Jesus's mother! Can Jesus come out and heal people?" I'm sure "Miss Mary" would have sent Jesus out the door. At the worst, she would have said, "Jesus can't come out right now. He's helping Mr. Joe build a cabinet." And from inside the hut maybe Miss Mary would tell Jesus, "Your disciples are outside. I don't want them wandering in and out. I just swept the dirt floor. I got a fish and a loaf of bread. This isn't a lunch counter in Jerusalem. And if they want a drink of water, tell 'em to go to the well."

Frankie finally strode out the basement door to the alley where we all stood.

"Hey, guys! What's going on?"

"We need your help, but we can't tell what we're going to do." Mark answered.

Mark had a way with his friends, able to talk them into almost anything, even when anything meant they would get in trouble when they returned home. And Frankie trusted Mark. You gotta love Frankie.

Mark outfitted Frankie with the pocket protector, a Parker pen and a sawed off version of the straw weapon we wanted to lift. Frankie was a bit bewildered as Mark and Dominic fit him for his unbeknownst role.

"Can I keep the pen?" He asked.

"No, that's my pen." Mark answered. Meanwhile, I walked down the alley about five yards and waited for Mark to give me a nod.

"Walk towards David." Mark said.

"Why?"

"Just do it, Frankie!"

Frankie walked towards me, Mark just a few steps behind. As the gap closed, Mark picked up his pace and bumped into Frankie's back just as I bumped into Frankie, stroking his hair, and lifting the straw.

"What's going on?" Frankie cried.

"You OK?" Mark asked.

"Yeah, but what happened?" he asked. "Hey, what's with you and my hair?"

I held the straw in my right hand. Frankie didn't have a clue. I had "kissed" him and he didn't know what happened. I think I was getting pretty good at this.

"Do it again." Mark said.

"Not if Dave is gonna fiddle with my hair."

"Just do it!"

Frankie did as told and we repeated the walk, bump and lift.

"You touch my hair again, I'll bop ya!" Frankie declared.

I had the straw in my hand, but backed up a few feet. Frankie was mad and since he was bigger and taller than me, I thought it wise not to be within reach of a roundhouse punch. Mark then explained to Frankie what we were doing, or trying to do. Frankie felt his empty left breast pocket and laughed.

"Youse two are sumpin else. I never wooda guessed and I didn't feel a thing." He laughed.

I breathed a sigh of relief. We were almost through with rehearsals. And the time to "kiss" Robert was almost at hand. We still had to tail him at recess and get an idea of his movements around the yard, but we were as ready as we ever would be.

We watched Robert for a couple of days, paying attention to when he sidled up to the nuns at recess, no doubt for brownie points; where he wandered around the yard and who he talked to. We noticed that he stayed away from Sister Knuckles, though. It wasn't a big deal, since Knuckles looked at him with the same contempt as she bestowed on all of us boys. But it was a card dealt in our favor. Once we lifted the weapon, we knew he couldn't run up to her and tell her he was robbed. "Robbed?" She would say. "You weren't robbed. You gave your soul to Satan a long time ago. Now go back to your seat and be quiet."

Each morning for a week Robert seemed to show up with a new straw. Each one sawed off to the right length for maximum accuracy. His targets now included not just choir boys, but anyone within range. Mark and I figured he was using two sheets of paper a day. That's a lot of ammo. His MO had grown not just in quantity and accuracy, but brazenness. All Knuckles had to do was turn around to the blackboard to write down two words and Robert fired off six shots. Oh, he was good. Really good.

Mark and I met in our outside office at recess to discuss Robert's flaunting the law and count causalities.

"This gink is out of control." Mark said to me.

"I know. The only ones who haven't been shot are the boys who sit behind him." I said.

"He shoot any dames, yet?" Mark asked me.

"Naw, not yet. He knows better. He shoots a dame; she's gonna finger him. And you know what that means." I said.

"Yeah. A trip to Sister Salvatore's office. They'd bring him out on a stretcher, for sure."

Sister Salvatore was the principal of the Shrine. She was eight feet tall, clad in a black Franciscan habit and her skin was stretched over her skeleton-like features. The angel of death would have cowered in front of her. This was no pious penguin anyone would want to mess with; not the parish priests, not parents, and I doubt even the pope would confront her. I heard reports from other kids that lightning bolts shot from her eyes when she got really mad. Her voice sounded like nails on a blackboard complete with vowel sounds. She carried a cricket clicker to get kids' attention and the mere sound made them freeze in mid leap. The clicker, no doubt, was brought back from the first crusades where she probably vanquished five hundred Saracens. I seem to remember an ancient painting depicting what hell looked like and I swear I saw her face in the painting, laughing at the souls who were descending into the depths of eternal fire, probably portraits of all the boys who ever attended her school. She was not a nun to trifle with.

It was at Thursday recess that we decided to bump and "kiss" Robert.

"You ready?" Mark asked.

"About as much as I can be. Let's do it." I answered.

Mark and I walked together towards Robert, who was jawing with Sister Bernie. Sister Bernie was the kind of nun who would talk to anybody with a soft voice and a smile on her face, even if she knew you were a lost cause and condemned to hell. They don't make nuns like that anymore. As we approached, I looked at Robert's pocket protector to make sure the weapon was sticking up a little and on which side his pen was. I didn't want to end up with a new pen, just the straw. We separated and fanned out, waiting for Robert to end his brown-nosing.

"Thank you sister, thank you!" We heard him say. We were about six feet away and slowly walking in opposite directions.

Oh, please! I thought. You're spitballing half the class and you're thanking her? For what? Not sewing your lips shut with thread that a priest had blessed? I didn't want to know why he was thanking her. I just wanted that straw… now.

Robert walked away in no particular direction and Mark and I circled him like two hungry wolves. We both needed clear avenues of approach, which is pretty hard to do with the crush of hundreds of people in a recess yard who also looked like they were going nowhere. The word chaos came to mind, but near collisions could work to our advantage. Mark nodded to me as he began his approach. We had rehearsed this so many times that I knew my role better than I knew how to be an altar boy at mass.

Mark's pace picked up as did mine with Robert squarely in our sites. We both had to get to him at the same time. And we did. As Mark bumped Robert from behind, my left hand touched his hair and my right hand went for the straw.

"Oh, sorry, Robert." I muttered.

"Watch where you're goin! You forget how to walk?" Robert reached into his back pocket for his comb to straighten his hair as he walked away in a huff.

"Didja get it?" Mark whispered to me.

I moved my right hand to my own pocket protector and slyly pointed. I had the weapon safely tucked away where it would never be used again in class, at least not today. Mark laughed.

"Man! That was great!" He exclaimed.

"Yeah, pretty cool." I said. But I wondered how many more times we would have to "kiss" Robert until he got the message.

That afternoon, during history, I noticed Robert was

looking around his desk and searching his pockets every time Knuckles turned towards the blackboard. He realized his weapon was gone, but didn't know where. Now he'd have to try and pay attention like the rest of us.

The lull in spitball shooting was short lived, though. It was another day, another weapon for Robert as he resumed his sharpshooting skills the next morning. The boys in the back of class were once again under rapid fire. We knew we would have to give Robert a second kiss and hope that some patron saint of gumshoes-turned-pickpockets would help us out.

Mark and I planned a different approach for recess. We would pick him out when he was distracted by the third grade dames. Robert had that budding Marlon Brando look that made the dames' eyes go woozy. Most of them would be planning a wedding with him, except I think we had to wait till eighth grade for that level of commitment. OK, we couldn't get married in eighth grade, but a bunch of dames already had their sights set on the best catch. Robert seemed to know it. He had a swagger, a timely wink in a dame's direction, and he wore the latest Army surplus clothes from Sunny Surplus which gave him a soldier of fortune look. What dame could resist that?

Mark and I mingled among the dames at recess. It wasn't easy. Going under cover in an altar robe was more our style. There was high pitched chatter, giggling, clucking and pointing that made me forget which way was North on a compass. How can anybody survive this mayhem of dames? It was like getting caught in a slow motion cattle stampede with bleating sheep for sound effects. The dames moved one way; then they moved another. It was a school of fish hell-bent on outer space and Mark and I were caught in the currents. I couldn't catch my breath as I tried to engage one dame in innocent banter so I knew I wasn't drowning.

"You always come to this side of the yard?" I asked as I fought the impulse to swim in a place without water.

"Yes! And did you see that dreamy guy who wears a parka? I'm going to marry him. What did you get in the history test?"

"I'm not sure what test you're talking…"

"And I'm going to be a nurse….and then we'll have three kids…and then…"

"A nurse, that's nice. But we're looking for a guy. His name is…."

"I want a house with a white picket fence. And it will have a second story that overlooks the garden."

"Great. But I'm looking for a guy named…"

"I'm gonna name our first son Sean, cuz I'm part Irish and I want all of our children to have Irish names. Are you Irish?"

"I'm part Irish. But I'm looking for Robert. You know him?"

"Robert!? Oh…my…God! I Love Robert! We're going to be married! "

I hit a collective nerve when I was able to say his name. It seems that Robert was the focus of matrimony by more than one dame. I wonder if he knew his future.

"You're not marrying Robert! I am!" Came a voice in the crowd.

"No, I am!" Came a cry from another tomato in the rear of the group.

"No! I am!" Another cry, but from a different side. This was about to get ugly.

It was time for me to exit this debate stage left, and the fury of women, find Mark and then Robert. I felt sorry for Robert, though. He had no idea what designs feminine fate had in store. He would probably be better off in the big house or maybe in a monastery.

I found Mark, almost on his knees, as he emerged from

the flock of dames. He was sweating, his shirt was wrinkled and half out of his pants, his brown tie cocked to one side, and obviously glad to escape.

"Don't ever ask me to do that again!" He yelled.

"Sorry. I thought it would be the best way to get to Robert."

"Robert! Are you kiddin me? Robert knows better than to get near that group. I got proposed to three times, had two dames tell me that we could have cute kids, had my hair rearranged. At least four dames almost gave me a going over like my doc did when I got a physical, and....!"

"And, what?"

"Well," Mark said with a sly smile. "I got the answers to tomorrow's arithmetic test."

"Who gave it to you?"

"Mary Margaret." Most of the time we had to use dames' first and second names to tell them apart since ninety percent of them had the first name Mary.

"You getting dizzy with that dame?" I asked. I had to ask, since Mark always asked me that same question whenever I had to talk to a dame.

"Are you crazy? No!"

"Must be your ruddy good looks, then." I laughed.

"I'm not ruddy, I'm Polish."

"Alright, then, Polish prince. Let's go find Robert." I said.

"Fine, but don't ever ask me to go into that herd of dames again. A guy could get seriously hurt. I'd rather play tackle football without pads than do that again. My ears are still ringing from their cackling."

"OK," I said laughing.

We spotted Robert in the center of the yard, schmoozing another nun. Mark and I went into our circling routine, waiting to see which way he would walk. I was pretty sure we could kiss him again, but I doubted we could keep this routine up. At some point he would catch on.

As Robert walked away, Mark and I closed in. We did this yesterday, and he already thinks I can't walk straight. Would he buy it a second time? As Mark bumped into him from behind, I collided with him from the front, once again stroking his hair and lifting the new weapon.

"What's wrong wit you two? I swear, you guys come near me again and I'll sock ya both in the jaw!"

"Sorry, Robert. I wasn't watching. It won't happen again." I answered.

"It better not!" He said as he once again reached for his comb to straighten his locks.

Once again I was successful in lifting the sawed off straw, quickly putting it in my pocket protector. I met Mark a few yards away.

"Oh, man! He seemed really mad." Mark declared.

"He'll be even madder once we're back in class and realizes he's lost his weapon two days in a row. He's going to put two and two together, and when he does, he'll be looking for us. We have to get him fingered."

"How? He'll beat the snot out of any kid he's shot who snitches on him." Mark said.

"Yeah, but he won't beat up a dame." I answered.

"Robert don't shoot at the dames. You know that."

"Then we'll have to set it up so it looks like he did." I said.

"And how do you think we can do that, Sherlock?" Mark answered in a sarcastic tone.

"Give me a minute. I'm thinking."

"Oh, is that what I smelled?" Mark laughed.

I had Robert's latest weapon so I was as armed as he was. If we could plant a rumor among the dames in the class that

Robert was about to expand his targets to include them, I might be able to create an advantage for us. I got it!

"Mark, old buddy old pal…" I began as I put my arm on his shoulder.

"Don't start that crap! I don't like how this is going and you haven't even told me the plan. The last time you gave me that 'old buddy, old pal' line Knuckles thought I was possessed by Satan and I had to spend three Saturday mornings in church and get drenched with holy water. My parents never believed what I told them about why I kept coming home wet."

"It's not like that time. All you have to do is talk to a dame." I said calmly.

"Are you nuts? At least it was quiet in church." Mark exclaimed.

"But you already know her." I said.

"Who?"

"Mary Margaret." I said with my hands in my pockets.

"OH NO! That's one of the dames who want to marry me!" Mark had taken his hands out of his pockets and was waving them around.

"She already gave you the test answers, so you're practically engaged, anyway."

"Says who? Look, I ain't dizzy with dat dame! If I talk to her again, she'll be drawing up wedding invitations." Mark was feeling threatened with marriage and I thought it was interfering with the case, but I couldn't blame him.

"Mark…old buddy, old pal…you can always back out of her plans later. Tell her you contracted a disease that won't let you get married since all your kids would look like poodles with mange. Or at the last minute, tell her you broke your earlobe and you'll be in a full head cast for a year. Just talk to her." I said trying to get him to stop walking in circles, waving his hands around, and just see the seriousness of the case.

"Why don't you do it?" Mark shouted at me.

"Dames don't seem to like me. I lack those Polish good looks you have." I said in the calmest voice I could.

"I hate flattery. It may be true, but I still don't like it." Mark sighed. "OK, what's up your sleeve?"

I outlined the plan to Mark. While he was still skittish about talking to Mary Margaret and what matrimony plans might come out of it, he understood the big chance he was taking. If he was successful we could stop Robert in his tracks, but then Mark could be married, in a sense, by the end of fourth grade.

"Alright, when are we gonna do this?" He finally said.

"We have to act fast. Robert will be in class tomorrow morning with a new sawed off weapon and probably another fifty sheets of ammo. Talk to her now, before the bell rings."

"I just escaped that flock of dames! Can't it wait till my nerves calm down?" He asked.

"No, Robert is too good with spitballs. He's been shooting every boy in class and he's no longer afraid he's gonna get caught. We need to stop him, now."

Mark tucked in his shirt, straightened his tie and ran his fingers through his disheveled hair. He took a few deep breathes like he was about to dive into an ocean of hungry sharks without a spear gun. The boy had moxie.

I saw him disappear into the crowd of dames like a farmer disappears into a corn field. Now you see him, now you don't. I heard the squeals, the clucking, and his name repeated over and over again. He was gone from view. I stood and waited for his exit, hoping that I wouldn't hear his cries of anguish as the dames tore him apart in their frenzy of affectionate kisses, hugs, and playing with his hair. There must be a medal for this type of bravery, but the only one that came to mind was a purple heart, and I didn't have one.

Just before Sister Salvatore's bell rang for the end of recess, Mark emerged from the herd. He looked like he hadn't slept in days, his school uniform was once again in disarray, and he struggled to talk.

"Are you OK?" I asked.

"Tell Knuckles I'm possessed. Anything…anything! Just don't ask me to do that again." Mark gasped.

"Did Mary Margaret go along with the plan?

"Oh, yeah, sure. She even told me that our first kid will be named after my granddad, because she gets the family heritage thing. I'm looking forward to a full head cast in plaster. You gotta get me outta this mess. "

"We'll worry about the marriage ceremony later. She's OK with the plan, right?" I wanted an answer as to why Mark put life and limb at risk, first.

"Yeah. All you gotta do is your part." Mark responded in a breathless voice.

The last piece of my plan was in place. I only had to show up in the morning armed just like Robert.

I spent the evening, after dinner and the dreaded vegetables my mom insisted on feeding me, working on my marksmanship. The plan was quite simple. I remembered on Saturday morning TV cowboy shows that the good guys always shot at the bad guys, but many of those shots seemed to ricochet off rocks. Sometimes though, the ricochet did the bad guys in. A well placed shot, off a rock the size of a small building usually hit the bad guy in the hand. He would then drop his gun, throw up his hands and surrender. Robert can't ricochet a spitball, but I could make it appear like he did.

Just like every other day in class, Robert resumed his shooting spree with a brand new weapon. Once again he was aiming at the boys in front of him scattering his shots to different rows. And this was a particularly good day since Knuckles seemed to be spending a lot of time with her back turned towards the board. It was English and she was introducing us to sentence structure all the while going through sentence diagrams, which confused me to no end. Nouns and pronouns, verbs and adverbs, straight lines, slanted lines going off in one direction or another, it looked like stick men engaged in mortal combat. I was watching Robert, trying to see if there was a rhyme or reason to his targets.

I finally figured it out. I noticed that if Knuckles turned to the right, Robert would shoot to the left when she turned towards the blackboard. If she turned left, he'd shoot right. Mary Margaret was one row to his left, three seats up and only two rows from me. I waited for Knuckles to turn, waited for Robert to shoot, and then I aimed directly at Mary Margaret.

BINGO! Luckily I hit her. I couldn't have made that shot again in a million years.

"Sister!!" She shouted.

Sister Knuckles spun around like a supersonic top. I think I heard a crack in the air as her movement must have broken the sound barrier; Knuckles was that fast. I wasn't surprised since getting whacked on the back of your hand with a ruler produced two identical sounds: the sound of the ruler breaking the speed of sound and then the impact on your hand.

"What is it Mary Margaret?"

"Somebody is shooting spitballs! And I can't learn if I'm being shot at." Oh, nice touch, Mary Margaret, I thought. I might even volunteer to be best man at your wedding. I forgot that I told Mark I would make him a full head cast so he could remain a single guy and escape her own well planned future of picket fences, three kids, a two story house and matrimonial bliss with my partner.

"Who's shooting spitballs?" She roared. Every kid in class froze, just like I suspected they would. I had already crumpled and stashed my straw in my pants cuff. I knew what was coming next.

"I want everybody to empty their pockets and put everything on their desks with your hands folded…now!" You can't refuse what sounded like the eleventh commandment. I figured Robert was getting careless, so he never anticipated being caught. It was just a matter of time and inspection of personal belongings. I wanted to follow Knuckles up and down the aisles with an evidence sheet. I'm sure Mark and I could solve a few more cases.

Knuckles walked up and down the aisles inspecting everything. When she got to Robert, she stopped.

"I said everything, Robert. Put your pocket protector on the desk and empty it out."

"Yes, 'ster." The entire class was now focused on Robert. Every boy in the class knew what he'd been doing and now most of the dames did, too, thanks to Mark. I thought Robert should be bleeding from multiple wounds inflicted by piercing eyes. I half expected him to get that look of someone about to meet the guillotine, but Robert was tough. He did what he was told and never uttered a word, but I think I caught his lips mouthing a final act of contrition.

On his desk lay his almost new Parker pen, the sawed off straw and twenty rounds of spitballs.

"He's the one! Robert shot me with a spitball!" Cried Mary Margaret. Calm down, sister, I thought. Don't overact. It's bad enough I see Bette Davis do it in the movies.

"Mary Margaret, sit down and be quiet." Sister Knuckles said.

"But, he's the one!"

"Mary Margaret!" Knuckles barked. She did what she was told and sat down. Mary Margaret looked over at Mark and winked. Mark looked over at me with a look on his face that said "Help!"

"Robert, gather your things and go to Sister Salvatore's office. Now!" A collective gasp came from the class, the same type of gasp I imagined that came from a crowd when the trap door on a gallows is released. Robert gathered his few worldly possessions and walked from the room.

At recess the yard was abuzz about the apprehension of the spitball shooter. Rumors swirled about Robert's fate. Some say he was immediately drawn and quartered pointing to a red paint stain on the second story of the building. Others said he was taken to a special room beside the auditorium where he was chained and then the wall was bricked up. A few others claimed that his parents were called and had to have a special meeting with Sister Salvatore. A few students said the first two rumors would be a preferable end rather than facing one's angry and embarrassed parents. Robert was not in class the next day, or the next week. In fact, we never saw Robert again.

"Well, we finally got him." Mark declared a week later.

"Yeah." I said. "But you know what they say in Westerns. Even if you think you're the fastest gun, somebody always comes along that's just a little bit faster."

"You think we'll face another spitballer?"

"Only a matter of time, Mark. Only a matter of time."

"Speaking of time, Mary Margaret is hounding me. She wants to tell all the other dames about us getting married. When are you going to buy the plaster to make me a head cast? I'm too young to get married."

Home of Deranged

I don't fully understand the twisted sense of humor that I see from the aspiring jailbirds, ginks and hoods in school. Their idea of fun always seems to have a dame as their target. What's even more confusing is that the dames seem to enjoy it once they get over the shock of surprise and terror. More often than I can count, some gink scares the daylights out of a dame, and then she's telling every other dame in her group that she and the said gink were meant for each other. I'm missing something here, but I just don't know what. Take this recent case.

A Shrine gink that I knew from recess was Marty. He loved practical jokes. I'm already in a dizzy since the words "practical" and "joke" just don't seem to fit together. But Marty loved to play them on everyone in the class. Once he ran out of boys who would fall for his pranks, he turned his attention to the dames. And with every squeal he heard, with every screech of his name, with every scamper of a chick who ran from him, he just got more and more bold.

Mark and I waited for his library of jokes to run out and, with it, a return to the general chaos of recess. Somehow, though, Marty kept coming up with new ideas to get squeals out of the dames. We knew we had to put the kibosh on his activities eventually.

Marty's latest joke was to run around at recess with a plastic snake and scare the dames. Marty was a master at making a plastic snake appear real in its movements. I even thought it was real the first time he showed it to me, but after being shot at with spitballs so many times, and the number of cuts I got from playing stretch and mumbly-peg with a pen knife, a snake bite didn't scare me.

"So, whadya think? Looks real, don't it?" Marty said with a wide grin.

"Yeah, Marty, looks almost alive."

"Just stand here and watch me scare the daylights out of those girls. "

"Aah, Marty, I'm not sure that's a good thing to do. The nuns are gonna take that snake from you."

"Naw. It fits in my pocket, see? The pious penguins won't ever catch me. And the chicks love it."

"That's not how it sounds, Marty."

"Sounds? Them chicks love it! They love squealin'!"

Marty's idea that dames love to squeal in terror and then forgive and forget didn't jive with what I knew about dames. Then again, what did I know about dames?

I walked away from Marty, his plastic snake making magical movements, and a herd of squealing dames at recess. I spent too much time with Marty already, and needed to get back to the crimes that were on the verge of being committed.

I walked to our recess yard office and unwrapped a butterscotch. It was just what I needed, not so much to calm my nerves, but to get a quick sugar jolt. Mark was already there, sitting on the ground with some dog-eared yellow paper looking them over. He looked a bit miffed.

"Anything wrong?" I asked.

"Naw, just the usual stuff here in the reports, but that squealin' from the dames on the other side of the yard is drivin' me nuts. Can't imagine what it sounds like if we were closer."

"I just came from there. I left Marty and his plastic snake and the dames to their own devices."

"And your ears ain't bleedin'?" Mark asked.

"I left before he got started with the dames." I answered.

"How does Marty stand it? You think he's deaf?"

"Not deaf. Deranged, maybe, but not deaf."

Mark's hands were moving quicker and quicker over the stack of papers every time he heard a high pitched squeal or heard Marty's name in a shrill voice. The recess yard was a noisy place anyway, with close to 250 kids running around, playing dodge ball, pitching cards, making deals and probably trading camels of questionable stock. After a year or two spent at recess you learned to ignore most of the noise. But this new high pitched sound, the kind that sounds like a hundred bad opera singers trying to hit a high C all at once was getting to Mark. I figured that once a few windows got shattered from the dames' squealing, life might return to normal, whatever normal was when it came to sound levels.

"Man! I can't take this anymore! We gotta do something about Marty." Mark finally said, as he ripped a few reports in half, obviously because of his nerves being frayed by the sounds. I didn't quite understand. I thought we wouldn't develop frayed nerves, or nerves of any kind, until we were in fifth grade. But Mark was always ahead of the rest of the class, anyway. He read books two grades ahead of everybody else, so maybe he'd already developed nerves.

"OK, you got any ideas?" I asked.

"Give him a taste of his own medicine." Mark's grin looked like a Cheshire cat bent on something diabolical, except his target wasn't some dame named Alice, but a gink called Marty.

"I like where you're coming from." I laughed. "Tell me more."

"He likes to scare the dames and hear them squeal, right? So why don't we see how high his own voice will go?"

Oh, this could be a lot of fun, I thought. I always love to give a gink a taste of his own criminal ways.

"My dad has an empty glass pickle jar on his workbench waiting to be filled with washers, nuts and bolts. But right now it's empty. Outside, under the porch, is a huge spider web. I've seen that spider. It's almost as big as a plate. Ugly, nasty, mean thing. I bet I can catch it in the jar, bring it to school, and we put it in Marty's lunchbox in the morning. When he opens it for lunch, the spider will be crawling all over his sammidge. I think that should cure him once and for all."

"I love it! All we have to do is figure out which lunch box is his. That might take a day or two, but we can do dat. Ya know, you have a bright future in crime, if you ever want to go there."

"I know." Mark laughed. "For now, I think I'll stick to fighting crime, though."

It all sounds easy enough on the surface. Catch a huge spider, put it in Marty's lunch box and wait for the results. But when you start counting the number of lunchboxes in a class of forty, and see how many are so alike, you don't want to put a spider in, say, Kevin's lunchbox, by mistake. That kid would probably keel over, or at the worst never eat a sammidge his mom packed in his lunchbox again, and then he'd prolly die of starvation in arithmetic class. We had to know exactly which lunchbox belonged to Marty.

Mark and I came up with a plan. We had to make sure which lunchbox was Marty's and where in the coatroom he put it. It called for a two pronged tail. Over the next few days, Mark would trail Marty into the coatroom. Then we would change places. We had to figure out how to mark his lunchbox, empty the spider into it, and be back in class before Sister Knuckles went wandering into the coatroom looking for Mark or me.

"OK, first we have to figure out what lunchbox he uses." I said. It sounds easy on the surface, except in third grade in 1959, boy's lunchboxes were either decorated with Davy Crockett, Roy Rogers or a cartoon character on Saturday morning TV. We could forget about all the pink Tinkerbell and Snow White lunchboxes. I had a Davy Crockett lunchbox, but so did a lot of other boys in class, same with good old Roy Rogers' lunchboxes. We knew we had to figure a way to mark the target, but in a way that wouldn't draw attention and wouldn't take a lot of time. The last thing we needed was Knuckles getting impatient with our dallying too long in the coatroom while we were working. I didn't even want to think about the possible punishment. If Knuckles caught us we'd probably have to stay after school and iron the priests' vestments with our bare hands, which they would heat over an open fire, all the while reciting the rosary. The pious penguins were never at a loss for unique punishments.

"Alright, tomorrow morning you tail Marty in the coatroom and tell me what lunchbox he uses and where he puts it. The gink doesn't have a big wardrobe, so I'm guessing he's gonna put it above his jacket. Tell me what jacket he wears and which lunchbox he uses. The next morning, we'll trade places, and we'll compare notes. Sound good?" I asked.

"Sounds good so far, but how are we gonna mark the lunchbox?" Mark said.

"I'm thinking about that."

"Is that what I smell?" Mark laughed.

"No, it's that sausage and sauerkraut sammidge you brought for lunch, wiseacre." I responded.

"I happen to like those sammidges. The bread gets soggy, but they taste really good." Mark said defensively.

"You really are Polish to the core, ain't you?"

"Hey! My busia makes 'em for my Uncle Met when he goes to work at the brewery. He says that with a few beers, you don't even remember the soggy bread."

"So how are we gonna mark Marty's lunchbox?" I asked, trying to bring our plan back to the front of our conversation and avoid a debate about how many beers it took to forget soggy sammidge bread.

"A crayon!" Mark exclaimed.

"I like it, but we have to pick the right color, ya know. If Marty's lunchbox is Davy Crockett, and we use a brown one, neither of us are gonna be able to see it in the dark. Same with a Roy Rogers lunchbox. There's too many brown colors. We have to come up with the right color, but not so obvious that he'll notice."

"Let's do red. We can put a red stripe on it and he probably won't notice." Mark said.

"What if he turns it around? We mark one side, then he puts it on the shelf the other way, we won't see it." I countered.

"OK, no problem, we mark his lunchbox three days in a row. If we see two red crayon marks, then we know it's his. On the fourth day, I'll plant the spider."

It sounded like a plan. It was easy-peasy. Before the week was out, the entire class would hear the highest note Marty could scream and maybe have to duck the shattering window glass.

"You have a red crayon?" I asked.

"No. You?"

"Aww, man!" I answered. "I know our sketch artist, Bobby, has a few. But he's still out with the mumps or typhoid fever or the black death, or sumpin. You sure you don't have a red crayon?"

"I did, but my brother went crazy drawing some pictures on construction paper and my mom wants them framed for the living room. He destroyed all my crayons. What about you?" He asked.

"My mom confiscated all of 'em. My brother was sitting on the floor in the living room trying to draw Mickey Mouse on the wall next to the TV. They were pretty bad, didn't look like a mouse or any animal for that matter, so I thought he might like to see a drawing of Woody Woodpecker. I took a few crayons from him and started to draw on the wall. I don't know what I was thinkin; don't ask me. My mom walked in and my brother and me, we were coloring the wall with cartoons. She threw a fit. She grabbed a SOS pad and started to scrub. She screamed something about my dad would have to paint the living room again. Anyway, I'm outta crayons."

"Rats!" Was all Mark said.

"Got any leads on how we can get a red crayon?"

"Nope. One of us is gonna haveta get some crayons. What about your brother? Doesn't he have crayons stowed away somewhere?" Mark asked as we were both scratching our heads.

"He may, but I have to see which ones he's eaten. I know he likes the taste of the blue ones. He won't eat black, says they taste too much like Good & Plenty's. I'll look at what he's chewed on."

"Doesn't he get sick?"

"Naw. After eating two pounds of sand downey oshun last

summer, I think he can eat anything. Even though, I think that scares the daylights out of my parents. They never know what he's gonna put in his mouth next."

"Any ideas? What about your sister? She got any red crayons?" Mark asked again.

"Are you kiddin' me? She's almost grown. She's like ready for high school. The only thing she owns in the color red is lipstick. And before you ask, I ain't pinchin' red lipstick and bringing it to school. I have a reputation to protect."

"Ok, ok. I was just askin'." Mark answered with his hands in the air.

"Looks like one of us is gonna haveta put out some dough for crayons. You got any scratch?" I asked.

"Me? I have a hard time just putting together enough for a pack of baseball cards."

"You need to work on your pitching, then. With enough practice, you could clean out half the pigeons in the yard, trade off your doubles, and you'd have a good stack and you wouldn't need to put out dough for cards. Hey! I got an idea!" I exclaimed.

"You scare me when you stop in mid-sentence. It always means you have an idea and I'm gonna have to do sumpin."

"What if you asked Mary Margaret?"

"Are you out of your mind? How many butterscotch candies have you had today? Ask Mary Margaret? No!" Mark was getting his back in the air at my suggestion to the point that he started to look taller.

"C'mon, Mark. All we need is a red crayon for a few days. What's the worst that can happen?"

"The worst that can happen!? OK, lemme tell ya the worst that can happen. I ask her if I can borrow a red crayon…she goes dizzy because I asked, see. She's gonna think I want it for a reason, like I want it to make a Valentine's card for her, or worse! I'm wanting to make wedding invitations. She's gonna tell all the other dames and they'll all be waiting for sumpin that I wrote with a red crayon. No! No! And one more time, No!"

"Tell her that you need it for a case you're working on." I was pressing him and I knew it.

"Like that's gonna do any good. She's gonna think I'm sayin it just to surprise her with a card or invitations."

"We need a red crayon. Won't ya do it just for me?" I asked in a voice that I use when I'm asking somebody if I can copy their homework. "Look if you won't do it for me, then do it for troof, justice and the Merican way."

Mark paced back and forth. He sighed, waved his hands in the air, walked around in a circle, sighed a bit more, looked at me like he wanted to sock me, walked away, walked back, then sighed again.

"OK, but you owe me." He finally said.

"I owe you, partner." I said. I was relieved.

"Don't give me that partner crap. Mary Margaret is gonna be all gushy when I ask her for a red crayon and you have to get me outta this. Unnerstaned?"

"I unnerstaned... But think how great you'll feel when Marty's screams break a window or two."

"I'm thinking how bad it's gonna get when I don't give Mary Margaret sumpin written in red crayon."

"We'll think up something for Mary Margaret and get you off the hook after we nail Marty."

Mark was always as good as his word. In less than five minutes he had a brand new red crayon in his hand.

"Wow!" I said. "Is that a new one?"

"Not only new, but she sharpened it for me, just in case

I need to draw some fine details in whatever she's expecting. And I'm tellin ya, she's expecting sumpin." Mark looked a bit frazzled and took out a root beer candy from his pocket. I'd never seen Mark indulge in that sort of thing before. He was more of a Bonamo Turkish Taffy kind of guy.

"Hey, are you starting to take after me?" I asked, half joking.

"Prolly. You're a bad influence, ya know dat?"

"I Prolly am. I've heard that since I was in first grade when Sister Monica told my mom that I needed a regular whippin' with a switch."

"What your mom say?"

"Nuttin. But when she got home she decided to trim the pussy willow tree of some long branches."

Mark and I were now set to trail Marty into the coatroom and mark his lunchbox. We had to be careful, though. Two Roy Rogers' lunchboxes sitting side by side in a dark coatroom could give us a major headache if we picked the wrong one three days in a row. It had to be a close tail, and that meant that we had to risk butting up in line in the morning to get behind Marty. One shout from an irate dame or some lazy mug complaining about line hopping, and one or both of us would be spending that evening with a 1,000 line "I will not butt up in line" task. Homework usually took us about an hour and a half. It took me about four hours almost every night. I think my parents had to get a loan so they could buy all the extra pencils and paper I used doing my "homework."

The first morning was Mark's turn to tail Marty. I lingered in the coatroom for a bit looking for a red crayon mark on a lunchbox. I saw nuttin.

At lunch I looked over at Marty as he wolfed down his sammidge and stuffed it with a bag of potato chips. Boy, he's pretty efficient, I thought. Maybe I could time him one day and see how long it takes that kid to devour his lunch. Maybe we could have a race with some other bozos and I could send the idea into some TV show like "Truth or Consequences." Naw, I thought. Competitive eating would never be a big deal.

Marty's lunchbox was like mine, Davy Crockett fighting Indians, bears and I think there was a forest fire going on too, but you had to look at all the sides of the lunchbox. Just out of detective habit, I looked at the outside of mine to make sure there wasn't a red crayon streak on it. Mine was clean, so I stared at Marty's. He was too busy stuffing his face for him to notice. The side that faced me was clean, but that didn't mean there wasn't crayon on the other side. I have to talk to Mark at recess.

"You mark Marty's lunchbox?" I asked.

"Yep. It's on the side with Davy fighting Indians. Might be hard to see, though. I tried to make it look like war paint. It's not a straight line, kind of a squiggle. But it's on there."

"OK, it's my turn tomorrow. Where's the red crayon?"

"I'm using it."

"For what?"

"Oltno. Sumpin. I can't tell ya, but I'll give it to ya after school."

"You gettin artistic like that Mike Angelo or that David Vinchie guy?"

"No! I just need it a little longer. I'll give it to ya after school." Mark seemed a bit secretive about the red crayon. What could he do with a red crayon, except maybe draw the symbol for a stop sign or a measles quarantine notice? OK, I thought, I'll wait and not press him and see if he can draw a masterpiece all in red.

"Here." Mark said as he handed me the red crayon after school.

"What happened to it?" I asked. Two days ago this was a sharp new red crayon when Mary Margaret gave it to Mark. It now looked like the lone survivor in a crayon sword fight. Half of the paper wrapper was gone, along with most of the crayon itself. If I didn't know better, I'd swear my brother was chewing on it.

"What?" Mark asked innocently.

"Look, if you're that hungry, just tell me. If you're putting face makeup on a dame, I'll understand. What happened? You haven't been coloring the statues in the church, have you?"

"Nuttin, no."

"But's it's almost used up!"

"Hey, crayons don't last forever, ya know."

"I coulda colored a whole coloring book with just a red crayon and I'd still have more than this." I answered as I looked at about an inch and a half of what remained of the new, sharpened and borrowed crayon.

"I had stuff to do, ok? There's still enough left that we can mark Marty's lunchbox. Besides, look at it as a concealed weapon. You can palm it and nobody's the wiser."

"OK." I answered. "But you'd tell me if you were hungry, right?"

"Yeah, sure."

"You ain't been coloring the church statues?"

"No!" Mark answered, laughing. But I wasn't so sure. Mark had this streak in him that gave grown-ups grey streaks in their hair. Sometimes he made me wonder if there was a Polish figure that was like an Irish Leprechaun. If there was, Mark could give either of them a run for their money.

I walked into school the next morning armed with the

remains of the red crayon and looking for Marty.

"Excuse me, sorry, 'cuse me." I said as I wiggled my way in the line of obedient kids headed for the coat room so I would be just behind Marty. The morning sunlight faded into a murky blackness as we walked single file into the cavern in the back of the class. I was right behind Marty and watched him shed and hang up his coat and reached up to put his Davy Crockett lunchbox on the shelf above it. I forgot one little detail. I'm the shortest kid in class and the shelf was a little beyond my reach. Sure, I could put my own lunchbox on the shelf, but I had to make sure it stuck out a few inches so that at lunch I could jump a little and get it back down. Marty was three inches taller, so his lunchbox would sit flush with the edge of the shelf. How was I supposed to mark it if I couldn't easily reach it? I was holding up the line as I pondered the challenge.

"Hey! Who's holding up the line?" Someone shouted.

"It's David." Came a reply. The response sounded all too familiar since the only time I hadn't heard that line from a crowd at the Shrine was in a Gregorian chant in church. As usual, it was directed at me and mostly in anger and frustration, which would explain why I hadn't heard it in a choir chant. I always expected, though, that the ancient music's lyrics would be changed, and interjected into a solemn Gregorian chant, would be something like "Who's holding us all up?" "It's David holding us up." It's probably not important, but to make it blend with the rest of the Gregorian chants who praise the saints, you'd have to go up one note (in harmony of course) on the word "all" and then descend a note on the word, "us." Once the solemn chant was concluded, the masses would feel free to light blazing torches and come after me.

"You get us all a task for not being at our desks on time, you maroon, I'll find you at recess!" Came another shout, which brought me back to reality.

I had to act fast. I pulled the tiny bit of crayon out of my pocket and jumped at the Davy Crockett lunchbox that Marty had placed on the shelf. I jumped up, aiming at the side of Marty's lunchbox, made a downward motion, and marked it. I could only hope that I made a mark that both Mark and I would recognize later.

I caught up with Mark at recess. I was confused, since Mark was able to mark the lunchbox and yet the unruly masses never shouted his name. And he had marked Marty's lunchbox the day before.

"How'd you get to Marty's lunchbox so fast?" I asked.

"I dropped my book bag on the floor and stood on it."

"Genius!" I said. Why hadn't I thought of that? It's not like we wanted to preserve our textbooks for the next generation. Even though I heard the voice in my head that declared "You know how much these books cost?" Mark realized that a badly creased or dented book wasn't going to affect its value very much. I, on the other hand, decided that it would be cool to create a series of drawings in the margins of the pages of my books like they do at Walt Disney, flip them rapidly and create my own cartoon. My textbooks never brought much dough when there was a used book sale, but that's the price you pay for being bored in class between September and May.

After school I handed the crayon back to Mark. "OK, it's your turn tomorrow." I remarked. Mark just stared at it for a minute.

"Was da matter?" I asked.

"It's kinda short."

"Short? It's the same size as it was this morning!"

"Yeah, yeah, I know, but it's kinda short. Think we could use a black crayon tomorrow?"

"I don't have a black crayon!"

"I know, but I think I can get one."

"OK, fine. Use a black crayon. Or use a blue one. I don't care as long as we know it's Marty's lunchbox."

"I'll tell ya the color in the morning."

"I know what you're doin. You're putting mustaches and lipstick on the statues in church, aren't ya?"

"Am not." Mark laughed. "But one of these days…" his voice trailed off. I could almost see Father Duck's hair turning to silver one day as he walked to the chapel altar and looked around. I'd have to go to confession just because I knew Mark.

The next morning Mark was right behind Marty as they entered the coatroom. I was five steps behind. I spied Marty's lunchbox which sported red, and now black, war paint. I was sure we'd both be able to single out the Davy Crockett lunchbox. At recess Mark and I compared notes.

"I can see the crayon marks on Marty's lunchbox. Can you?" I said.

"Yep. All I have to do now is get that spider in the jar." Mark responded.

"Need help?" I asked.

"You got a whip and a chair?"

"Nope. My knapsack ain't big enough." I answered.

"Just askin." Mark laughed. "I should be able to get it with no problem. Hey! You seen me chase down rats at the Run. A spider won't be a problem. You'll have to create a diversion in line tomorrow and hold everybody up while I put that critter in Marty's lunchbox, though."

"I can do dat." I answered. I figured I could fake a fit of Saint Vitus dance, whatever that looked like, and hold up the line for about thirty seconds. I knew I'd hear that Gregorian chant. "Who's holding us up? David is holding us up. What would the saints want? Throw him out the window." It would be complete with harmony and "Ahh…ahh…ahh…Amen." Some nice organ music to go with it would be nice, but I knew I couldn't get our organist on such short notice.

I met Mark first thing in the morning to see how his spider capture had gone.

"How'd it go?" I asked, expecting him to be wearing a pith helmet and a big grin.

"I got it. But, boy, is this thing mad! If it had teeth, it woulda chewed through the glass already. Marty's gonna love his new pet." Mark was almost beside himself with laughter.

"Then we're set. You go first. I'll follow you by a bit and distract the crowd."

"How ya gonna do dat?"

"I figured I'd fake a fit of Saint Vitus dance."

"What's that look like?"

"I dunno. Don't worry 'bout it. You'll have about thirty seconds to give that spider a new home. Any longer and Sister Knuckles will be racing to the coatroom, and to me. You gotta act fast."

"Got it under control. Marty won't have control at lunch time, though." We both laughed at our diabolical plan which would unfold in just a few hours.

Mark was positioned just behind Marty in single file entering the coatroom and I was standing just behind Mark. I walked slowly, giving Mark some distance in the morning ritual cattle parade of hanging up your coat and stowing your lunch. When Marty had hung up his coat and placed his lunchbox on the shelf, I stopped. Mark was already getting the jar out of his knapsack. I hadn't practiced my version of

Saint Vitus dance the night before because I still didn't know what it was, but I figured if it was named after a saint and it was called a dance it must look like something holy and unholy at the same time.

My first move was to wave my hands in the air and then bring them down like they were propellers. My next move was to spin around in a circle. Next I joined the two movements and started to swivel what I think was my hips. My older sister taught me that hip move but I wasn't sure I was swiveling the right way. It didn't matter, though. I dropped my knapsack on the floor, rolled my head, clawed at imaginary flying bugs, spun around and made faces at the kid behind me. That Gregorian chant was about to begin and I was hoping Mark was on schedule.

"Hey! Who's holding up the line?" Someone asked. I began counting to thirty.

"It's David." Came another voice in the mob.

"What's his problem? Hey, stupid! Move it!" I knew that voice and vowed that I'd never share a candy with him again as long as I lived.

"He don't look too good."

"He never looks good." I was still counting to thirty and waiting for Mark to give me a signal.

"Ster, Ster, I think something's the matter with David." Oh, drat! If Knuckles comes back here now I'm sunk. Mark needs to hurry up.

Just then Mark let out a short whistle and I knew that he'd planted the spider. I stopped my jerky movements, turned around to the crowd and in a nonchalant voice said, "So, how's everybody today?" I casually walked into the coatroom, hung my jacket up and put up my lunchbox on the shelf and took my seat in class. Knuckles had heard the commotion but was a little slow getting to the back of the room in time to see my act in person. She walked up to me with a stern look on her face.

"David, are you ok?" She asked.

"He's never ok!" came a retort from two aisles away, which caused Knuckles to spin around to find who made that verbal jab. The class giggled, and it was just the time I needed to compose myself, put an innocent look on my face and reply.

"I'm fine, 'Ster. How are you?" Knuckles walked back to the front of the class in exasperation.

We had three hours of classes before lunch. We ate lunch every day at our desk, no doubt to prepare us all for a later time in our lives when we would always be eating lunch at our desks at work. I anxiously watched the clock tick away the minutes to lunch time, just like I'd probably be doing when I grew up and had a job. Some things in life don't change much.

At 11:25 AM Sister Knuckles announced that it was lunch time, and row by row, we returned to the coatroom to retrieve whatever our moms had prepared, wrapped, and stuffed in our lunchboxes. Mark and I looked at each other as we made our way back to our desks. We wouldn't open our lunches until Marty had opened his, because we didn't want flying glass to shower our sammidges. We both looked at the windows and waited.

Screams come in all octaves. There's middle "C" and sometimes there's maybe an "F sharp minor" scream. I heard that a high "C" could break glass, but I'd never heard it. One of our buddies even told us that if somebody screams loud enough, dogs would bark from two blocks away because there's a pitch that only dogs can hear. I'd never heard anybody hit every note, all at the same time, with that kind of volume. The windows didn't shatter, but they shook. My pencil rolled down my desk because of the vibration, as did everybody else's in class. Knuckle's eyes rolled back in her head and she looked like someone had just punched her. In the distance we could hear dogs bark.

Marty? Well, Marty's hair seemed to go grey as we watched him. His skin color changed from white, to blue, and then back to white. His eyes looked like they sunk in his head. His arms and legs went stiff for a second or two; then they looked like rubber. And just before he lost his ability to speak, he was saying something that sounded like "I hate you, Mom." But I couldn't be sure since he started drooling.

I met up with Mark at recess to get his opinion on how we stopped Marty's antics.

"So, whaddya think? Think Marty learned his lesson?" I asked.

"Who knows? His mom came and picked him up. She put a blanket around his shoulders and carted him away a little while ago. But as soon as she did, he took the blanket off and shook it. He was babbling about spiders coming to suck his blood and it was all her fault. I dunno, maybe after he spends some time in a hospital ward, he'll be back to his old self. Then again, he may be a changed man. I heard Sister Bernie say something about months of therapy and he may not be back at school this year."

"I know this much, though." He added. "His screams were heard all the way to the third floor, Father Duck heard it in the rectory and the dames in the class are happy."

"Good." I answered. I looked at his right hand and he was carrying a white sheet of folded paper.

"Watcha got there?" I asked.

"Nuttin important. Just sumpin for Mary Margaret."

"Can I see it?"

"No! I gotta give it to her. You don't need to see it."

I had spied the red and black crayon showing through the white paper. I couldn't make out what it was. It could have been a heart with a lot of writing, but it kinda looked like something else. I wasn't sure. I decided to let it go.

"See ya tomorrow." I said.

"Yep." Mark answered, as he walked towards where the dames congregated.

You and What Army?

Along with being the youngest gumshoe at the Shrine, I'm also one of the shortest kids in class. Most of the boys in my grade are already almost as tall as the Franciscan nuns. Not me. I still have to look up at them. What I lack in height I try to make up in attitude and hustle. I don't have any more brain cells colliding in my head than the next guy. But take a gink, with an almost empty noggin, add in a set of parents who believe more in the law of the jungle than they do in troof, justice and the Merican way, and you can quickly hatch yourself a bully.

I don't want to say that bullies are born or made. They just show up in class without a clue how to act in public. Almost every class has a bully, be it a gink or a dame. And almost every class has a target for bullying without regard for gender, hair color, size, or what's been said at recess. I've always tried to keep my sense of humor when dealing with ginks, hoods and jailbirds at recess. Seems there's always a bully nearby when somebody within arm's reach isn't up to a bully's height or weight. Needless to say, as one of the shortest kids in school, I hate bullies.

None of us were the perfect picture of heath in the late 1950's. Besides getting a cold or flu, our parents were always on the lookout for chickenpox, measles, mumps, scarlet fever, smallpox, yellow fever, malaria, leprosy, typhoid fever, along with walking in the back door covered in locusts because somehow we offended God. I watched Charlton Heston as Moses in the Vilma Movies. I knew what the word "smote" meant, ok? However, the biggest fear of both parents and kids was that we would be infected with polio. It must have been a tough time to be a parent.

Most of us escaped the dreaded polio virus, but not everyone. If you were born in 1949, like I was, there was a chance you could get it. Stiffening of the muscles, can't control walking, can't breathe, and might die were all phrases I'd heard. "Iron lung," "wheelchair," and "leg braces" were scary possibilities even if you were running around in the Shrine school yard; because one day, without warning, you may get it and life would change forever.

Not all of us were fortunate to escape childhood polio.

There was a sweet good-natured tomato at recess named Melissa. While she escaped the Calf Lick required "Mary" as her first name, she didn't escape polio. She obviously got polio before the first grade because by third grade she was able to get around with the help of steel leg braces that resembled the scaffolding on a house, along with two crutches. For somebody like me, if I had to endure what she did when it came to just walking, I'd probably be the last person humanity would want to be around. But Melissa was different. She was smart and funny and quick to answer a lot of stupid questions.

"Gee, Melissa, what happened to you?" Would come the obvious stupid question.

"'Oh, I forgot. I musta left my good legs at home." She'd answer.

"Isn't it hard to walk with those braces and crutches?" came the next stupid question.

"Is it hard for you to walk and chew gum at the same time?" She'd answer.

Just because almost all of us liked Melissa because of her spunk and moxie didn't mean everybody liked her. She became a target of one of the cruelest bullies at the Shrine. His name was Henry, Hank for short. Hank would bully a butterfly off your finger simply because he thought he could and he would laugh when it happened.

Mark and I weren't aware of what was going on at recess until Mary Margaret barged into our office one afternoon in a state of tomato huff. Boy, was she mad!

"Listen, you two! You've got to do sumpin bout Hank. He's been tormenting Melissa every day and he won't let up. She took the magnets Hank attached to her leg braces with a laugh. She even listened to him joke about her being crippled. But today...." Mark and me watched her rosy face turn to beet red, "Today! He ran up to her and stole one of her crutches! It's the last straw! As great as Melissa is, losing her crutches along with everything else she's had to live through....she's in tears. You gotta stop Hank."

Mark and I looked at each other because we hadn't heard about Hank's bullying behavior before.

"Oh, and Mark. If you don't do sumpin about this...I'm gonna stop writing invitations about us of any kind right now. Got it?" She was glaring at Mark so hard that I thought he'd need sunglasses and suntan lotion. The sun may give you a tan, but the angry glare from a dame is gonna burn you to a crisp.

"Fill us in, Mary Margaret. " I said.

She went into detail about how this hood, Hank, went out of his way every day at recess to torment Melissa. The more Mary Margaret talked, the more I wanted to bury this lug's face in the mud. I have to admit I have a soft spot for dames of any sort, but when a dame gets tormented and bullied I start to lose my cool. My fuse gets even shorter when it's a chick like Melissa.

"Melissa talk to the 'sters?" I asked.

"Who?"

"You know, the pious penguins, the nuns." I responded.

"Oh yeah… them. Yeah, sure, Melissa has told a few of them. Know what they told her?"

"Buy some heat?"

"No! That would have solved everything! But…No! They told her to smile, turn the other cheek, ignore Hank and he'll stop and go away, and say some prayers to St. Jude. Guess what? Melissa's done all that and Hank is just getting worse."

I was never a fan of the "turn the other cheek" idea. How many cheeks does a person have? And besides, while you're turning your face how do you keep smiling? I imagine with so much going on in the world, Saint Jude, the patron saint of hopeless causes, probably had a very long list and Melissa might be at the bottom. The nuns might have their hands full with the rest of the unruly students in class and at recess, I just didn't think it was jake to leave Melissa to hang out to dry and twist in the wind. This hood, Hank, was not about to go away anytime soon. I've seen his kind before. Even if he did get tired of tormenting Melissa, he'd just find someone else to bully and start all over again.

"What grade is this Hank guy in, Mary Margaret? You know?" I asked.

"Sixth. But he looks like he should be in high school. I mean, he's got hairs on his lip! I think he's been held back a few times. He's even got hair on his knuckles!"

"He a big lug?" Mark asked, as we both looked at our hands to see if we had hair growing there yet.

"Yeah! Dontcha think if he was our size that me and my friends would have taken care of him? No, he's pretty big."

"OK, Mary Margaret, we'll get right on it." I said as I slid my hairless hands in my jacket pockets.

"You better." She said as she started to walk away. She stopped and turned to us. "Hank's over at the fence with one of Melissa's crutches, in case you wanted a head start."

Mark and I took a stroll towards the far fence of the school yard to confront Hank and get Melissa's crutch back. At least that would be a start.

Hank was twirling the crutch like it was a lacrosse stick, joking with a few clueless friends and showing off. He definitely looked like he should be in high school because the cuffs of his pants were about five inches above the ground and his shirt sleeves were half way up his arms. His antics with the crutch just confirmed he'd been held back more than a few grades. And boy was he a big hood, one of the biggest I'd seen at recess! I'd have to sit on Mark's shoulders just to look him in the eye. He had crazy curly brown hair and eyes that matched. Mark and I walked up to Hank and I spoke up.

"Hank, you don't look like you need a crutch, with all your dancing around. And besides, we know that it belongs to a chick named Melissa. We came to get it back."

"Yeah? You want it? Come and get it." As Hank twirled it above our heads.

Mark and me knew this keep-away routine so well that we knew what to do. As I stepped towards Hank, Mark went to the right, jumped and snatched the crutch in midair. Without a word, Mark walked back to my side, crutch in hand, and we both stared at Hank.

"Pretty slick, youse guys. So you got the crutch. Big deal. I'll just get it again tomorrow."

"Think so, Hank? I asked.

"Who's gonna stop me? You two runts? You and what army?"

Mark and I walked away from Hank, refusing to take the bait on an all-out fight in the recess yard. But what Hank just said made the wheels in my head start to turn. That's exactly what Melissa needs to protect herself from the likes of hoods like Hank - an army, and we were going to build one.

"Got any bright ideas spinning in your noggin?" I asked Mark.

"Nuttin yet. You?"

"Yeah. Hank told us we'd need an army to stop him. We're going into the recruiting bizness."

"Oh… great. You see how big that lug is? I know Melissa needs help, but even if we got half the third grade to join up, it's just not going to be enough to stop him."

"I know dat! I also know that if we went down that avenue every third grader would get charged by the nuns for starting a riot. It's just like in football; it's the second guy who throws the punch that gets flagged for a penalty. No, we're gonna get some eighth grade guys to help us out."

"And like you know so many of 'em."

"I don't, but my sister is in the eighth grade. Remember?" I answered.

"So you gotta recruit her first." Mark responded.

"Shouldn't be a problem. She was teased and tormented when she was our age. I'm gonna talk to her."

After we had finished the ritual Lenten Friday dinner of coddies, pierogies and green beans (with a watery Junket dessert), I knocked on my sister's door.

"Go away!" Came the response through the tightly latched door.

"It's me, Sis." I called back.

"I know. That's why I said go away."

"I need to talk to ya. I need some help and you're the only one who can help me." I knew my sister would take this bait and years later might hold it over my head with a story that would begin with "Do you remember when you said I was the only one who could help you?" But I wasn't trying to weasel anything out of her for myself. If she'd let me in her room and give me a few minutes to explain, I'd probably never hear the beginning of that story.

The door opened and my sister stood there, face covered in what I think was concrete and a look of frustration. Sometimes big sisters can look really scary.

"Ahh, Sis, it ain't Halloween, it's Lent."

"Look, make it quick. I still have homework to finish." She said.

It was the high broiling heated voice used by older sisters on younger brothers that was just below the proper temperature to serve up a kid brother for a proper French dinner, complete with cousins on the side. I had no idea what the proper wine might be, since my dad drank beer, but I was pretty sure my mom would have an idea for dessert.

"Mmm…what is this dish, again?" My dad might ask my sister, who by the way hated to cook but was learning French.

"Mon frère l'insecte du mutard, Father." (My brother the insect with mustard) My sister would respond. "I learned the words in French class."

"Nice touch, daughter. Hand me another Natty Boh, will ya, hon?" He'd holler to my mom. "Seems a bit bland, though. Some Old Bay would help. And what you did with your cousin… I like the red sauce. Whatdya call it? Le cousins de rouge? (Cousins in red sauce) Hey, Ev! What's for dessert? Too bad your brother isn't here to enjoy this dinner."

OK, this was knocking around in my head and my imag-ination. But I bet other students learning French didn't like their younger brother, either. While the heat from my sister's eyes would make the sun put on a pair of shades, budding cooks prolly used a bit of French cooking on their little brother, added some mustard and nobody was any the wiser.

Anyway, I recounted the day's case about Melissa, her having to wear leg braces and walking with crutches, and then being teased, tormented and bullied by a sixth grader named Hank. I didn't mean to get my sister upset as I told her this, but I noticed that the face cream had hardened and as her face took on a look of anger, the face mask began to crack. Sometimes big sisters can look even scarier than you first thought.

"And the nuns told her…what?" She interrupted.

"Smile, ignore him, and say a prayer to Saint Jude."

"Typical nun response. Oohh, this makes me so mad! They never helped me either. Unless one of them catches this guy in the act, to them it just sounds like a third grader tattling on a sixth grader." She was almost shouting. And some dried concrete face mask began to fall to the floor. I didn't think it was wise for me to point out that she looked like somebody in the last scenes from "The House of Wax." Just when you think your older sister couldn't look scarier….

"OK, you think you and Mark can snatch Melissa's crutch Monday, in case he does it again?" she asked me.

"Yeah, we know the moves. But a second time means that he'll come after us. Know what I mean?"

"I know that. I need two days to talk to some of my friends. You gotta do something else. I need to know which way Hank walks home."

"Mark and me know how to tail a suspect. We'll do dat."

"Fine. Tell me so I can get my friends in the right place at the right time."

"Thanks, Sis. I knew you'd understand." I answered.

"It's ok. Just let me know by Monday. By the middle of next week Melissa will never have to feel scared by this guy Hank again. Oh, and by the way, don't even think about knocking on my door until then. Got it?" The heat from her gaze made me want to find the leftover suntan lotion to protect myself from basting and make sure the jar of mustard was still in the fridge.

"Yeah, I got it. Oh, and by the way, your face is falling off." I said as I quickly walked away from her. As her door slammed shut I scampered back to my room lest I find parts of myself on a platter and my parents praising my sister for coming up with such a unique supper.

It was Monday recess and Mark and me were circling around the recess yard trying to keep an eye on Melissa and Hank's whereabouts. It was a very noisy recess what with camel trading, deals going on, baseball card pitching and dodge ball in full swing. Our heads were on swivels so we could keep an eye on everything.

A third grade classmate named Jeremy ran up to us and spun us around.

"Youse guys gotta come and investigate this!" He panted.

"What's the problem?" Mark asked.

"There's this fourth grader, see. He's pitchin cards like a ringer, ya know. He's cleaned me out and two other guys. Nobody can pitch cards that good. Nobody! He's gotta have an edge, ya know, like weights or spit or sumpin. You gotta come now."

This kid was yammering like he was a stool pigeon under the third degree lights and it was his last confession or his first night on stage. As try as I might to give this kid the shoulder, he was in our face, up close and personal; a bit too personal.

Suddenly, a few dames let out screams and a big kid ran past us with what looked like a long stick in his hands.

"Hank's got another of Melissa's crutches!" Mark shouted. We took off after him toward the opposite corner of the yard. I woulda smacked Jeremy for getting in the way of a stakeout, but I was focused on getting Melissa's crutch back.

Instead of a lacrosse stick, Hank decided that Melissa's crutch was an almost perfect pretend sword. He was twirling it, but his movements with the crutch were more pointed towards Mark and me. We watched his quick flurry upward, then towards us, then towards the ground. I have no idea what sounds he was making as he did this, but it sounded like he was squealing like a pig. I think he expected Mark and me to walk away because he was acting so strange. Not a chance.

We watched Hank flail the crutch around for a few seconds and tried not to laugh. As he was squealing and spinning Melissa's crutch in some kind of show, I turned to Mark. Errol Flynn never made sounds like that as Robin Hood in the movies. What was wrong with this gink?

"You want me to kick his arm, or do you?" I asked Mark.

"No, you rush him, get his attention. I'll kick his arm as he raises Melissa's crutch. But don't go too fast, cuz when I do kick it, you gotta be ready to snatch the crutch. On three. Ready?

"Ready"

Mark and I squared up against Hank. The move we were about to make was done so many times by Raymond Berry and another Colt's wide receiver that to us it looked almost routine, except for the kicking the crutch part. Otherwise it felt natural.

"One, two, three! Hike!" We said together.

I charged Hank head-on expecting him to lower the crutch while Mark rushed to his left. Just as we expected, Hank lowered the crutch as he caught sight of Mark. Hank wasn't sure which side to defend, and that gave us the window we were going for. I was rushing Hank head-on and then veered to my right as Mark placed a perfect kick near Hank's hands that sent the crutch into the air. Five yards from Hank's right, I snagged the crutch midair and then ran towards where Melissa and her friends hung out. Mark had already broken off his post pattern and was following me.

"I'm tellin! Hear me?" Hank screamed.

I stopped running and as Mark ran up to me, I lateralled the crutch to him. "Get this back to Melissa. I'm going back to have a short talk with Hank." I walked back to within twelve feet of Hank, just to give me some room in case he decided it might be better to give me some chin music than tell a nun what we just did.

"Hank, I think you should go tell a nun right now." I began. "It's a good idea. In fact I'll go with you, if you like" I continued. "I want to hear how you explain to one of them what you're doing with a crutch that belongs to a third grade girl, seeing that you don't have polio or even a broken leg. C'mon, let's go." I was feeling pretty cocky. "Wait! There's Sister Bernie! Want me to flag her over here for ya?" OK, I was feeling really cocky.

One day the look of hate might be a crime, but it isn't yet. Right now, right here in the recess yard it's probably a venial sin. Of course in Hank's case it might be a mortal sin, but I'm no priest so I don't know which list it's on. There's probably a sin list, complete with suggested penance to be handed out, tacked up in the priest's confessional so they can keep it straight. If hate were bullets, I'd be dead right now, gunned down by Hank's stare.

"You ain't stopping me, runt. Ya hear?" Hank screamed at me.

"I know, I know. It'll take an army."

"That's right, runt! An army." Hank responded, as if he knew an army would never show up at the Shrine.

I joined Mark who was in the middle of a crowd of dames. He was trying to straighten his hair and escape the arms of grateful females. But no matter how many times he twisted and turned, ducked and covered, he was immediately hugged by another chick. He just couldn't seem to break the tackles. Poor kid, I thought. I made the mistake of walking into it all.

"Mark, leave the girls alone. We gotta get back to work." I said.

"There's your hero! Wasn't just me! Go hug him!" Mark exclaimed as he pointed in my direction. So many big brown, blue and green eyes turned to me that I wasn't sure what to do. Running away sounded good, but as I looked around, I realized there just wasn't any way out. I was surrounded. In an instant I was being pawed, hugged, kissed, and cooed at. Now I understood what Mark had been going through for the last several months. And I got what he said to me: next time just send me into combat. Even grandmothers and aunts who hadn't seen you in months didn't act like this.

"Ok, ladies!" I yelled. "You're welcome!"

Mary Margaret walked up with Melissa just behind. I'd heard the word "beaming" before, but never remember seeing it in person, until now. Mary Margaret had a tight grip on Mark's arm, but released it as she threw her arms around me. Mark immediately started to brush his arm like he was trying to get rid of female cooties.

"Our heroes!" She cried out as her arms around my neck cut off my ability to breathe, and Mark's brushing his arm became more rapid. Mary Margaret finally relaxed her grip on me and I was able to catch a breath.

"Thanks, you guys." Melissa said.

"Don't thank us yet, Melissa." I gasped. "We're going to put an end to this, though."

Mark was still brushing his sleeve of "girl cooties" but he looked at Melissa and said, "We're gonna put an end to this soon. Be patient." However he wasn't patient in his frenzied stroking of his shirt sleeve that Mary Margaret had released just a minute before.

Mark and I walked back to our corner office in the recess yard, having just escaped a crowd of grateful dames. Recess was about to end, but Mark was still brushing his shirt sleeve. I figured he'd rip the shirt on purpose, just to make sure he'd never have to wear it again.

"Would you stop that?" I asked, as Mark continued brushing his sleeve.

"I can still feel it! It's itchy!" Mark seemed determined to scratch away Mary Margaret's touch.

"Leave it alone! You won't croak."

"How do you know?" Mark asked.

"Just leave your shirt alone, OK?"

I knocked at my sister's door that night to give her an update on Hank and his continued teasing of Melissa, along with what Mark and I had done to recover her crutch and hopefully she could give me some news on her end.

"Go away!" Came the usual angry response from the other side of the door.

"C'mon, sis, it's me. You said I should report back to you."

The door opened and once again my sister's face was

covered in some kind of plaster. If that white goo was con-crete, the harbor tunnel would have been paved in a silky smooth white roadbed.

"You get a bunch of guys to stop this hood, Hank?" I asked.

"Yeah, I got'em. "

"Is it an army?"

"How many boys do you want me to get? Look, I went through this. You may want twenty guys, but, I'm tellin ya, it won't take that many. Trust me."

"So what's the next move?"

"You go up to this Hank guy tomorrow and tell him to meet you at 3:30 in the parking lot behind Read's."

"Sounds like a suicide mission."

"Trust me. I'm your sister. I already have your army in place. "

"How big is this army?"

"Three, so far. Maybe four. Don't worry, it'll work out. I'm your sister. Trust me."

"And you have names that belong to this army?"

"Yes. There's Dickie B, Steven and Mario. We may get a few more, but, believe me, those three will be more than enough. Trust me."

I walked out of my sister's room not very confident in what she wanted me to do tomorrow. I wasn't even sure I'd recognize her tomorrow, what with the white face paint she was wearing. What is it with older sisters?

I brought Mark up to date at recess. He was wearing a new shirt and wasn't brushing his sleeve, so he paid attention to what I was sayin."

"And you're gonna say what? " He asked.

"I'm gonna tell Hank to meet us behind Read's at 3:30."

"You, me, and what army?" He asked.

"My sister said she's got it covered. We'll have an army that will stop Hank." I said with confidence, except I wasn't feeling very confident.

"Listen," I continued. "You get Mary Margaret and her crowd to huddle around Melissa so we don't have to get her crutch back. I'll talk to Hank. Just be behind Read's at 3:30." I said as I walked away and into the crowd of the Shrine's recess yard.

I found Hank leaning against the fence acting like the sun, moon and the stars were shining down on him. I still kept about twelve feet away just in case he decided I was an easy target.

"Hank, meet me behind Read's at 3:30 today. We're gonna settle this once and for all."

"Got your army, runt?"

"Just be there." I said.

"OK, it'll be a pleasure to pound you into a pulp, runt."

At 3:15 Mark and I walked onto the parking lot behind Read's Drug Store. There were probably ten cars parked at different angles since the parking lines were so faded that nobody knew exactly where to park. Close to the back door of Read's sat the huge dumpster. My sister was standing next to a '53 Plymouth that looked like someone had painted it baby blue with a toothbrush. Next to her were two of her girlfriends. Hopefully one of them knew first aid. I was getting nervous.

"Ah, Sis, this doesn't look like an army." My voice was starting to get shaky.

"Guys!" My sister shouted, and she smiled at me. "I told you to trust me."

Six of the biggest guys in school popped up from behind different cars. I looked around and felt relieved. I looked at Mark and he had this wide grin on his face. I guess our faces said it all as we looked at our army. My sister motioned over the two biggest kids to join us.

"David, this is Dickie B and Steve. I think you know Steve, he lives down the street. These are my girlfriends, Susan and you know Mary Jane." She said. I shook hands with both guys and realized they had hair on their knuckles. One day I might get hair there.

Both Dickie B and Steve looked like they could play defense for the Colts. I knew Mary Jane since she almost lived at our house every weekend for the last two years. I still hoped that my sister's friend Susan knew first aid, just in case.

"Dave, right?" Said Dicklie B "Listen, Dave, we got this planned out. We're gonna use the element of surprise on Hank, OK? I want you and Mark; its Mark ain't it, to stand this guy down for just a minute. We wanna hear him spill the beans about tormenting this girl Melissa. She's in your class, right? Don't worry. Me and the boys will take care of him and this chick Melissa will never have to be afraid again."

"I don't know what to say." I said. "Thanks, guys." Was about the best my brain and mouth could come up with.

"Don't have to thank us, kid. None of us like bullies. We'll take care of this Hank bizness."

Our makeshift army disappeared behind the cars and Mark and I were left standing in the late afternoon sunshine behind Read's Drug. My sister and her two friends were standing just behind us. I realized the reason they were there was for diversion as well as support, not Mark and my support, but to support a defenseless third grade chick named Melissa.

Hank strode into the parking lot, his book bag hanging on one shoulder, and both his face and his hands were clenched. This was a kid bent on making sure he could bully kids at the Shrine, and since only Mark and me had outfoxed him over the previous week, pounding both of us into a pulp would just make him appear stronger at recess. Hank was about ten feet from us when he dropped his book bag and laughed.

"So that's your army, huh. Two third grade runts and three chicks. This is gonna be more fun than stealing that crippled chick's crutches at recess. I'm gonna enjoy this." Hank said.

"You really like to steal Melissa's crutches, Hank? You know how that feels?" I asked.

"I don't care! She's a weak, crippled little third grader."

"You told me that I needed an army to stop you, Hank." I said defiantly.

Hank didn't just laugh, he laughed in a way that made a person's blood boil, like in a Vincent Price horror movie. I knew now that he thought that two third graders and three girls was the army he thought Mark and I had mustered.

I looked over at my sister. "Call 'em out, Sis."

"Guys!" my sister shouted.

Six guys rose from behind the parked cars and formed a circle, with Dickie B and Steve on either side of Hank. Hank lost his scowl as Steve grabbed his left arm and put it in a hammerlock behind his back and Dickie B stood on his right.

"Well… well… well." Dickie began. "Hello….Henry. Remember us? We were in the first and second grade together, remember? You don't? Well we were, and then you got held back. You failed second grade and then in fourth, right? And now you're in the sixth grade and you think it's OK to torment, tease and bully a third grade chick who has polio. You're real brave, Henry. Real brave. You're a big man at recess, ain't ya?"

Steve was pushing Hank's left arm up higher and higher behind his back with every sentence from Dickie B. I looked at both of them with a feeling of wonder. These two guys were doing what I wanted to do, except I'm too short and too young. They were fighting the right fight, not just for Melissa, but for every kid at recess who was the victim of a bully.

Dickie B continued. "My friends here tell me that you keep taking Melissa's crutches. Tell me….Henry. Would you like the chance to use some crutches? Look around you…Henry. We'd be more than happy to help you learn. Wouldcha like dat….Henry?"

"Hey, Dickie, it'll only take a second to break one of his legs. Mario!" Steve called out to one of the guys. "You got that Louisville Slugger wit ya?"

A tall olive skin kid reached into his knapsack and tossed a Mickey Mantle bat to Steve, who caught it one-handed without releasing his grip on Hank's left arm. Hank's face turned to pure terror, faced with the prospect that he would not only have to crawl home, but the sheer pain he was possibly facing. Steve twirled the bat like a drum major handles a baton in front of Hank's face.

"Easy, Steve." Dickie B said. "If we break his leg and he has to use crutches, we're worse than he is."

"Break his arm!" Mary Jane shouted.

Both Dickie and Steve looked at her and smiled.

"Henry…Henry…Henry" Dickie began as he turned Hank's face toward his. "As you can see I got more than a few friends who would love to see you with a broken leg, maybe both legs. They might even be satisfied with your arm in a cast. At least they'd like to see you in some kind of sling for the rest of the school year. I even have a notion to send you home with your teeth in your lunchbox. Are you listening to me, Henry? Henry, look at me. Ya know, Steve just got a 60 on his history test. He's pretty angry right now. He'd love to break sumpin. Right, Steve?"

"Yeah. Just one whack, Dickie. C'mon. I'll feel better after one swing. I swear, there won't be any blood. OK, not a lot of blood." Steve said and his face brightened at the idea of letting out his frustration.

The color had drained out of Hank's face. He looked more like a first winter's Bawlmer snowman than a human. Steve still was pressing Hank's arm higher, all the while twirling the bat, while Dickie B kept talking in his ear. Mark and I looked at each other hoping that one of us was taking notes. The other four guys in this army were keeping close watch. My sister and her friends had a look like they couldn't decide whether this gink should be allowed to walk home or left with the rest of the garbage in Read's dumpster.

"Henry….Henry!"Dickie B exclaimed. Hank's fear of probable injury and trying to get him to focus on the army that surrounded him and his inability to move an inch because of Steve's hammerlock made listening to Dickie a major challenge.

"You're not gonna bully another kid at recess, right? Or any other time, right?" Dickie almost whispered in Hank's ear.

Hank's gaze shifted from the baseball bat, still being twirled by Steve, then towards Dickie.

"No. Never." He finally said.

"Just in case you forget, Henry, or you think we may, Steve and me will be going to high school next year. Our four friends here will be in the eighth grade next year. I have a sister in fifth grade and Steve here has a brother in fifth, also. And Dave and Mark will be keeping an eye on you, too. If me or Steve hear you've gone back to your old ways…it's gonna be you who will need an army, not to mention a trip to the hospital and crutches of your own. Got it?"

I heard a loud gulp from Hank. "Got it."

Dickie and Steve released Hank and he quickly snatched up his book bag and ran from the parking lot. As Hank faded into the afternoon sun, my sister and her two friends hugged each guy. I wanted to know how Steve was able to twirl a baseball bat in one hand, but I was also grateful to my sister for recruiting the army I needed to stop a bully.

I walked up to both Dickie B and Steve to shake their hands and thank them for all they'd done, not so much to save Mark and me from getting a beating, but because we knew Melissa would never have to worry about being bullied.

"You guys really have a brother and sister in fifth grade?" I asked Dickie B.

"Naw, but Henry doesn't know dat."

"On behalf of Melissa, Mark and me want to thank you." I said.

"It's ok, shrimp. Steve and me and the rest of these guys hate bullies and after what your sister told us, we knew we had to stop this idget in his tracks .You wanna do me a favor?" Dickie asked. "Talk to your sister about Friday's CYO. See if you can get her to dance with me." He said and smiled.

"Sure, Dickie." I said .

Because of Dickie's request I was gonna brave a closed and locked door, not gag when my sister opened it with white concrete on her face, and even brush off everything hateful she might say to me in the second story hallway of our row house. I felt like I owed it to Dickie…and I owed it Melissa.

The next day at recess was relatively quiet. We kept an eye on Hank, who was now playing politely in a game of dodge ball, and Melissa and her friends were still huddled around her like mother hens protecting their chicks.

"You think we should tell Melissa what happened?" Mark asked.

"Naw. It'll sink in in a few days that she doesn't have to be afraid of Hank. Besides, you wanna go over there and give those dames the news? Haven't you been hugged enough?" I asked.

"Oh, yeah! I've had enough of that!" Mark exclaimed.

I unwrapped a peppermint candy and popped it in my mouth.

"Peppermint? Really, peppermint?" Mark exclaimed.

"What? I like peppermint." I responded.

"Yeah! You like peppermint ever since my dad handed you a shot of peppermint schnapps last Christmas!" Mark laughed.

"I happen to like the taste." I said, as I could feel the cool rush of sugar going straight to my brain.

The Last Bus to Gwynn Oak

If we made it through the school year without a serious injury at recess, hadn't shot at Father Duck, the archbishop or the pope, and had decent grades, there came a Friday in late May when the Franciscan pious penguins at the Shrine would decide to reward us with a day trip to Bawlmer's Gwynn Oak Amusement Park.

It was a strange end to the events of a school year. After the "almost, it's finally here" celebrations of Advent and Christmas, the forty days of denial of Lent, the yearlong preaching about starving children in other countries, the endless extra envelopes at mass collecting for someone who was destitute, starving, oppressed, naked, as well as all of those who were less fortunate than we were because we attended a Calf Lick school, we were carted off to Gwynn Oak Amusement Park just to show us that hard work had its payoff.

What better way to celebrate doing our part in saving all those starving children and oppressed villagers in some far flung country than to go to an amusement park? We did our share and it was time for self-indulgence. I imagine that missionary nuns and priests in some far off land, after a year of helping the starving, the naked, the oppressed and the unwashed masses, looked at each other and said, "Let's all go to an amusement park and ride the roller coaster and carousel and eat hot dogs all day. The poor unwashed naked heathen peasants will still be here when we get back. We can get back to converting them to the Lord tomorrow. But today, it's time for a party!"

I never got the connection.

Amusement parks never made sense to me. Too many rides resembled my life. A merry-go-round reminded me of my life going in circles. A roller coaster (with its long steep climb to a top, then experience a high speed plunge into depths that always felt out of control) reminded me of the highs and lows of my life. Even a ride on a small scale train that took a scenic route around the area just told me that where I started is where I would end up. No thank you.

I seemed to be in the minority as so many friends giggled and swooned over what lay ahead. To them, this day trip was a reward for hard work in and out of the classroom. It was a time to wear your street clothes on a school day, a day long recess in a kind of yard that had bells, whistles, as well as rides that made you realize you had motion sickness(and ended up puking), loud noises and all kinds of shenanigans. Except for the motion sickness, that was every day at the Shrine. Maybe there was an up-side to all this. The Franciscans wouldn't be pointing out every sin you committed once you were let loose at Gwynn Oak.

Once we reported to class and were given our papers, like refugees from some communist country, we were cleared to go. Everyone sat at their desk squirming in giddy anticipation waiting for the buses to arrive. Sister Knuckles patrolled the aisles making sure giddy didn't turn into unbridled happiness. Publicans are allowed unbridled happiness. Calf Licks were supposed to be a bit more reserved, like feeling guilty for something that happened on the other side of the world. I think unbridled happiness was a venial sin, but it may depend on the way you talked and how much leg twitching went on under your desk.

Finally, yellow school buses pulled up to the Brendan Avenue curb. The random chatter among students reached a level I hadn't heard since Marty screamed when he was surprised by a spider in his lunch box. Sister Knuckles quickly stopped the near riot of students.

"Everybody! Back in your seats! Now! I will tell you when it's time to get on the bus." She screamed.

The chaos reminded me of what it may have looked like when the Titanic was sinking. If only the Titanic had a few Franciscan nuns as passengers, more people would probably have survived. Maybe the Hindenburg would have had more survivors had the Franciscan nuns been on board. Maybe there wouldn't be a Cold War going on since if anybody can get two sides to stop what they're doing, it would be Franciscan nuns armed with a high caliber cricket. And really, I've seen grown men back away when a pious penguin was twirling a yardstick in their direction. Maybe more chicks would have made a full recovery to sanity after watching Elvis on the Ed Sullivan Show.

The yellow Bawlmer public school buses sat at the curb with engines running. My classmates were almost sitting in their seats inside the building. It was a stampede waiting to happen. The only thing holding back an all-out offensive to take over the buses was a few nuns, crickets in hand and yardsticks at the ready.

"OK, class, I want you to line up in rows and walk two-by-two out the door and board the bus." Said Knuckles.

What we heard instead was, "It's every man for himself!" Even the cowboys on the "Rawhide," TV show, firing off six shooters, yelling, snapping whips and hollering "get along little doggie," wouldn't have been able to contain this mad dash through the classroom doors, down the hall and out the doors to the waiting buses.

Seats were claimed and seats were reserved, as the early settlers on the buses staked their claims like gold miners in California. Pretty quickly, one would find out who their real friends were. This was not a pretty sight as more than a few found out that who they thought were their best friends were nothing more than convenient stooges who probably supplied answers on the previous night's homework. The wandering of the confused students who thought they had a best friend to share the day at Gwynn Oak, looked from front to back on the bus without a welcomed nod from a friend, and stood amid classmates who were beckoned to "sit here." Not a pretty sight, but it was mostly done by the dames in class. For us guys, all we needed to know if we were somebody's best friend, was to get pounded in the arm or given a charley horse in the thigh by them. For guys, it was pretty simple. If I hurt you in fun, I liked you. Some lugs thought that worked with the girls in class, too. It never worked out like they thought it would, though.

Mark and I walked onto the third yellow bus and tried to find an open seat. I looked around the interior of the bus. No wonder publicans acted like they did. The interior resembled a cattle car, except with seats. The interior was an even worse shade of drab yellow than the outside: steel handrails, no ads that proclaimed the virtues of hair spray or toothpaste above the seats to brighten your day, and a driver whose vocabulary never went beyond five letters. "Humph," "grunt," "burp," and "a-yep." Our driver sounded like my next door neighbor who always struggled to put three words together in a sentence.

"Mr. Ed, how are you this morning?" "Burp, ok, a-yep." I just hoped this yahoo knew how to drive.

Mark looked at me and said, "I think we should sing a song while we're on our way. Whadya think of '99 Bottles of Beer on The Wall'? That ought to get the crowd going."

"It may get the crowd going, but the nuns would be going for you."

"Yeah, prolly right. Not everybody is a Cub Scout on this bus." He replied.

Besides going through the tame army boot camp of Cub Scouts, we also learned a variety of drinking songs on our outings. As scouts we were being trained in basic survival skills as well as preparing us for loud, friendly heavy drinking at each den meeting. You could get a scout badge for just about anything except for heavy drinking in Cub Scouts. I didn't know what badges were handed out once you became a Boy Scout. Heavy drinking and singing the associated songs at the top of your lungs might be a badge worth working on. Since I wasn't a full-fledged Boy Scout yet I'd have to wait to find out, though.

As soon as the buses pulled away from Brendan Avenue, Knuckles stood up at the front of our bus. Well, I thought, here it comes. I wasn't disappointed.

"I expect all of you to be on your best behavior today. There will be a lot of people at Gwynn Oak and I want all of you to conduct yourselves properly. I expect you to be proper representatives of The Shrine of the Large Flower. Does everybody understand?"

"Yes, 'Ster." Came the reply from the excited, but now deflated, mass of humanity on the bus.

"Good. By the way, confessions will be heard tomorrow afternoon."

The jibber jabber on the bus almost made my ears hurt. Mark kept coming up with ideas for a sing-a-long but each one was a drinking song. Meanwhile Knuckles walked up and down the aisle of the bus, pointing her cricket at anybody who looked like they were descending into out-of-control happiness. Among a few riders were the chicks and the guys who were holding hands during the ride, obviously caught up in a nine year old romantic moment.

"Robert! Take your hands off that girl! We'll have none of that here! Teresa, you know better than that. What would your mother say, not to mention our Blessed Virgin Mary, if I told them you were holding Robert's hand?" All in all, the trip resembled any other day in class, except we were winding our way through the streets of Bawlmer on a yellow public school bus.

At last the buses pulled onto the grounds of Gwynn Oak Amusement Park. You could tell you finally arrived at Gwynn Oak because the Dip Racer's old wooden roller coaster stared you in the face and its rickety sounds filled your ears. While the buses sat idling, my classmates were anything but. They were ready to bust out and make a break for it as soon as the doors of the bus opened. I looked at Mark and he looked at me as squeals began to rattle the windows.

"We in a hurry to join this stampede?" I asked.

"Nope. Far as I know, this place will be open all day."

"You got any place in particular you want to go first?"

"I got a few in mind. But like I said, we got the whole day."

I know a bomb didn't go off in the back of the bus because I'd have heard it. But as the doors opened next to the driver, it looked like everybody was shot out of a cannon toward the front of the bus. Even Knuckles, who stepped out of the bus just a second before, had a look on her face that resembled astonishment. It was the first time in my life that I saw any nun look like that.

A large red round sign greeted us as our feet hit solid ground. "Welcome to Gwynn Oak" it read. Mark and I walked beyond the sign and were greeted with noise. I'm not talking about recess yard noise like we heard every day, but it was mingled with different music coming from every corner of the park. The carousel was playing one kind of music, the Ferris wheel had a different tune playing, and the whip ride was playing something different altogether. Along with this was the rattle of the Dip Racer rollercoaster racing on a wooden trestle with screams coming from it. I wasn't sure if it was terror or joy that I heard. The first stop in Gwynn Oak was the ticket booth where you traded hard cash for tickets so you could get on the rides. Obviously, the big guns of Gwynn Oak didn't want their carnies handling cash and challenging their math skills.

"So where do you want to go first, Mark?" I asked after we had a small roll of orange tickets tucked into our pants.

"The line at the Whip isn't very long, let's do that."

We stood in line and were shown our barrel in which we'd ride. The Whip began slowly then picked up speed. As it did, and my head and body were snapped in one direction, then another, my mind tried to make a connection between ride and life.

"David! Conjugate the Latin verb 'habere,' to hold." Came the message in my head.

"Haberit?"

"Wrong!" And my head was snapped around.

"David! What was the first capital of the US?" As the Whip hit the curve.

"Washington, D.C."

"Wrong!" And my head snapped around.

"David! If a train leaves Chicago heading east at 30 miles per hour, and another train leaves New York heading west at 50 mile per hour, what will be the most popular lunch on each train?"

"I'm working on it. Gimme a minute. Egg salad?"

"Wrong!" And once again, my head snapped around.

"David! Do you walk to school or carry your lunch?"

"Huh?"

"Wrong, again!" At this point both my head and neck hurt.

As Mark and I got off the ride I felt like I'd been put through a ringer. This was one of the most innocent rides in the park and yet I felt exhausted.

"Hey! That was pretty cool. What say we go for the Dip Racer?" Mark exclaimed.

"Thanks, partner, but no thanks." I answered as I rubbed my neck.

"OK, I'm going for it, though."

As Mark wandered towards the Dip Racer, I tried to clear my head. Since the carousel didn't have a long line, I thought a short ride in a circle might help. After I handed my two tickets to the Gwynn Oak guard and operator, who wore a look like he was employed by the gubmint looking for counterfeit twenty dollar bills, I climbed aboard a blue painted horse on the outside and waited for the ride to begin. Just before the ride began a large woman with a small child climbed aboard and the kid was deposited one row over on a lion next to me.

"I don't wanna be on a lion!" the kid wailed.

"Now, Bobby, every other animal is taken. Lions are nice."

"I hate lions!" the kid screamed.

The ride began moving and some strange music played;

my horse moving up and down and the lion next to me doing the same, except the kid's screaming went up and down with every move.

"Mommy! I want off! I hate lions!"

"Now, Bobby."

I know I'm not making this up, but the carousel spun for five minutes and the entire time little Bobby complained about riding a lion. As the carousel slowed down I looked around to see if I could feed Bobby to a real life lion. The Bawlmer Zoo at "Droodle Park" was too far away, but had it been inside Gwynn Oak, I would have hauled the whining tyke over to the closest wild animal cage.

As I got off the carousel, I wondered about the idea of this place being called an amusement park. For whose amusement was it? I wasn't amused, so it must be for the workers.

I began to walk down the midway where all the games of skill were. There was a pretty large crowd at something called the "Kentucky Derby." I stood for a minute looking for local bookies since the cheering of spectators made it resemble something my dad would have tossed two bucks at in a bet. The race of eight make-believe horses along a peeling painted race course ended with a mix of emotions. Obviously one guy who was whooping and hollering was the winner, while a few others walked away mumbling about the race being fixed.

I walked past the shooting gallery, called the "Rifleman's Range" where it seemed like most of the Shrine's ginks and hoods were waiting in lines to pony up some tickets, taking pot shots at different targets and trying to earn some kind of marksmanship award. I looked over the lugs, so eager to try their hand at shooting something and thought: this doesn't look good. You just don't hand a loaded weapon to a Calf

Lick boy, especially a day before confession.

There wasn't much else to see as I wandered around the grounds and under the trees that gave shade to an area that looked like a permanent carnival. With so many Shrine students darting back and forth, I was constantly dodging arms and legs attached to bodies in a rush to get to the next ride.

I decided to sit on the steps of the "Dixie Ballroom" and wait for everything in front of me to calm down, except it didn't look like it would any time soon. I glanced behind me and read the cardboard signs near the doors. "Appearing this Saturday" it said in bold black print on an orange background. "The Lafayettes" and "The Admirals" along with some guy named "Fats Something" who was getting top billing. I had no idea who he was, but I'm sure my sister would know, since there was a line at the top of the sign that read "As Seen on The Buddy Deane Show."

I guess I coulda stayed home, but who would I play with? Everybody I knew was here. Since it was past noon I opened my brown paper sack and pulled out the sandwich bag of Utz Potato Chips that my mom had packed and sat on the Dixie Ballroom steps to wait for Mark.

Mark sauntered up to me as I was munching on my last chip and sat beside me on the step.

"Why so glum, chum?" He laughed. "Get it? Glum? Chum? I'm a poet and don't know it."

"Yeah, I get it. We'll give you an 'A' in English." I answered.

"Seriously, what's the matter? You ain't gonna puke, are ya?" Mark said as he sat four feet away, just in case I was gonna puke.

"What are we doin here?" I asked.

"Having a good time, in case you hadn't noticed."

"Yeah, I see it all around me. So many dames and palookas

are just running every which way. They look like they're having a good time. I'm just not getting it."

"Know what your problem is? You think it's all up to you."

"Ain't it?" I asked. Not all up to me? Since when?

"No. Look, partner, there's more nuns here than a convent can hold. We got more parents on the grounds than can fit in the chapel and the pleese are right out there on Liberty Heights Avenue. If anything goes wrong, we got cover. It ain't all up to us."

"Can I ax you sumpin?" I asked.

"Sure."

"You think we'll always be gumshoes?" I asked.

"Don't know about you, but I don't think I will. Oh, sure, it's been fun putting the bracelets on some ginks at recess. I love strong-arming a hood as much as the next guy, but..." Mark's voice trailed off.

"Not your calling?" I asked.

"No. Not my calling. But what about you?"

"Oltno." I answered.

"How many rides you been on since we got here?" Mark asked.

"That stupid Whip. All I got was a pain in my neck and a lot of questions rattling in my head. And then I rode the merry-go-round with a kid named Bobby who hates lions and wailed the entire time."

"How about we take the train? A trip around the park might help." Mark answered.

Mark and I walked through the midway where so many ginks were still trying to win some big fuzzy animal at a game of skill and impress some dame who stood a few feet behind. Even I knew that none of these games involved skill. It was all luck and chance, but the odds of winning didn't seem to discourage the ginks who were tossing tickets like confetti. They'd take the chance, just to appear better than the rest of the class.

We passed the "Rifleman's Range" and the number of hoods standing in line to let loose some slugs seemed to have grown since last I saw. You just don't hand some kid heat after he's been hemmed in by nuns for an entire school year.

"You think any of 'em can hit a target?" Mark laughed.

"I doubt it, but I hope not." I answered.

We got on the replica of the B&O train that would take us on some kind of scenic trip around Gwynn Oak. That whinny little tyke Bobby that I suffered with on the carousel wasn't on this ride, so I began to relax as Mark and I sat in the second car. Maybe what I needed was some breeze in my hair. No, that couldn't be true since my parents decided to have my hair cut into something that resembled the first day in basic training. I just didn't have hair that a breeze could blow through. Maybe what I needed was some sunshine after sitting so long in the shade of the Dixie Ballroom.

Mark and I rode the train around the grounds. While Mark seemed to enjoy the breeze, I was looking down at the tracks and wheels as the newly mowed grass passed by beneath me. Yep, I thought, same green grass, same scenery, and I'm gonna end up where I began. At least I didn't hear some kid complain about the rocking of the cars as we took the ride.

Once the train stopped Mark and I got off. "Feel better?" He asked me.

I shrugged my shoulders. I got on here. I got off here. Why should I feel better?

"Know what you need?" Mark asked.

"A butterscotch?"

"You need a change in altitude." Mark declared.

"You mean attitude."

"No, altitude. You're living too close to the ground." Mark observed.

"Hey, I'm almost four foot tall, which makes me an inch taller than you! Just because everybody else in class is taller than me doesn't mean anything!"

"I'm not talking about that, you maroon! You need to see life at a higher level."

"Great! Find me a chair and then I'll see everything." I replied.

"You ain't gettin it. What I'm sayin is, maybe we need to get really high up, like on the Ferris wheel, so you can look down and see that everything, for the most part, is jake." Mark said in a tone that sounded like he was concerned, which I guess he was.

"You want me to take a ride on the Ferris wheel. So I feel better and see life at a higher altitude?"

"Yeah. Won't hurt." Mark quipped.

"You think that ride would help, huh."

"How many tickets you got left?"

I reached in my pocket to count the tickets. I counted twenty. With an average cost of two or three tickets per ride, I could have been on every ride at least once. What a waste, I thought. I'd never use all of these tickets.

"C'mon, partner. Let's take a ride on the Ferris wheel." He said.

Mark led the way to the Ferris wheel near the entrance to the park. He seemed excited to get a bird's eye view of the happy mayhem that was going on. All I saw was mayhem. We stood in a short line to get some altitude as the operator asked for tickets.

"Tree tickets, youse guys." A carney who looked like a Bawlmer panhandler declared.

We handed over the tickets and sat in a hard worn steel bench that was flaking paint like one of my sister's boyfriends with dandruff, except this was green stuff. The guy in charge closed the bar as we sat down and nudged a lever forward. The Ferris wheel swung forward about ten feet.

"Don't none of youse lean forward! No rockin! And leave that bar where it is." He said as the next empty flaking steel green bench came to sit at the boarding area and a couple of dames climbed in.

This herky-jerky movement continued until all twelve benches were loaded and we'd heard the instructions shouted over and over again. Finally, the Ferris wheel began its ride from street level to stories above in a lazy circular motion with the sounds of the park growing louder and then fading away as we traveled close to the ground and then again to its heights. I was almost beginning to enjoy the ride until suddenly the Ferris wheel stopped and Mark and I were at the top.

"Pop, pop…pop, pop, pop" Is what we heard.

"What was that? It sounded like gunfire!" I shouted.

"Prolly was. Anybody hit?" Mark said as he turned around in the bench.

"How do I know? We gotta get down there!" I said.

We had no idea why the Ferris wheel suddenly stopped, with us perched at the very top. What we heard were cries and shouts. Kids on the ground were running in all directions. It looked like every ride was frozen in time as I leaned forward to see what the problem was as our bench rocked forward and Mark grabbed me.

"You crazy? We almost fell out! Don't do dat!" Mark yelled at me.

"Pop, pop…pop" came another burst.

"Look!" I shouted as I pointed over my left shoulder towards the ground and to the midway below. It might have been the biggest flock of Franciscan nuns I'd ever seen running in the same direction. It was a huge crowd of black and white robes, rosaries trailing behind, and a cloud of dust like I'd seen in the movie, "Grapes of Wrath." Something was going on and Mark and me were stuck at the very top of the Ferris wheel.

"We gotta get down there!" I shouted.

"How? We're stuck!" Mark answered.

I looked around, since I had a bird's eye view of the park. Whatever was happening, I knew this was big. And I realized that I was perched atop a frozen Ferris wheel almost four stories above the ground. I was powerless.

"Pop…pop." As a few more rounds echoed in my ears.

"We gotta get down there!" I repeated.

"Dave, we ain't gettin down any time soon." Mark responded. He was right. Some yokel who operated the Ferris wheel below was standing close to the handles and he looked like a bad wax figure in an old horror movie. He wasn't moving.

"Hey!" I yelled. "Let us down!" I may as well be yelling at a stuffed bear; he never moved.

"Look we're private eyes! We need to get off!" I said.

The bad wax figure of a ride operator looked up at us with a smile on his face. "Private eyes, huh? Good! Cuz I'm the King of Siam. Nuttin moves until I'm told it's all clear, see. Sit tight."

Mark and I watched the cloud of black and white robes sailing inches above the ground, trailing rosaries and white waist ropes, scamper into the area of the midway. I learned that penguins couldn't fly on a recent "Disney Presents" TV show, but you couldn't convince me of that as I watched a flock of pious penguins fly towards the sound of gunfire. As they flew towards the sounds of commotion, three black cop cars, red lights on the roof twirling, pulled up and six pleese jumped out and ran into Gwynn Oak to join the chase into the dust. I was missing out on one of the biggest collars of my life.

I was hopping up and down on my green flaking steel bench, no doubt showering the riders below me with paint dandruff. This is what a private eye lives for – putting the bracelets on a real criminal in the act. I wasn't about to climb down the beams of the Ferris wheel, though.

We sat at the top of the Ferris wheel, feeling helpless. As the shouts of the pleese and nuns, who obviously had surrounded the hood with the rifle, screams of classmates, parents and assorted wayward children filled the air, I was still trying to figure out a way to get to ground level. But it just wasn't going to happen.

The noise below subsided and most kids stopped running and began to walk. Between two flatfoots was a hood with his hands behind his back and a nun walking behind him holding the rifle above her head like a trophy, pumping her arms up and down. I missed it all. I missed one of the biggest collars of my life

The Ferris wheel began to move downward to its boarding spot. As Mark and I jumped off I looked at the lug that had left us at the top. I was hopping mad at this galoot, and decided to express my anger.

"King of Siam, huh. You couldn't let us off?." I sneered.

"A private dick. You shoulda known better, kid." Was his reply. This guy wasn't even sorry!

There was a very different air on the grounds of Gwynn Oak as Mark and I began to walk away from the Ferris wheel. Gone were the squeals and laughter I'd heard just a half hour before. Gone was the unbridled happiness of a few hundred Calf Lick kids set free who acted like their publican counterparts. There was a hush among the kids as some walked towards open rides, but no longer screams of delight to get on a Gwynn Oak ride.

I looked at the subdued and now quiet crowd of my classmates. They all had a look of shame and guilt even though none of what just happened was their fault. I thought, My God! We really are Calf Licks!

"Who was that kid that wanted to shoot up Gwynn Oak?" I asked Mark.

"Oltno. Never got a good look at him."

"We gotta find out." I said.

"You really think it's important right now?" Mark asked.

"I wanna know." I responded.

"He got carted off by the pleese. I don't think the pious penguins will be yammering about who it was. Besides, you think we missed somebody in our rounds?" He asked me.

"Oltno. I'd just feel better if we knew after we spent an afternoon stewing and sitting at the top of the Ferris wheel."

"OK, let's start asking questions. Ya know that this is gonna cut into my ride time, right?" Mark said.

I reached into my pocket and brought out all the ride tickets I had and put them in Mark's hands.

"You're right. Here. Take'em. I'll go ax questions." I said.

I decided to find Steven somewhere among the crowd because I figured he would have been in the middle of the hoopla and could fill me in. I doubted he had anything to do with the crime, but he might know something. I found Steven playing the pretend horse race and waited until the game ended. Steven walked away from the "Kentucky Derby" muttering about how the game must be fixed, since he didn't win.

"Steven, we need to talk. I just spent half my life stuck at the top of the Ferris wheel while some kid went haywire with a rifle down here. I figured you'd know sumpin."

"Look, wasn't me or any of my boys, see. I don't let any of em pack heat. I'm more into gentle persuasion and…. watchacallit…salesmanship. Yeah I saw it, though. You see how fast those nuns were? Man! Almost ran me over. I think the pleese showed up to make sure that the kid wasn't beaten to a pulp by the nuns."

"Know what grade he was in?" I asked.

"Wasn't one of our grades. He looked like he was maybe a sixth or seventh grader. Ya just don't let a loose cannon from those upper grades anywhere near a weapon, ya know? Maybe it's just the education we get, ya know? All that homework and stuff. It wears ya down and then somebody snaps, ya know."

"You're prolly right." I answered.

"Got stuck at the top of the Ferris wheel, huh." Steven asked with a smile on his face that said to me – serves ya right.

"Yeah. I really wanted to be in on the collar, though."

"You couldn't have done anything anyway. The nuns and the pleese took care of it. Not all up to you, ya know."

"Yeah, I heard that before." I answered as I left Steven with his crowd of goons.

The Franciscan nuns seemed to have vanished close to the park entrance along with the suspect and the pleese whose black cars sat idling even though the red lights never stopped twirling. No chance anytime soon that I'd be able to ask them questions. But I decided to try anyway. I tracked down Sister Bernie.

"'Scuse me, Sister Bernie. I was stuck at the top of the Ferris wheel with Mark and we missed the excitement. Can you tell me what happened?"

"There was no excitement, David. Just a very unfortunate incident. The boy does, or did, attend the Shrine. Nobody was injured."

"Was he in our class?" I asked, trying to get a line on the suspect.

"No, he was a few classes up. Nothing you need to concern yourself about. We had it under control. Nothing you could have done."

"Just askin, 'Ster." I answered. That's the third time I'd heard that line: nothing I could do, not all up to me. If it wasn't up to me and there was nothing I could do…exactly what was I supposed to do?

It was getting late in the afternoon and the day's events, both big and small, were drawing to a close. I, along with most of my class, began to wander towards the entrance and, just beyond, the yellow school buses that would return us to the Shrine.

Mark tapped me on the left shoulder, even though he was on my right. It was an old trick we'd learned at recess to figure out who was smart and who still had difficulty trying to choose between right and left. Normally, I would have laughed.

"So, partner, you have a good time?" Mark asked.

"Oltno." I said as I shrugged my shoulders.

Mark and I climbed onto the third bus and sat in one of the last rows. I was glad to be shut of this place. I just wanted to endure the ride back to the Shrine and walk home and reclaim a few parts of life that I'd come to know. If I ever see another amusement park in my life, it'll be too soon.

Sister Knuckles was the last person to climb onto the bus. She looked up and down the aisle, looked up to heaven and didn't say a word. Obviously, we were on the last bus to leave Gwynn Oak.

Once the bus turned onto Liberty Heights Avenue, Mark stood up and shouted a question that had bugged him since the morning.

"So…does everybody know '99 Bottles of Beer on the Wall'? Let's all sing….99 bottles of beer on the wall, 99 bottle of beer…"

The Bottle Deposit Mystery

It was a Friday morning in early June as I walked up Pelham Avenue to stop at the Pelham Bakery for a cuppa chocit moo and a Bismarck pastry before I had to serve as an altar boy at a requiem mass at the Shrine. The school year's end was just a few days away but sending off the dearly departed to heaven never jived with class schedules anyway. Mornings are not the best time of day for me but I seemed to have wandered into the morning constitution of a flock of pigeons on my way to the bakery and there was no way to escape.

Lucrative detective work for a 9 year old gumshoe just doesn't fall out of the trees. Bird poop falls out of trees, but that shower of plenty won't keep you in donuts even if you're playing the sympathy card at the local bakery. Believe me, I've tried that gambit and it doesn't work. It also doesn't help when the obvious questions thrown at you while you're waiting to buy a donut is "Hey, Hon! Where you been? Take your coat off! You're stinking up the place, Hon!" What can I say? "I think I have a few enemies that have trained pigeons and their aim has improved." Sometimes you just wear what life drops on you and you work to make ends meet, no matter what it smells like.

A steady source of income for me is pulling a wagon around my Bawlmer neighborhood beat and collecting glass soda bottles to be redeemed at the supermarket for the deposit. It's the well-heeled who ignore the 2 cent deposit on their soda and just toss the empty. The same kind of folk who can afford to buy a dozen donuts and their coats aren't soiled when they walk into the bakery.

My beat has a good number of these wealthy kids who dress clean but dirty up the alleys and sidewalks. On an average day I can pick up 20 bottles, enough to maintain my habits of buying baseball cards, comics and butterscotch candy. I told my mom I would quit those disgusting vices, but it's pretty hard to ditch the bubblegum and the butterscotch all at once.

It was a warm and humid Bawlmer Saturday morning. We had all been told we were going onto the next grade the day before and I knew that the revelry and binge drinking had been in full swing last night. All I had to do was wait as the sugar induced comas set in and classmates slept in late. Empty Coke, Pepsi and Royal Crown bottles would be there for the taking. I might even be able to buy some baseball cards and a few extra butterscotch. Sometimes I can be as bad as the next sugar junky.

I walked down the alley, a wagon with a loud squeaky wheel in toe. The wagon wasn't always squeaky. That noise started right after I took my little brother for a ride a month ago. My mom thought I was Mister Wonderful when I suggested it. What she didn't know was that I had put signs on the sides that read "brother for sale - make offer." We got caught in a spring shower and returned soaking wet, the ink on the signs smeared, and a very angry mom who accused me of trying to get my brother hit by lightning. Since I didn't make a big score by peddling my brother off, I was again pulling my wagon and looking for signs of the out of control drinking of my classmates from the day before.

Nothing.

I turned a corner where two alleys met. It was a well-known fact that a congregation of students would have assembled in a high spirited celebration of their release from prison....'scuse me, school.

Still nothing. Even among all the candy wrappers that lay around like fall leaves, there were no bottles.

Something wasn't right. I knew most of the parents in the area and meticulous garbage pickup in the Bawlmer alleys was not one of their priorities. I also knew the character of the party goers. The last day of school was not the time to become neatniks. After being berated into neat and orderly for an entire school year, this was the time to thumb our noses at being careful, organized and neat. Since it was early June, soaping car windows and TP'ing the neighborhood was postponed until Halloween. As odd as it may sound, there was an order to misbehavior based on the calendar.

I walked down the alley behind Lyndale Avenue then trekked up the alley behind Elmora Avenue. Even though my red Radio Flyer wagon was empty its weight started to resemble a reluctant dog that doesn't want to be lead on a leash. The squeaking wheels of the wagon were echoing off the backs of the row houses as I trudged up the hill. While the neighbors were used to hearing the Cloverland Milk and Rice's Bakery Pie trucks making their usual deliveries on the front street at this time of the morning, a squeaking wagon behind their houses would most likely put many of them in a bad mood. It's the difference between waking up to the comforting sounds of clinking glass milk bottles on your front porch and the obnoxious sound of the bell of an alarm clock next to your bed. The neighborhood dogs were a different matter. I had no sooner started to walk down the alley, squeaky wagon in tow, than the dogs began to bark at me. Once one dog barks, every pooch within five blocks joined in the chorus. It didn't drown out the sound of the wheels on my wagon, though. Somewhere within all this noise was a song, I thought. Not a very good song. No, it sounded more like a title fight that was headed into the tenth round with a crowd going wild.

"Hey, kid! I'm tryin to get some sleep here!" Came a voice from a second story, and recently opened window.

Sorry, sir." I called out.

"I just got off the third shift down da point at Bethlum Steel! I need some sleep. You got every dog yapping in the neighborhood. Whadya doin?"

"I'm collecting bottles for the deposit so I can help a poor kid I know." I answered back. What I didn't tell him was that I was that poor kid.

"Oh…OK…but can you take that wagon someplace else?"

"Yes, sir. I was looking around for a few bottles, though."

"Look in the can, kid. There's a few in there you can have."

"Thank you." I answered as I flipped the shiny aluminum lid of his garbage cans, the metal lids clattering to the ground which caused the neighborhood dogs to bark even louder, and searched around. I pulled three Coke bottles out from among used tissues, some tin foil TV dinner plates, a Hellman's mayonnaise jar, and a few well chewed corn cobs.

"Hey, kid!" The man called out. "For God's sake, put some grease on dem wheels! You sound like you're dragging six cats around."

"Yes, sir." I answered.

Before the window was fully closed, I heard the man call

out to someone else in the second story room. "I'm tellin' ya, Mabel, I don't know what's with deese kids today. A man's gotta get his sleep. There ain't no…" And the window closed tightly and I heard nothing more from the window. However, the dogs barking, and the sound of my wagon's wheels still filled my ears.

I scoured the alleys and curbs for tossed bottles and still found nothing. I even looked under the cars parked at the curb, hoping to find a bottle that had rolled. I could feel my sugar dropping and felt a queasy feeling. Somebody had patrolled the area before me which left me with bupkis, zilch, nada. I'd heard those words before but didn't quite know what they meant, but they were always in the same sentence with the word nothing.

I walked down Ravenwood. I even walked up Bonview Avenue.

Still nothing.

I had covered more than five blocks, walking up and down alleys, looking under cars, rummaging around bushes, and still all I had was three Coke bottles. If barking dogs were worth anything I'd be a rich kid. I decided to trek to Pantry Pride and collect my deposit.

I was an almost regular at the Pantry Pride Supermarket which anchored the strip shopping center at the corner of Sinclair Lane and Erdman Avenue and the store manager would probably be wondering where I was. I'm sure he had a load of change in his pants pocket just waiting for me to show up and redeem the empties I'd collected in my rounds.

I left my wagon at the front door of the supermarket figuring that I could hunt it down by the creaking sounds if anybody was stupid enough to steal it. As the automatic doors opened I looked to the left where empty glass bottles were kept. Stacked neatly along the outer wall, in wooden cases, were at least 60 empties. Obviously, somebody beat me to a bonanza.

I walked up to Mr. Freeland, the store manager, and held out my three empty bottles.

Mr. Freeland was a very tall man with perfectly combed hair but a haphazard look. He was clean shaven but his shirt hung over his belt and the shirt tail flopped over his rump. The tips of his shoes looked like he spent most of his day crawling on his knees. While he barked at the cashiers constantly, he schmoozed customers like they were great aunts with a large inheritance destined for his pockets. He always treated me well when I brought in empty bottles but I guess he expected me to talk to my aunt to include him in her will.

"Good morning, young man!" He said as he bounded out of his elevated office and onto the floor of the market. He took a quick glance to his left where the cashiers were busy ringing up groceries.

"Those are leeks, Helen, not scallions!" He roared. "I swear, these broads don't know the difference between grapes and watermelons…what I have to put up with…no wonder I don't get a bonus." He muttered.

"Morning, Mr. Freeland." I said. Mr. Freeland turned to me, his scowl turning to a smile in an instant.

"You have some bottles for me?"

"Yes,sir. But not many. Seems somebody beat me here with a pretty big load." I said as I eyed the stack of crates that seemed to grow even bigger as I looked at them. I began counting the empty bottles and instead of 60, it now looked like there were 160. I looked back at Mr. Freeland because I didn't want to see 360 empty soda bottles. It's the same reason that when you play football or baseball, you never want to look at the scoreboard.

"Only three?" Mr. Freeland asked.

"Yes, sir. Just three." I replied. "How many people brought in all those empties?"

"Just one. He had them stacked up next to the door when I opened this morning. Musta taken him all night, though." He handed me six cents for walking ten blocks, listening to at least a hundred barking dogs, being cussed out by a third shift adult who needed sleep and a wagon that reminded me that silence is golden.

Yeah, I thought. All night. One guy worked pretty hard on a graveyard shift. By the looks of the crates, I guessed whoever it was had made somewhere between three and four trips. I had to find out who this person was.

"You know him?" I asked.

"Naw, some kid with ambition, though."

"Didja get a name?" I asked.

Mr. Freeland looked up to the ceiling, obviously trying to remember an early morning encounter that occurred before his morning cuppa joe. I followed his gaze, almost expecting a banner that looked like something I would have seen at Memorial Stadium. Instead of a blue and white banner that decreed the Colts championship of 1958, I was looking for something like "Most empty bottles returned for 2 cents each" with some kid's name on it. I know it sounds crazy and it doesn't make any sense, but I looked up anyway.

"Something…water." He mumbled. "Flush water. No that's not it. Toilet water, no, that's not it either. Pee water, no, that's just silly. It was something water."

"It's ok, Mr. Freeland. I was just askin." Actually I wanted to know who this kid was and if I had serious competition in the bottle return industry. Some night owl with serious drive could put a big dent in my own bad habits. I was still too young for a legit job like delivering "The Noosemerican" or "The Balwmer Sun" and like I said, steady income working as a gumshoe doesn't fall from trees.

I walked out of Pantry Pride, a whole six cents to my name for almost two hours of work. I figured I'd grab my wagon, walk home and try and find some 3-in-1 oil buried somewhere on my dad's workbench.

My Radio Flyer was still sitting where I left it. I wasn't surprised since any wagon thief would leave it behind once he rolled it a foot in either direction and heard the squeal from the wheels. Just like car thieves, wagon and bike thieves wanted the newest model without major problems. It just made the job of fencing a lot easier. However, sitting in my wagon were four bags of groceries and standing next to it all was an older gent. He was tall and thin with a grim look on his face and a pair of glasses on the end of his nose that looked like they just didn't want to be any part of the conversation about looks or age. His gray hair was well combed, no doubt due to a generous amount of Vitalis which just added to his look of grumpy. He was well dressed with freshly ironed pants that had a crease on them that were arrow straight and a plaid shirt to match.

"Your wagon?" He asked.

"Yes sir"

"You got some important meeting at Pleese headquarters this morning?"

"No sir." How could this old man know I was a gumshoe? Maybe it was just a guess.

"Look, you haul these groceries for me and I'll make it worth your time. It's better than me pushing a shopping cart home and then bringing it back. You game?"

"Sure." I answered. I didn't have anything on my calendar for the first day of summer vacation and a tip might make up for what I lost in bottle deposits.

"OK" he answered. "By the way, your fly is down."

I looked down at my pants and he laughed. "Gotcha lookin!"

He led the way towards Erdman Avenue where we had to wait for a break in early Saturday morning traffic so we could cross. The old man was probably as old as my granddad, and while he walked pretty well, he didn't walk very fast.

"Your dad in the war?" he asked as we had crossed the very dangerous abyss called Erdman Avenue.

"Yes sir."

"He ever talk about it to you?"

I had to think a minute. The squealing wheels were interrupting my thoughts. "He only talked about the funny stuff that happened to him and his buddies. He never really went into details about the Battle of The Bulge, though."

"Good man. You don't need to know all the details, son. I was in the Great War myself in France and I'd rather remember the good times with my guys than how many friends I lost. If you're lucky you'll never know war first hand."

"Yes, sir." I answered.

We had begun the walk down Ravenwood Avenue and he commented on the neighbors, the Arabbers who still walked the alleys hawking all manner of things from marsh rabbits to fresh fruits, the knife sharpening guy who rang a bell as he walked around trying to summon housewives out of their kitchens, and how the Good Humor man seemed to come just before supper to spoil a kid's appetite.

"By the way, you know somebody tied a cat under your wagon while you were in Pantry Pride? That's why it sounds so God-awful." He remarked.

I stopped walking and got on my knees to look under the Radio Flyer.

"Hah! Made you look!" he laughed. Somehow, this old man was trying to teach me something, or maybe a lot of things. I wasn't sure which. I wasn't sure what. And I wasn't sure why, either.

"So, what do you wanna be when you grow up?" He asked in a wistful matter of fact way.

"A private detective." I blurted out before I even gave his question much thought. Had I not had both hands on the wagon I was dragging, I probably would have slapped myself on the forehead. Man, such a stupid answer! I shoulda said something like accountant or engineer or even janitor…now I was open to such answers like "you could get shot," or "nobody makes a living doing that sort of work," or "what would your mother think?" Once you open your trap, you can't take it back. I looked at the ground waiting for the inevitable "you'll never make any money" response.

"Private eye, huh?" was all he said.

"Yes, sir." I responded. What could I say? I was just waiting to be shot down.

"You know, 90% of the cases you'd get would bore you to tears. Too many of them are just routine grunt work. But… that other 10%…" He looked up at the clouds. "That other 10% will get your blood pumping, you'd have trouble sleeping, you'd lose your appetite until you solved the case, and none of your friends would want to be near you while you were working on a case."

"Would it be that bad?"

"Yep. But late at night, after you went over every clue for the umpteenth time, and after you finally figured it out… you wouldn't trade it for all the tea in China."

"So…you don't think I'm stupid, right?" I asked.

"Not at all. If you can get attached to the Bawlmer Pleese Department, you should do ok. Just study hard and get good grades."

He finally stopped in the middle of the Ravenwood alley behind a neatly kept row home with a back yard filled with rose bushes and opened the chain link gate. As he opened the screen door to unlock the basement door I noticed that the screen was painted with a scene of a river, a few trees and an old farm house. It didn't look like anything I'd seen on family Sunday drives. Maybe it was a picture of some place in France, recalled from memories of a time long ago.

"We've arrived." He said. "Drag that sorry excuse for a wagon to the back door and help me in with the groceries and I'll find you some 3-in-1 so the dogs bark at you and not that…thing." As he pointed to my Radio Flyer.

I helped him carry the sacks of groceries into the small but tidy kitchen and then returned to the wagon which was a major roadblock on his back yard walkway. Just to make sure there wasn't a cat under the wagon, I quickly looked again.

The old man came out of the back door carrying a can of 3-in-1 and handed it to me. I squirted a healthy dose of oil on all the wheels, pushed the wagon back and forth a few times to work the oil in, and the squeaking stopped.

"Thank you." I said.

"Can't alert the enemy to your position, ya know." He answered, smiling. He handed me a quarter and a dime. Holy cow! I hit pay dirt! All my early morning trudging up and down neighborhood alleys trying to find empty bottles without success seemed like a distant memory. Home delivery of groceries might be the way to go from rags to riches.

"Thank you!" I exclaimed.

"It's alright. I enjoyed the company and the help. If you're ever back at Pantry Pride on an early Saturday morning, maybe we can do it again. What rank did your dad hold, by the way?"

"Corporal, of some sort. His stripes had a 'T' on it."

"Well, you tell your dad that Sergeant Dennison from the 29th Blue and Gray division thanks him."

The look of confusion on my face was obvious. "Just tell him what I said. He'll understand." He said.

"OK, Sergeant Dennison. I'll tell him. Thank you for the tip, too."

"Oh! One more thing. Your shoe is untied." He said in a matter of fact tone.

I resisted the urge to look down. I knew my Keds were tied and just stared at Sergeant Dennison with a smile on my face.

"You catch on quick, kid. You'll do ok in life. Hope to see you again." He chuckled.

I walked out of the yard towing a now quiet Radio Flyer with two thoughts in my head. Deliver a message from a World War One veteran to my dad and find out who the kid was that ransacked the neighborhood alleys of the empty bottles for the deposits the night before.

The message for my dad could wait till supper. Right now I needed to lean on every kid in the neighborhood to find out who the kid with "water" as part of his last name might be. I knew I couldn't repeat Mr. Freeland's mumblings about "pee-water" or "toilet-water." Even if I repeated them and it made sense to a stool pigeon, they'd be laughing so hard I'd probably never understand them.

It was time to scour six square blocks to find out who this ambitious "water" kid was. Somebody would know, somebody would make the connection and then I could confront him about territorial boundaries and the proper etiquette of picking up empty bottles that were out of his realm. There might not be anything written down about who can pick up what, but a little chutzpah can go a long way sometimes.

I decided to work my way outward from my own alley and hope that I would get a name before I ended up on the edge of mankind. First I would talk to the locals, the wayward Calf Lick souls who had been involved in the previous night's shenanigans. I decided to ask the neighborhood gossip, a dame named Amanda.

"Glad to see you recovered from last night. You see anything suspicious? Like some kid going behind you picking up your empty bottles?" I asked her.

"What day of the week was last night?" She responded with eyes so wide that I thought her eyeballs would pop out.

"Friday. You remember, the last day of school."

"The last day of school? Did I pass? Oh my god! Really? Did I pass? It was such a blur, ya know, with all the drinking and dancing. I remember being here in the alley, but after you have a few Cokes, you just lose all track of time, ya know. Did I pass? Did I graduate?"

"Do you remember some kid picking up the empty bottles?" I asked.

"I seem to remember somebody pulling up my jumper and I slapped his hand down. A bunch of us were autographing each other's shirts. Wait! I remember!…No, I don't remember. Did I pass?" she asked again.

"Never mind." I answered. I should know better than to ask a dame about what happened the night before when she'd been drinking. She ain't gonna remember. But, that same dame could tell me how many Valentine's Day cards, how many birthday cards and how many Christmas cards she got in the last ten years. And to boot, she'd be able to tell me the names of every palooka who ever sent 'em. Go figure. I'd have to ask some guys if I wanted an answer.

I met up with Johnny Helarya the next alley over a few minutes later. Maybe Johnny Helarya could give me a lead on this mysterious ambitious kid.

"Hey, Johnny, how the hell are ya?" We always greeted Johnny like that since it included both his first and last name.

"Cool, Dave. What's up?"

"I'm looking for a kid. Maybe you know who he is. His last name is sumpin-water. He was up late last night collecting empties, patrolling the neighborhood. You see anybody like that?"

"I saw this guy late last night." He began.

"Yeah?"

"He was walking around suspicious like. Looking at the ground like he was seeing gold or sumpin."

"Yeah? You know his name?" I asked, trying to keep my excitement secret.

"Gerry. Gerry Stankowich. Strange kid, always looking down."

"Johnny, I was asking about a kid whose last name was sumpin-water. Stankowich ain't got nothing to do with water."

"Oh. Sorry. I got nuttin, then." Johnny replied.

I kept walking up and down the neighborhood alleys and asking questions. After getting so many answers referring to old Polish, Italian and German names I thought about going to the library to find translations hoping that I'd get an answer to"'sumpin-water."

I finally met up with David K, who lived a block beyond where I lived. You wouldn't know it by talking to him, but he knew everything that was happening from Edison Highway all the way to Parkside Drive.

"David! How are ya?" I exclaimed.

"Hey, Dave. I'm good. How are you?"

"I'm looking for somebody and I'm betting that you know who it is."

"You laying some scratch on that?" He asked.

"It's a figure of speech."

"Oh. Well, there goes my extra baseball cards for the week. Anyway, who ya looking for?"

"A guy whose last name ends in 'water.' Mr. Freeland at the Pantry Pride said his name was sumpin like 'flush-water' or 'pee-water.' He wiped out almost six blocks of empty soda bottles last night before I had a chance this morning. I just want to hunt this guy down. You know who I'm talking about?"

David K was laughing. "Pee-water." He kept saying over and over.

"When you stop laughing, you can tell me what you know, David."

"Sorry. Sorry. Pee-water. That's so funny. Sorry. I know who you're looking for. His name is Clearwater. Chad Clearwater. He says he's an American Indian, but you'd never know it by looking at him. He's got an older brother and they live near the end of Brendan Avenue, close to Sinclair Lane. Nice guy, unless you cross him. You say he cleaned out the neighborhood of empty bottles? Could be him. If it was, he probably had a reason."

"Thanks, David. I owe you a pack of cards if this is the guy." I said as I walked away.

Now I had a lead and a location, of sorts. The name was Clearwater, he was an American Indian, he had on older brother and he lived close to Pantry Pride. I started to canvass the area close to Sinclair Lane and asked everyone who walked pass me about this suspect.

"You know a kid named Clearwater?" I asked an older lady who was dragging her Chihuahua around. When I spoke to her the fuzzy feisty canine began barking and she looked like she was ready to have the wagons turned in a circle. She immediately turned and walked away, the whole time the pooch was giving me a what-for even as the lead was tightening around its neck.

I kept walking along Brendan Avenue looking for a lead into this mysterious kid.

I finally spied a little girl playing at the top of the alley where Bonview and Brendan Avenues met. She had an angelic face and was playing with a couple of dolls and was maybe four years old. I decided that maybe she might know something. Maybe she would know where Chad Clearwater lived.

"Hi, little girl. Do you have any idea where the Clearwaters live? I've been told it's close by."

She looked up at me, slowly twisting the head off a Barbie doll she was playing with and with a really strange voice said, "Go away." I did what I was told, thankful that I may have escaped some kind of spontaneous combustion.

Four year old little girls that play with dolls aren't supposed to have a voice like some 70 year old woman with a four pack a day smoking habit that started 60 years ago. For that matter, little girls shouldn't have red glowing eyes. That look comes later, after mothers have a kid like me.

I walked back and forth on Brendan Avenue looking for something next to the doors that might indicate the Clearwaters lived here. There was nothing on either side of the street. Just then I spied the mailman on his morning rounds. He walked lazily from house to house until he arrived on one particular porch. At that house, he looked around, took a deep breath and quickly stuffed the mail into the door slot. He then bounded down the seven steps in two leaps, wiping his brow when he hit the "payment." He obviously dreaded delivering mail to this address, looking like he had escaped dragon's claws that were about to grab not only the mail, but him in the process. I thought asking him would give me a clue.

"Excuse me, but do you know where the Clearwater family lives?"

I expected an answer, but what I got was a trembling finger pointed at the house that he'd just delivered mail to. What do you say to the mailman who looks like he'd just escaped certain death?

"Thanks."

I now had an address, so all I had to do was wait for some kid that looked like, or kinda looked like, an American Indian. It shouldn't be too hard, I thought. All I had to look for was somebody wearing moccasins and a few feathers stuck in a headband.

After a two hour stakeout looking for anybody wearing feathers, a kid sauntered up to the house. He had shaggy blond hair, dressed in blue jeans and a denim jacket. I figured he probably knew Chad Clearwater, so I raced across the street to question him.

"Excuse me, but do you know Chad Clearwater?"

"Who wants to know?" Came the response.

"Nobody important, just me."

"I'm Chad. What can I do for ya?"

I guess the look on my face gave away my surprise. I was looking for a headband with feathers, buckskin pants, maybe even trailing a painted pony. He looked like half my class.

"I was out early this morning, trying to pick up empty bottles, see. And when I got to Pantry Pride, they told me some kid had already done it. Was that you?" I asked him.

"Yeah, that was me. I had to do it, ya know. My brother barged into my room last night and took all my money. I was outta smokes and I needed bird food. He told me he had this hot chick on the line. I made six trips last night just to get some dough. Sorry, squirt."

I was still looking at him, trying to get something straight in my head and it just wasn't coming together. Chad looked at me.

"What?" He asked.

"I dunno, Chad. I'm still tee'd off that you took every bottle in a six block area, but I kinda understand." I said. "At least I think I do."

"So…what's the beef?"

"Not sure. See, I got contacts who told me you were an Indian, and all. But," I sputtered, "You don't look like an Indian." At that outburst, I half expected this older kid to pound me into the dirt. He laughed.

"Powhatan"

"Pow-what?" I answered.

"My dad's dad was Powhatan. My dad married a girl from Germany. The Powhatans used to live around the Chesapeake Bay, and while I'm part Indian, I guess I got my mom's looks. My brother got his looks from my dad's side of the family. What were you expecting? Me prancing around in some sort of long feather headdress around a campfire?"

"Well, no." I stammered. "It's just…"

"I just don't look like an Indian." He said with a smile on his face.

"Sorry, Chad. It just took me by surprise. You ain't gonna pound me in the dirt for askin that, are ya?"

"Naw." He laughed. "At least you're honest about it."

"So can I ask you a question?"

"Sure."

"How come the mailman is afraid to deliver mail to your house?"

"Oh, that was my brother's thing. A few months ago he got really drunk and decided to put on war paint. When the mailman showed up the next day, my brother was yelling at him. My brother actually followed him around, dancing and chanting. He laughed about it later, but I guess the mailman is still afraid."

"You know anything about a little girl a few streets over? She seems to know who you are, but she's got these weird eyes and…"

"Jennifer." He quickly answered. "Lemme give you a piece of advice. Stay away from Jennifer. She was twisting the heads off of Barbie dolls, wasn't she? Sounds like an old man when she talks? Just do yourself a favor, keep your distance. You really don't want to see what she does to a Ken doll. Man to man, just between you and me, it hurts just to see her do it."

"So why did you walk six blocks and pick up every empty for the deposits? I'm tryin to support all my bad habits, and had it not been for an old guy who I helped this morning, and the tip he gave me, I'd be getting the shakes about now."

"I told you. My brother had a hot date with some chick. He needed dough for a movie, a cheap bottle of Port, and a steak sub after the movie. He cleaned me out. I was down to my last three Winstons and I'd run out of bird food. I had to do sumpin. He said he was gonna pay me back, but he wouldn't say when. You sore about the bottles I picked up?"

"No. I was just wonderin if this was gonna be a regular thing, that's all."

"Man! I hope not. I haven't slept yet, ya know. I get an allowance from my parents, but sometimes an older brother walks into your room, looking like he's ready to rearrange your face and telling you he needs dough. What would you do? Anyway, if you go out and find the alleys empty, you know that my brother robbed me again."

"Bird food?" I said.

"What?"

"Bird food." I repeated. "You said you needed to buy bird food."

"Oh yeah. I have, or at least I had, a flock of pigeons that I was training out in the back yard. It was a pretty good group. They stuck together, pretty much. But with all the construction on Sinclair Lane, I guess they got spooked, what with all the noise of the trucks and steam shovels and such. I heard they're building a new high school over there. They flew off about a week ago and I don't know where."

"I think I might know where they are." I answered.

Bawlmer Lexicon
(English is my Second Language)

A short glossary of "Balmerese" complete with pronunciation help and an English translation.

Arabbers…(A-rabbers) – Street and alley vendors who use horse drawn wagons selling fruits like warmelons and canlopes, and vegetables like maters, taters and other stuff like marsh rabbits.

Ax…(AX) – Ask - as in lemme ax you sumpin.

Bawlmer…(BAWL-mer) – Baltimore, Maryland. Depending on the area, it can also be pronounced "Balamer" or "Baldamore." Still our home town, just a bit uptown or maybe downtown or when you're trying not to sound like you're from Dundock, Hollantown or Hamden (all neighborhoods in the area).

Bethlum…(BETH-lum) – Bethlehem Steel Mill in Sparrows Point, MD.

Bidness…(BID-ness) – Business - as in none of your bidness. Sometimes pronounced "Bi-ness."

Bizness…(BIZ-ness) – You own the company, it's your bizness.

Brefist…(BREF-ist) – Breakfast - First meal of the day.

Calf Lick…(CALF-lick) – Catholic – You're either Protestant Jewish, or…

Canlopes…(CAN-lopes) – Fresh melons of summer with an orange flesh. Called out by the Arabbers as they travelled the streets and alleys.

Chimley…(CHIM-ley) – Chimney - How Santa Claus gets in your house.

Chocet…(CHOK-it) – Chocolate - The brown sweet stuff you get on Bergers cookies and most cakes as well as in milk.

Coddies…(COD-ees) – Potato and cod fish cakes. In 1960 the price was 5 cents which included two crackers and some mustard. A must have on Fridays if you were Calf Lick.

Down A Point…(DOWN A POINT) – Down the point - Sparrows Point, MD. A shorthand phrase for travelling to Bethlehem Steel in Sparrows Point, MD where you worked.

Downey Oshun…(DOWN-e O-shun) – Down the Ocean - Ocean City, Maryland where most Maryland locals go for summer vacation.

Droodle Park…(DROOD-le Park) – Druid Hill Park, home of the Baltimore Zoo.

Duddney…(DUD-nee) – A contraction of the phrase "doesn't he."

Dundock…(DUN-dawk) – Dundalk - One of the first suburbs of Baltimore. Named after Dundalk, Ireland. A blue collar area of workers who work down a point or at the (now closed) General Motors factory.

Far…(FAR) – Fire - Anything that's going up in flames. Usually handled by the Bawlmer Far Department to put out da far.

Gubmint…(GUB-mint) – government - It can be local, state or federal.

Hollantown…(HOLLIN-town) – Highlandtown - A Baltimore City neighborhood.

Hon…(HUN) – The most common name you're called in Baltimore - like sir or miss…Interchangeable with any name or title in greeting and conversation. Geographical equivalent in the US Deep South might be "sugar."

Init…(IN-it) – Isn't it - A contraction of an contraction.

Jeet…(JEET) – Did you eat?- Usually answered by "nojew?" It's a contraction of "No, did you?"

Marsh Rabbits…Muskrats, large aquatic rodents usually skinned so they look like rabbit.

Maters…(MATE-ers) – Fresh tomatoes.

Merica…(MER-i-ca) – America - Used in the phrase "Troof, Justice and the Merican way."

Merlin…(MER-lin) – Maryland, the Free State.

Noosemerican…(NOOSE-mer-i-can) – A news broadsheet that closed in 1986.

Noosepaper…(NOOSE-PAPE-er) – General reference to either the "Baltimore Sun" or the "News American."

Oltno…(ALT-know) – I don't know - Another contraction of a phrase into a single word.

Payment…(PAY-mint) – paved surface usually of concrete.

Pockeybook…(Pah-key-book) – Pocketbook or purse carried by women.

Po-leese…(PO-leese) – a single police officer.

Pleese…(PLEESE) – two or more police officers.

Proly…(PRAH-lee) – Probably.

Sammidges…(SAM-idges) – sandwiches.

Spars…(SPARS) – Sparrows - Refers to Sparrows Point, MD.

Troof …(TRUFE) – Rhymes with roof, but not like "ruf" which are the shingles on top of a house. Common phrase - " Troof, justice and the Merican way."

Unnerstand…(UNNER-stand) – understand.

Warmelons…(WAR-melons) – Watermelons - Seedy, red

fleshed melons of summer that help you refine the art of spitting. Sometimes called a woodermelon. Also called out by the Arabbers on their journey.

Wayment…(WAY-mint) – wait a minute.

Wooder…(WOOD-er) – Water.

Wurjagitdat?…(WER-ji-get-dat) – Where did you get that? A contraction of a phrase into a single word.

Hard Boiled Lexicon

Babe: Woman
Big house: Jail
Blower: Telephone
Broad: Woman
Cabbage: Money
Copper: Policeman.
Dame: Woman
Dizzy with a dame, to be: To be deeply in love with a woman
Doll: Woman
Dough: Money
Finder: Finger Man
Flatfoot: Police officer
Gams: Legs
Gink: Man
Goon: Thug
Gumshoe: Detective
Hatchet men: Killers/gunmen
Heat: A gun
Hood: Criminal
Hoosegow: Jail
In stir: In jail
Jake: Okay
Kiss The Dog: Work face to face with a mark
Lettuce: Folding money

Lousy With: To have a lot of
Lug: Dumb Guy
Moll: Girlfriend
Palooka: Man, probably a little stupid
Pigeon: Stool-pigeon. A person without a clue and/or an informer
Punk: Hood, thug
Rat: Inform
Scratch: Money
Screws: Prison Guards
Sister: Woman
Ticket: Private Investigator's license
Tomato: Pretty woman
Trouble boys: Gangster

About the Author
(Yeah, like you're really interested)

David was born and raised in "The Land of Pleasant Living," Baltimore, Maryland. The product of twelve years of Catholic education, he graduated from the University of Baltimore with a B.S. degree and set out to change the world. The world wasn't ready. After 45 years in the food industry in various roles (business owner, produce consultant, helping local farmers transition to food from tobacco by orchestrating local auctions). He always encouraged people to chew slower and enjoy their meals. Eventually, David dropped out, tuned in and began his career in writing.

In a pen and ink on velum type of world, David is a crayons on construction paper kind of guy. And the world still doesn't appear ready.

David currently lives in a small town in the foothills of North Carolina's Blue Ridge Mountains with his wife and their miniature Schnauzer, Guinness.

You can complain about or applaud David's book directly to JuggledWords@gmail.com.